ANY
SURVIVORS?

ANY SURVIVORS?

A LOST NOVEL OF WORLD WAR II

MARTIN FREUD

TRANSLATED BY ANETTE FUHRMEISTER
EDITED BY HELEN FRY

Front Cover: U-boat commander (Mary Evans Picture Library)

First published 2010

The History Press
The Mill, Brimscombe Port
Stroud, Gloucestershire, GL5 2QG
www.thehistorypress.co.uk

British Library Cataloguing in Publication Data.
A catalogue record for this book is available from the British Library.

ISBN 978 0 7524 5344 6

Typesetting and origination by The History Press
Printed in Great Britain

CONTENTS

PREFACE

It is every historian's dream to stumble across something significant in a battered old case in a forgotten attic. However, that is precisely what happened with Martin Freud's unpublished novel *Any Survivors?* I discovered it quite by chance whilst rummaging through papers which the family had lent me for writing *Freuds' War*. The manuscript was amongst several papers in a tatty briefcase, both of which had seen better days. The novel, which ran to over 330 typed pages, was written in German except for the opening scene which was in English. When I read the opening scene, I wanted to read on – who was the survivor pulled out of the freezing water by men on a British destroyer? And what was his connection to the U-boat crew that had perished? Whilst my German was not sufficient to understand the bulk of the text, I knew already from my study of Martin Freud's life that much of what he had written in the past was strongly autobiographical and I suspected that this might be true of this novel which is set in the Second World War. During his lifetime Martin Freud published two books: the first his autobiography *Glory Reflected* and second, his novel *Parole d'Honneur* which is heavily based on his experiences in the Austro-Hungarian Royal Horse Artillery in the First World War.

The manuscript has been translated from the German and edited in such a way as to keep closely to the style and ambiance of the original.

Martin Freud was the eldest son of Sigmund Freud, the founder of psychoanalysis. Born in Vienna on 7 December 1889, Martin grew up in an environment where he was aware of his father's international reputation and fame, and spoke of being 'content to bask in reflected glory'. Martin was close to his father, whom he described as having '*ein froehliches herz*' (a merry heart). From 1914 until 1918 he fought for his country on the Russian and Italian front lines during the First World War, during which time he was awarded seven medals for bravery, two of which were Military Crosses. Just days before the Armistice was signed in November 1918 he was taken as a prisoner of war by the British in Italy and spent nearly a year in an Italian prisoner-of-war camp until the summer of 1919. When he was finally released he returned to Vienna and trained as a lawyer. On his thirtieth birthday in 1919 he married Ernestine Drucker and settled into married life. They had two children: Anton Walter (1921) and Sophie (1924). During the 1930s Martin ran his father's press as Director of International Psychoanalytical Press (Verlag). The offices of the Verlag had moved to 7 Berggasse, just down the street from the family home. In March 1938 Freud's world and that of Austrian Jews was turned upside down when Hitler marched his troops over the border into Austria and annexed the country. After a period of house arrest and two tense months in which it was not obvious the family would get out, visas were finally secured. Martin left for England a month before his parents and settled in London. His marriage had deteriorated and so Martin and Esti separated. Esti stayed in France with their daughter Sophie until forced to flee from the Nazis again, eventually settling in America.

With the outbreak of war in September 1939, Martin and son Walter (now in England) were classified as 'enemy aliens'. In June 1940 Martin was interned by the British government at Huyton near Liverpool, from where a few months later he enlisted in the British army's Pioneer Corps. Disillusioned with life in a labour corps, he was eventually invalided out in June 1941 and took up reserved war work travelling the country as an auditor for the National Dock Labour Corporation. It was during this particular work that he may have gained the inspiration which forms the basis of parts of this novel. This is not an unreasonable assumption because most of his unpublished short stories which exist amongst the family papers are largely based on his personal experiences; likewise his autobiographical first novel *Parole d'Honneur*. Martin worked for the National Dock Labour Corporation until *c.* 1948. When he left, he opened a tobacconist shop near the British Museum. Later he moved to Hove in Sussex where he lived with his partner Margaret, until his death on 25 April 1967. His ashes are interred in the family section at Golders Green crematorium.

During his lifetime Martin had no success in getting *Any Survivors?* published. However, four decades after his death this has come to fruition and is a welcome addition to the Freud family contribution to the literary world.

Dr Helen Fry, author of *Freuds' War*

PROLOGUE

'Are there any survivors? Any survivors?' asked the commander of the British destroyer.

'Just the one, sir. A young sailor. He is conscious and unhurt. Spitting a little blood, the poor chap. I don't think his lungs could cope with the *Davisapparat*.'

'What is he saying?'

'Well sir, he won't stop talking. His English is terrible but he insists he is not part of the U-boat crew.'

'What a cheek! He appeared at exactly the spot where we sank the U-boat. And who does he pretend to be? A cruise passenger or a leisure traveller …?'

'Sir, I don't think he means any harm. He's just expressing himself a little awkwardly in our language. He's saying: "I am supposed to be a member of the crew but I am not a member." He may well be confused from the shock of being submerged in the icy water. He keeps repeating that he must tell his story. Would you like to hear it, sir?'

'Nonsense! Not now. The man should be taken to quarters, given some warm clothes and put to bed with a hot toddy. Tomorrow, as soon as we land, he will be taken to hospital.'

'Yes sir!'

What a dirty trick to pretend he is not a member of the crew.

Well, here is the story …

1

LIGHTS OUT!

September 1939

I was thinking … and when I was thinking simple things, I thought in English. I had been living in London for over a year. Although I was not exactly a maharajah in my home town, I was at least a young man with a profession and the opportunity to progress in my career. A dental technician is a useful and reputable occupation and even well paid. And here I was now living as a refugee in England with no work permit, forgetting the little I had learnt in my previous life. People treated me like one half of a pair of gloves found lying on the street – of no commercial value.

I'm sure my mother was right to persuade me to leave the country. I can divulge only a little of my past as my mother is still in my home country and anything I say, write down or do, could harm her. I will say only this much: I am from a country that used to be free and happy until Hitler came along and forced us into submission with arms and no resistance.

I received some aid here in London but not to the extent that I could live it up in the Grosvenor House or even anywhere in Mayfair; I was living in King's Cross in a basic boarding house. Unfortunately it so happened that

I was the only young man in the house. The other guests, mainly elderly ladies, were also from countries that Hitler had already occupied – or was going to in the near future. The more prudent amongst us did not wait but emigrated well before he seized power.

My room was a tiny garret on the top floor, just big enough to sleep in but with no real space in which to live during the day. Once, when I was in the communal living room, I had no time to relax because all the ladies started bossing me around and asking me to do things for them. As they were older than I, and female too, they believed this was their right. If they had their own way I might have spent all day on ladders, hanging blackout curtains and filling gaps with black paper to achieve perfect darkness.

I should have started with the fact that war had just broken out. As I headed for the lounge, I could overhear one of the ladies saying: 'Where is that insolent lazy-bones hiding?' It was one of the elderly ladies with a very deep voice. 'I've been looking for him all day. I want him to go to the W.W. for me to get some more drawing pins before they run out.'

'I don't know what you mean,' said a lady with a much higher voice. 'I don't think he's insolent. He is modest and shy and often looks at one with his kind eyes. I tell you it makes me feel quite motherly towards him.'

'That's only when he wants something from you; some toast made or some trousers ironed.' Now this was slightly unfair in my opinion; it was over a week since anyone had made me any toast or ironed my trousers.

I came into the room. 'Please excuse me,' I said. 'You were speaking about me.'

I don't think I put that quite right; I should have said 'Excuse me for listening in' but I wanted to be as polite as possible. My aim was to take a book from the shelf, and there was the danger that they would come up with another thing for me to do, as in: 'Leave the book there and go and fill some sandbags instead.'

All this took place yesterday. As I came into the room today, there was no one there. It was unusually quiet. I took out a book on Charlotte Corday since I was researching the history of famous murderers of tyrants. Not that I wanted to murder a tyrant myself. Personally, I didn't feel I could murder anyone, even less a tyrant, but I was interested in the method: how to plan grand deeds and how to execute them, peaceful deeds that are not murderous ones.

I was daydreaming, pleasantly seated on the biggest and most comfortable sofa. The only good reading light was to my left. The Charlotte Corday book was on my lap, with my thumb marking the spot where the beautiful murderess buys a kitchen knife from an ironmonger near the Palais Royal at the crack of dawn. My legs were dangling down the side of the seat and to my right there was a glass of water. I gazed at the cheap clock on the mantelpiece, its hands gratifyingly inching towards 7 p.m. Any minute the dinner gong would sound. I was only on half board, entitled to breakfast and dinner. This arrangement was more appropriate for those who worked and lunched in the city. Shouldn't the gong have sounded by now? Earlier today there had been some unrest: furniture was shifted, doors banged and phones rang. The silence now was pleasant in contrast.

I heard footsteps and quickly sat up straight, removing my legs from the cushion. It was only the chambermaid with whom I was having a minor feud. My circumstances dictated that I could not tip her but that was no reason for her to treat me with contempt and not speak to me in her mother tongue, which was Scottish. She came in, took the clock off the mantelpiece, stuck it under her arm and left the room without saying a word. *Aha*, I thought, *we're having soft-boiled eggs for dinner or something that needs to be timed accurately*. She came back in. This time she took my half-empty glass of water without a word of apology and disappeared again. *Aha*, I thought. *Frau Pokorny has visitors and they are serving orangeade for which they need more glasses*. Frau Pokorny lived comfortably – her daughters were married and living in the United States and sent her money regularly. The boarding house charged 6*d* per glass which was surely a 100 per cent mark-up since sugar and fruit were still cheap.

The girl came back again, this time approaching me directly. I clutched my book resolutely. She grabbed the reading lamp, unscrewed the light bulb and stuck it in her apron pocket. She used a cloth to hold the bulb so as not to burn her hands; then left me behind in complete darkness. This seemed to me to overstep the mark of what I could endure. I was a paying customer even if I was being helped financially. Besides, I was no more than three days behind with the rent. Ready to complain to the chambermaid, I carefully felt my way out of the room.

The hallway was full of boxes. The chambermaid was now unscrewing the bulbs from the lamps in reception and filling a basket with them. The doors to the bedroom on the ground floor were wide open and all the rooms empty. There was no sign of the landlady. On the desk I found a letter addressed to me. It was the weekly bill which was normally due in four days time. I owed 15/4 and this morning's breakfast was the last meal they were charging me for. Underneath the bill I found the following:

Dear Mr …, I trust that you will pay the outstanding amount of 15/4 as soon as you receive your next benefit payment. We are closing here and are moving to a new site. I am only able to take the ladies with me, as we are

already at full capacity. I'm sure you will find somewhere
else to stay.
Yours sincerely,
...

It was not only water and light that had been taken from
me; it was now the roof over my head. I could just about see
into the kitchen downstairs. The crockery and cutlery was
all packed up and there was no sign of the gong either.

'When are you closing up?' I asked the chambermaid.
She shrugged and remained silent. I may as well have
spoken to her in Farsi. The sooner I left, the sooner I would
find somewhere else to stay. Two men came in and started
to remove the suitcases. Emergency lighting on the stairs
enabled me to make my way up to my room to pack. Only
when I had opened and closed all the cupboard drawers
did I realise that there was nothing I could pack because
I had no possessions. There was no point in taking a pile of
old papers and magazines. My spare shirt and second pair
of socks were in the wash with little chance of retrieving
them now that I owed laundry money. I put on my shoes
with the bitter feeling that horses and cows could grow
new hooves but the heels on my shoes would not grow
back. They would only wear down further. My slippers
weren't worth taking either. I packed only my razor and
toothbrush. The towel and bedding were part of the hostel
inventory. My flute was already in my trouser pocket and
I had sold my coat last April. I had never owned a hat. I was
as ready as I could ever be.

But ... where were my documents?

I remembered they were being held at the central office
responsible for refugees, and since they were in the process
of moving premises as well, my papers had been deposited
safely. In case we were interned, they promised they would

send the documents straight to the *Lagerkommando*. My mother can't write to me now the war has broken out so she won't mind if I don't have an address for the time being.

'*Adieu, Mansarde*,' I called. 'Goodbye to all you mice! You'll miss me when you look for cheese rinds under the bed.' At dinner I liked to save a piece of cheese to eat in bed at night. I went back downstairs and deposited the Charlotte Corday in one of the baskets the maid was now filling with books. There was little hope that these items would arrive in one piece, as there were light bulbs at the bottom and books on top. But what can you expect from a chambermaid who won't even speak to you in her native tongue?

If I hadn't walked the route to King's Cross so often in daylight, I would have been lost. The darkness was merciless. It was a blackout because of the war. From time to time, when I could see nothing at all, I stood still and waited. When cars passed and shed their lights on the streets for a few seconds I got up and moved a few metres further on. I had no real plans of where to go. Five pennies was all I had. If only I owned luggage or better clothes I could have stayed in a boarding house and lived on credit until my next payment. But from the way I looked, I could expect no courtesy. My only item of respectable clothing was the immaculately kept gas mask with a brand-new white hemp cord; but everyone knew that these were free, not for sale and compulsory to carry around. I had a few telephone numbers of fellow emigrants who lived in posh hotels but I wasn't brave enough to invest my few pennies in the risky venture of a phone call. And how would they treat me in reception? My heels were worn and my tie was pieced together from bits of one of the ladies' old dressing gowns.

It had been some time since the last car had passed me to cast a faint light on my path. I should have spent less time thinking and more time paying attention. Now I was truly lost. I could hear cars passing in the distance but I must have landed in a side street with no traffic. I rationalised – I may be lost but even if it seems like I'm in the midst of a deserted mine, I am in a million-strong city. Within a few metres of here there must be people in their dressing gowns and slippers, playing with their offspring, making toast and reading the *Evening Standard*. If it weren't for the blackout curtains I could make them out, I was sure of it. Someone had to come by and help me out sooner or later. I felt around for something solid and sat down. Something crashed to the ground. I must have knocked over an empty milk bottle in the darkness. It shattered but luckily I was unaffected as there was no dampness and the stones remained dry and warm. As I was seated comfortably I thought that I might as well continue my train of thought …

I came from a country that used to be free and happy. We spoke German at home, that much was true, but was that reason enough for Herr Hitler to come along and take over? I was almost always a good boy and often stayed at home to help my mother, although she did send me to the mountains to live with her brother for a while to build up my strength because I was a weak child. I wondered why my mother, teacher and priest all tried to convince me to be a good and honest young man and put up with no injustice from others? When this was put to the test and I followed these directives, it caused only shock and dismay. The first time this happened was when I was buying a new exercise book. This was immediately after the invasion of the German troops and in the midst of jubilation. The window display of the stationers with the funny name was almost empty. Only the owner, an old man with a grey beard, sat there with a sign around his neck – *Saujud*, swine of a Jew. It was written with no orthographic errors unlike the other signs in similar shops, and this was rare. An SA man guarded the shop. It was already obvious to me that no one would be able to buy an exercise book in the foreseeable future. I didn't walk on. It was a disgrace to humanity; and I felt sorry for the man in the window display with the sign around his neck. He had always been so kind to me and friendly. Perhaps I could help.

'Why don't you let me sit in the window in his place?' I asked the SA man. A few people who had been eyeing the display came a little closer so that they could follow what was happening. 'Just think,' I continued, loud enough for the others to hear, 'how embarrassing it must be for the old man. Imagine if it was your father.'

One of the women said, 'Really, what is the point? Why should an old Jew sit in the window like that?' The other women murmured their approval. At this time and location it wasn't unusual for the crowd to change their opinion. It resulted in the SA officer setting the old man free. People weren't really that bad; they were easily led astray. One only has to lead them on the right path again. With these comforting thoughts in my mind I fell asleep.

The next attempt was less successful. Two days later, quite early in the morning, I passed a group of elderly women who were being led away by the SA for cleaning duties. I think they were mainly wives of old officers and aristocrats, loyal to the emperor. They were carrying heavy buckets filled to the brim with lye, brushes, brooms and cleaning rags. A particularly unsavoury rabble who had recently converted to the new regime followed them, scoffing and jeering loudly. One old lady with snow-white hair stopped to rest. She could go no further with the amount she was carrying. I stepped in, took her bucket and said: '*Gnaedige Frau*' ('Madam, let me carry that for you'). I was not sure why they felt they had to beat me to a pulp for this act of politeness. If I had not pretended to be dead, they would have carried on relentlessly. My poor mother hardly recognised me. I had to stay at home for a few days so my wounds could heal.

I was disappointed – I had no chance! How could I change the mind of 80 million people? I had to change my methods. I would either need several hundred kind helpers or I would have to speak to larger groups of people at one time. It would not be easy recruiting helpers, so I chose the alternative – to speak to the masses. Sadly, this was not as easy as I had imagined. The masses that gathered to hear the speech of a bigwig might have listened to what I had to say. The speech they had come to hear was to be about the extermination of the inner enemy. I got no further than 'In the name of humanity' before the Gestapo grabbed me by the collar of my overcoat. I managed to free myself by slipping out of the coat and darting between their legs. I then was able to get through to the next street by running into a house with two exits, and then jumped onto a tram.

I remembered my coat pocket held the deposit receipt for my *faltboot*, my collapsible boat. Here I had left a copy of a book from the library. The author was a Jewish philosopher and it was about the freedom of speech. There was a register showing who the current holder of the copy was. If the Gestapo followed this lead, they would track me down within a few hours. When I got home, I told my friends and family. Everyone was shocked. My friends all contributed money to enable me to cross the border straight away. Once out of the country I was passed from pillar to post until I finally ended up here in England.

A car finally approached. It was heavy and moving very slowly. I got up and ran towards it, waving my arms in the headlights. I hoped this car would give me a lift, at least to somewhere I had a chance of finding my way from. It stopped. It was a Rolls Royce with a slightly unusual shape. The bonnet was exceptionally wide and the roof was very high. The driver and his partner were wearing top hats and there was a large black box behind them – it was a hearse. I decided against the lift. 'Sorry,' I called out and stepped back on to the pavement. The car with the sombre profession appeared to have gotten lost in the blackout; the headlights were aimed towards the houses and walls, on the lookout for a clue to their current position – a street sign perhaps or something else. This proved to be fortuitous for me because the gloomy memory of the hearse was soon replaced by something far more pleasant. A larger-than-life image of a beautiful girl with long flowing hair and rosy cheeks was glowing in the darkness. Her white neck was shimmering and her shapely arms were beckoning me. For a few seconds I thought I was witnessing a miracle, but then I understood. The headlights were directed at a large poster and had singled out this perfectly sharp image. I could not make out what her sweet smile was extolling: soap, toothpaste or shampoo? Something to eat or strengthen the nerves or perhaps washing powder? The fair image disappeared. The searchlights found a clue to our whereabouts. We were only a few hundred metres away from Upper Regent Street.

As I walked on I asked myself: why was I not only without a home country but also without a home and poorer than I had ever been? Was I being penalised for the fact that I had spent recent months following my personal interests and only worrying about satisfying my creature comforts? Should I travel back to the Reich and continue with the fruitless task of trying to persuade 80 million people to change their opinion as one single soul labouring against the masses? That was the error. What a ridiculous mistake to think that I could influence millions of people when their individual opinion counted for nothing. In the whole of the Reich there was only one man whose opinion counted – and that was Hitler himself. I should have tried to persuade *him* instead so that he would see the error of his ways and end this war that was both wrong and unjust. This insight came a little late as I was now in England and there was no opportunity for me to get back to Germany and penetrate the Führer's inner circle. Disillusioned and a little bitter, I told myself: just give up! There is no point in fantasising. You need to think about yourself and the future. And right now you need a bed for the night!

I decided to head for the West End. This is where I would normally find my friends and acquaintances. There was a good chance I would bump into one of them, start talking and then be invited to stay the night. I did not think I would even have to beg or complain about my situation too much. It was generally enough to look a little sad and despairing. The darkness made things difficult. If only I had a big illuminated sign or something to hang around my neck, but even then no one would be able to see what kind of face I was pulling.

People of various shapes and sizes were running into me, as I had been standing still for a few moments. I could sense by their prods that this was no ordinary flow. People were heading in more than one direction. An entrance covered with a heavy black curtain became clear to me. On it red neon letters proclaimed: OPEN ALL NIGHT, MUSIC.

Thank God for that! Music was allowed again.

People pushed in and out as the flow led me towards the entrance and I found myself heading inside. It must have been fate. I didn't suppose I could invest my 5*d* in a profit-making way so I thought I might as well spend it. Why wait until I got even hungrier and more tired? Judging by the raincoats, packages and dialects my neighbours in the human stream called their own, this was more a haven for the common people, not the upper classes. I would rather avoid being somewhere where custom would dictate that I tip half a crown in the absence of having the right change to hand.

Despite my resolution not to be impressed, and although I had been here before, I took in the lavish luxury of the establishment. Marble, cut-glass mirrors, concealed lighting illuminating the vaulted ceiling, porters in uniform ... Had the flow of people not carried me, I might have turned around and ended up in a cheap pub eating fish and chips or sausages and cabbage instead. The stream carried me past the reception desk. I reached into my pocket and counted the coins by feeling with my fingers. They were all still there. At the other end of the hall there was a podium with white-suited musicians, instruments at the ready. The conductor was just raising the bow of the violin as I tiptoed past as quiet as I could. I had just taken my seat when the dulcet tones began. If only the other customers had been as considerate. They spoke in loud voices, rattled their cutlery and plates, shouting their orders loudly to the waiters. I, for my part, had no wish but to remain invisible for the time being and surrender fully to the rhythm of the melodies.

The band was playing the Intermezzo from *Cavalleria*, a piece of music that in the best of times could move me to tears. It was either that or take out my flute and play along; both options sadly out of the question. People were still coming and going, getting awkwardly in and out of their coats. A new experience for me: the aim of many was not to listen to music, talk to friends, or eat and drink, but rather to find the most complicated way of shedding their parcels, gas masks, umbrellas, hats and coats. How complicated life was for the well-heeled! I was much better off, I thought. I had nothing to stash away under seats and behind tables. Full of enthusiasm I listened to the music, determined to reach the most paradisiacal state of bliss that my 5*d* would buy, regardless of what the waiters thought of me. And who knows, I thought; they might even play *La Bohème* or *Butterfly*.

It was not possible to remain invisible. The waiters were already attempting to take my order, approaching me from all possible sides. Finally I had to acknowledge their presence. I took the menu as if I had never looked at it before. It was a smallish leather-bound booklet with multi-coloured print. I explained to him that I needed more time. My English was improving. He seemed to understand and left me in peace to make my choice.

There were two pennies on the table which I could have swiped without anyone noticing. My assets would have increased to 7*d*; enough for a proper meal of bread and butter, for example, with two sardines or bangers and mash or even soup and an egg. However, 5*d* did not yield quite as much. I could not bring myself to order a mere cup of tea when water would do just as well to quench my thirst. The waiter returned. I pointed to the 2*d*, for I was and wanted to remain, an honest man. He seemed to misunderstand and disappeared, reappearing with a fresh tablecloth. A few practised movements and the old tablecloth, by no means pristine, was gone and replaced by a new one. He then removed the 2*d* from under my eyes. I could hear the rattling in his pockets and the coins were gone. It was time for me to order. It was a good thing my hearing was what it was. 'Chicken liver is out,' I heard another waiter say. Perhaps my waiter had not been into the kitchen for a while. I ordered the liver; he noted it and went off. Another fifteen minutes of paradise passed. The band still did not play *La Bohème* or *Butterfly* but *We're Going to Hang out the Washing on the Siegfried Line*, not a piece I particularly enjoyed but I tried to memorise it because I thought it might work well on the flute. I tried with little success to ignore two gentlemen and a lady behind me who were speaking loudly and unabashedly in German. But they were beginning to interest me. To turn around and stare at them would have been impolite and was unnecessary. I could observe their table in one of the many mirrors if I looked straight ahead. Admittedly, I could only see them the wrong way around. There was a young man with broad shoulders and a smart haircut, a greying older gentleman and a younger lady with platinum-blonde hair. They must have had a few drinks before they came in because they were definitely in 'high spirits', but here they were only drinking coffee. Finally the band finished *We're Going to Hang out the Washing* and was silent. I could now hear every word they were saying and paid full attention.

'How much have we earned all in?' asked a bass voice, probably the greying man.

'I haven't counted it,' replied the metallic tenor voice, undoubtedly belonging to the young man with the mass of hair. 'Here,' he was beating his breast pocket. 'You can hear the rustling noise. Loads of £10 notes. And the timing was perfect! If the war had broken out twenty-four hours later I would have lost it all to the Portuguese agent who disappeared to South America. Poor German bigwig in Berlin! I can see him now, tears rolling down his fat cheeks. But I don't dare let the money out of the country. Rather than risk coming into conflict with the Defence Finance Regulations I'd prefer to waste it and drink on my own. I mean with you guys, ha ha!' He was sounding merrier by the minute.

'Leo,' said the man with the deeper voice. 'I hardly recognise you, pull yourself together. Yes, it is an achievement to receive a handsome sum in English currency as a result of the outbreak of war, and I have no sympathy with the

German bigwig. But that's no reason to lose control of yourself like this!'

'Oh, you and your self-control, *Herr Doktor*,' the girl squealed. She probably hadn't had the most to drink but seemed to tolerate the least. She also had a rather off-putting speech impediment. 'Come on, Leo,' she lisped. 'Celebrate (*th-elebrate*) with me. I'm a bird, flying high in the sky (*thky*), high as a kite. Tweet, tweet!'

In the mirror I could see she was getting up and trying to use the seat as a step onto the table. People began to stare.

'Sit down, Angelica!' the tenor hissed, 'or I'll feed you to the dogs.' She put up some resistance but fell back into her seat, throwing her things to the floor in the process. Her hat, handbag and umbrella rolled towards my feet. I could no longer ignore the situation and turned towards them. The music was changing: Troubadour, *Schon naht die Todesstunde* (*The Hour of our Death is Approaching*). Not quite appropriate but I had no time to enjoy the melody. I could only make out the skinny back of the girl in her ill-fitting suit. She was crawling on the floor, looking for her treasures.

By now I was looking right at the man with the tenor voice; he had a pleasing, well-balanced and well-fed face with a strong chin. Sparkling blue eyes were staring back at me. His complexion was like milk and blood, a dimple in his cheek, his smooth forehead set off by the well-coiffed light brown curls. He left me no time to admire him further. He grabbed the lapel of my jacket. I was none too pleased about his rough treatment. He pulled me up, shouting: 'You old crook! Have you finally escaped? You see – you managed it without my help. But I'm pleased. I'm really pleased!'

How could I escape this sudden outburst of unwanted attention?

I responded coolly: 'Sir, I am neither old, nor a crook, escaped or otherwise. Besides, I don't even know you. Please be so kind as to let go of my jacket.'

His reaction was one of unfeigned surprise. Despite being the victim of a misunderstanding, I was playing a manly and dignified role. The waiter had returned and was standing behind me: 'Chicken liver is out, sir.'

The girl by the name of Angelica had packed her things and was ready to leave. 'You know what he's like, full of fun and jokes!' Once again she demonstrated her speech impediment. I looked at the girl more closely. There wasn't much of her. Without the make-up, the platinum-blonde hair, false eyelashes and the speech defect, she was very ordinary – and this girl was called Angelica!

Now the bass-voiced man got involved. 'You know, I don't think it's him, Leo. He must be five years younger, but what a resemblance!' he said quietly to the tenor. 'We should make the most of this opportunity.' The man with the grey hair was grim-looking and serious, his glasses thick, mouth small and malicious.

'Leo … honey,' Angelica begged, 'but we promised our friends …'

The grey-haired man added quietly, 'And what we promised we should keep. And besides, someone with such technical knowledge is a good investment.'

I had no idea what they were talking about but I was starting to feel a bit uncomfortable. It was a bit like being in a madhouse. The rosy-cheeked man was still holding me by the lapel of my coat and the waiter was still waiting for my order.

'Do give us the pleasure of joining our table,' said the man called Leo. The other man pulled out a chair for me. I hesitated.

'I would be pleased if you could clarify, Mr Leo,' I said. 'I don't know your surname, so please excuse me for calling you Leo. Is this an invitation? Then I would gladly accept. I'm afraid I do not possess the means to get involved in such unclear situations where I do not know what is expected of me.'

Now they were all laughing.

'Of course we are inviting you,' Leo said, as he signalled to the waiter. 'You haven't eaten dinner? One should really eat at seven o'clock, several hours before going to bed. That's much healthier. Anyway, we will have … er … soup, mixed grill with all the trimmings, sweets and coffee.' The waiter could hardly keep up. I listened without feeling obliged to protest; the man had grabbed me and called me a crook so he could pay.

'My name is Leopold Karner,' the young man introduced himself whilst I was already greedily spooning my soup. 'From Vienna,' he continued. 'I was a former illegal; an SS man in the *Vitztum* legion. You are from Vienna too judging by your accent? Or at least Austrian?'

I ignored the question. 'I've heard of the legion,' I interjected. 'But to be perfectly honest it doesn't win my sympathy vote.' I went no further as I didn't want to lose my new friends before they had served me the meat course.

'Excellent,' said my new benefactor. 'I have also liquidated my relationship with them and think it's time we both came clean with each other.'

Thank goodness – here was the mixed grill.

'Now, I'm not saying I've lost touch completely – on the contrary, I still have some lucrative contacts. But I want nothing more to do with the Gestapo. They are after me. Now let me tell you the story. And you, you are an enemy alien, aren't you?'

Ah, I thought, *he's interrogating me*. I nodded.

'Your permit? Is it for residence only, not for work? And where do you live? Do you have any friends or relations? What about your documents?'

'At the moment I have nowhere to stay,' I disclosed. 'Hardly any friends, no relations and no documents.' The music had stopped. There was lukewarm applause from the more good-natured people in the audience. Then quiet.

'How would you like to …' Mr Leo began. Judging by his face he was about to say something of great importance and I forgot to breathe. At the same time I felt someone kicking me under the table; then, somewhat annoyed, they apologised. It seemed that Leo also received a similar kick that prompted him to stop mid-sentence. After an awkward pause he continued: 'Some cheese?'

'Yes please,' I said. But the question was not a serious one. Instead of ordering some cheese he said to the waiter, 'The bill please', and the three of them watched silently as I finished my meal. Even the girl pulled herself together. It seemed the drunkenness of the party was wearing off. I was in good spirits. Things had been going wrong for months and now it was time for my luck to change. My first stroke of good fortune was already consumed. The bill was on the table and I was just polishing off my last piece of apple torte. I was ready to go.

'If it's okay with you we will finish our conversation elsewhere.'

I nodded.

'Gather your things,' he ordered, upon which I shrugged. 'I have no things.'

We marched past reception, Leo in front; I was the last. Leo paid with a pound note and then the four of us were in complete darkness. Whilst our eyes had got used to the bright lights inside, it was now impossible to see anything. Leo called for a taxi and a shadow appeared, its faint light getting brighter. All three got into the taxi.

'I fear I won't be able to find the way, even if you describe it to me,' I said, in what I thought was the direction of the window of the taxi.

'Don't be a fool; you're coming with us,' the tenor voice said, his strong fists pulling me into the taxi where I stumbled into some very sharp girlish knees. The thought of getting into a taxi was so far from what I was used to, it was hard to imagine. I hadn't set foot in one since leaving my home country. After only a few minutes' drive the cab stopped at a big block of flats and Leo and I got out. We must have been on Edgware Road from what I could make out by the faint glow of the traffic lights. The girl was preparing to get out too. 'No. You stay here Angelica,' said Leo. 'I don't think you will lose a pearl from your crown if you have to sleep in your own bed for a change.' The greying man also remained in the taxi, which had now pulled away and was rolling off into the darkness at a snail's pace.

Leo grabbed me under the arm and led me into his bachelor's flat where he dumped me in a comfortable leather armchair. It didn't bother me that the horsehair was visible in parts. I was sitting comfortably and would have liked a smoke, preferably a pipe but a cigarette would do. Sadly Leo was not inclined to offer. He came straight to the point. 'Well Herr …'

I remained silent.

'Okay,' he said, 'if you won't tell me your name, I don't need to know. It really isn't important. You have no papers, you already mentioned that. That's fine by me. However, one thing I do need to know is this – are you pure Aryan?'

I decided to wind him up. 'According to our family history,' I said, 'which we can follow back several centuries, a distant ancestor of mine had an intimate relationship with the devil. He was accused, tried and burnt at the stake as a witch – but as far as I'm aware we never had anything to do with the Jews.'

He smiled. 'Thank you. That's enough. You ought to be careful with jokes like that! So Herr Nameless, how would you like to travel to Germany for me?' Now fate was resting her hand firmly on my shoulder. The circle was closed. This was my chance to do my bit for humanity.

I composed myself and said with feigned nonchalance: 'If the conditions are right, then why not?'

'Well sir,' he answered, 'these are the conditions: free travel in second class, pocket money, documents, newly kitted out from head to toe – and I do believe you are in dire need of the latter. We'll head to the West End tomorrow. And from you I expect the following: discipline – complete soldierly discipline, to obey orders and ask no questions. You will stay in contact with my sub-agent in the Reich. He will provide advice and supervision. No heroic feats or assassinations either. No Aryan would think of such a thing! If you should happen to come across military intelligence then you will notify me via my sub-agent and take your 40 per cent share in any profits. And the reason I am sending you shall remain a secret for now but will soon become apparent.'

What followed was purely technical. 'Do you speak any Cuban?'

'No.'

'Estonian?'

'No.'

'Chinese?'

'Afraid not.'

He was getting out his collection of passports. 'What about Danish?'

'Sorry,' I replied meekly.

'Would you be able to tell if anyone was speaking Danish to you?'

I had to concede that I couldn't tell the difference between Danish and Hungarian or even Japanese. 'I will have to give you the Danish passport,' he said, shaking his head, 'and perhaps a travel companion for part of the way.' Then he went on to instruct me. 'If anyone tries to speak any other language than the one you're familiar with, even English, then you are to answer with the following: "I admire the Third Reich so much that I cannot bear to speak any language other than German when I am a guest on this holy ground – heil Hitler!"' This was one sentence I was going to have to practise.

'And take care! If you let your mask slip for one moment it could cost you not only your acting career but also your life. But don't worry! It can get no worse than decapitation. Spies don't end up in Buchenwald. I should also add: the organisation for which you are subordinating yourself is called the *Geheime Macht*, the secret force.'

'Here,' I said, happily remembering, 'are two passport photos I have been carrying. This will save you taking new ones.' He took them off me, studied them carefully and said 'completely useless', tearing them cleanly in half. This angered me. When you own so little, two photographs mean a lot. Admittedly, the meal I had recently consumed was worth three times as much as new pictures; I shouldn't be feeling aggrieved.

'I can take new ones here,' said Leo taking out a Leica camera and setting up two bulbs. There was only one other light on.

'That's impossible,' I protested, even though I knew nothing of photography. 'There isn't enough light.'

'Nonsense, you don't know what you're talking about. With this modern equipment I can take a picture of a galloping horse in candlelight. Smile please, thank you!' I had to remind him to wind the camera. He was yawning now, though it was not surprising since it was past midnight.

'You can put the two chairs together or sleep on the floor tonight,' he said. 'Whatever you prefer. Here's a blanket.' It was a leopard-print throw. 'You can take all the cushions as well. Can I get you a night cap?'

I declined. He took a generous drink with a little soda.

'Herr Karner,' I said, still curious from his earlier remark. 'You were going to tell me the story of the *Leibstandarte Vitztum.*' The drink had loosened his tongue and he obliged ...

'The biggest hounding we had since the Turks and congress in Vienna was the public outrage against the murder of a certain Herr vom Rath. It was organised meticulously but the SS had to keep a close eye on the SA. I was also on duty in the Karntnerstrasse. I had just thrown out a unit of SA men as they were taking a suspiciously long time inside a Jewish jewellers. There I was alone in the midst of boxes that had been broken into and with the smashed display windows when a messenger entered wearing *Hitlerjugend* uniform. He made me jump such that I almost dropped the golden watch I had picked up as I wanted to check the make. I remember well, it was a Warscheron. If I forget the name, I can always dig it out again and check. Anyway, the messenger handed over the note:

The Vitztum would like you to know that everything is discovered and you must disappear at once.

'As it was signed by my best friend, I really did fall for it and left the country the same day with forged papers. It turned out to be a complete lie. Nothing was discovered at all. The *Vitztum* did not send me a message. He is still chief constable despite the rumours that circulate about him. My so-called friend just wanted me out of the way so he could take over my position. I decided not to go back. Not only because my false papers were a little obvious and would not have got me very far, but also because I had got into the habit of reading the newspapers here and by reading neutral papers it was easy to see that something unpleasant was going on. Did I really want to be part of it? Things are not so bad here – I really cannot complain. As long as I am not interned I will be okay. But somehow I don't think it would happen because I am a political refugee. Anyway, that's all for today. Goodnight!'

He disappeared behind a door that must have led into his bedroom. I pushed the two sofas together to create a wonderful bed. The door opened again and a black piece of fur was thrown out, hissing. It was a little black cat. I took her in. She was quite content with only a tiny piece of my blanket. I would have slept like a log had I not been worrying about whether the passport photograph would turn out okay.

2

SEALED ORDER

Leo got up late but soon made up for the lost time with feverish activity. He pulled me from shop to shop and made calls to travel agents, friends and agencies. In short, he was paving the way for my travels. I naturally admired him and his enthusiastic bustle, although I did begin to wonder why there was no further mention of the passport photo. When we were in the taxi on our way to Liverpool Street Station, I plucked up the courage to ask him.

'It's all done,' he replied, 'developed, stuck in and stamped. My, you are a worrier! You must have had some bad experience as a child.'

I declined to answer. His bedroom must have had a secret exit or been connected to a dark room. I had not left his side all morning. When did he have time to get it developed?

'Here is your passport, you can stop fretting now.' He passed me the thin booklet, looking slightly worried. I opened it to the first page and nodded, satisfied. It was me but it was not exactly flattering. I looked more closely and contemplated: what had I done to deserve these wonders? I was ready to accept the miracle of a walking stick bearing blossom or a songbird starting to speak, but they were old fashioned compared to this. A photograph that was taken of a man in sole possession of a dark blue shirt and spotted tie had developed into a gentleman with white dress shirt and tuxedo. This was too much to take in. I nudged Leo with the passport. 'Please, Mr Leo. Something's not quite right.'

He became angry and shouted, 'Enough of this Talmudian sophistry! If that's all you can come up with then we can stop right here. I thought you had discipline!' To give up because of this small matter didn't seem worth the risk of having to hand back the new clothes, the travel money and, most importantly, having to give up the mission that fate had sent to me. As a result, our farewell at the station was far less heartfelt than we might have expected it to be.

I had company during the short journey from Esbjerg in Denmark to Flensburg. It was a fellow conspirator from the *Geheime Macht*, sent to see me through the Danish-speaking area. He was an unattractive man with black fingernails and a chubby, red face. He must have been Danish as I couldn't seem to communicate with him. According to Leo he was part of the organisation but in all likelihood he was badly paid and seized the opportunity to vent his bad mood on me. We didn't even need the secret signs we had agreed on. I was the only passenger leaving the rickety cargo steamer and he was the only one waiting at the pier. His greeting consisted of pulling my thick woollen scarf around my mouth and chin, making me look like someone suffering from severe toothache. I could scarcely breathe, much less talk, which must have been the aim of the procedure. I was to be silent and inconspicuous. Unfortunately I forgot to ask Leo, amongst other important details, who was in charge of paying expenses. At every opportunity my companion gestured menacingly that I had to pay and at one point he snatched my wallet from me. Thank goodness it only contained Danish loose change. After paying he pocketed the wallet. I felt stupid but could not protest, being forced to remain mute. It was a small country and we soon crossed it. The expenditure on beer, ham sandwiches, cheese sandwiches and cigarettes remained negligible. All the same, if on my next mission by any chance I had to travel through Asia on the Trans-Siberian Railway, I would be sure to insist on a more amicable companion.

Entering Germany was easy and posed so little danger I felt ashamed of myself for not visiting before. I envisaged crawling over fences, sneaking through barriers, swimming through channels. I was almost disappointed to find there was no need for further deception or skill. My guide left me at the border, just after passport control, with no further pleasantries such as a goodbye or handshake. I gave him a friendly nod. He spat out and mumbled something in Danish, more than four words. I suddenly felt I understood the language after all, although I'd rather not translate what he said. I had a second-class ticket to Kiel and was one of those people who, in possession of a window seat in direction of travel and a valid ticket, could feel nothing other than happiness and satisfaction. My scarf was where it belonged, around my neck, and I no longer resembled someone fearing a visit to the dentist. My miserable friend was gone and Reichsmark notes were rustling in my pocket. From head to toe I was dressed in fine clothes and had the air of a tourist on a pleasant leisure trip. Leo had bought everything in a large London department store, not in the cheap basement area, but where the upper classes shopped. He instructed me to sew in all the Danish labels from his extensive collection but was no longer in a position to control how far I had got with this. In the overhead luggage compartment my suitcase was swaying, filled as it was with further unexplored delights. When had life ever been so good to me? And I was so free! In my button hole there was a large enamel symbol with the white Danish cross on a red background, upon which stood *Danimarca* for those who were not so good at recognising flags. I was humming with pleasure '*Ein freies leben fuhren wir, ein Leben voller Wonne*' ('a free life we lead and a happy one') from Schiller's *Räuber*. The man opposite me, an SS man with the Führer's insignia, accompanied by his *soignée* mother, smiled indulgently with tolerant sympathy; probably thinking that the man from the neutral country is feeling good in Germany.

Leading a free life was an exaggeration, as I soon found out when I began to receive instructions from the *Geheime Macht* almost immediately. When I got to Kiel I felt in my pocket for my ticket and discovered a sealed envelope. The miserable guide must have left it there. In typewritten letters I found the name of a hotel where I was to stay. In Vienna I would never have dreamed of entering one of the fine hotels and they would probably have turned me away. But shyness was one of the characteristics I was shedding with age. In London, where the hotels are more imposing from the outside, I had once arranged a rendezvous in the reception hall. Another time I was almost invited to have tea in the Savoy. But all the same, to enter a hotel like this and book a room was a novel sensation and almost as fantastically exciting as a train journey in a sleeper or seat in an opera box at a gala performance. I was suitably excited; even sweating. The cover of the Baedeker guidebook I was clinging to desperately was rubbing off on my hands – fortunately no one would notice since my hands are naturally red.

The hotel in Kiel was no marble palace with endless columned halls and multiple floors, but instead was a narrow two-storey building, bourgeois and dignified. I was happy to see that there was only one counter. At least they wouldn't send me from one to the next – a favourite pastime of those in public buildings with multiple counters, whether a railway station or unemployment office. I am convinced that if there are counters at the gates of heaven then the waiting souls will be sent back and forth endlessly. The hotelier, the porter and the room waiter, all three no longer in the prime of their youth, sprang to attention and started clucking like hens to receive me with full honour. I immediately began to recite my little saying about the holy German language because everyone was attempting to extend their welcome in various languages I could not understand. When they proceeded to speak to me in German, I had to pretend I could understand only snippets of their ramblings. The hotelier, who also happened to be the chief receptionist, asked me how he could help me. Although my arrival was not unexpected, they had not made a firm reservation because they had so many vacant rooms. I could choose between a single room with running water, a double bedroom with street-facing balcony or an apartment with an en-suite bathroom. I took my time, leafing carefully through the language section of my Baedeker and responded with feigned concentration and some mispronunciation: 'Without doubt, *mein Herr*, I prefer the latter.' The clucking increased, as did their activity and they began to tread on each other's toes. To be more precise, the hotel manager took advantage of his position as an entrepreneur by treading repeatedly on his employees' toes without once apologising. It became apparent to me within a few minutes in the society of the new regime that their maxim of transcending class barriers was a myth. In the most convoluted way I could manage and in my very best German I asked the porter, who was also my room waiter, to take my luggage into my suite. I then went out into the blacked-out night to buy a beer.

My first outing was not particularly successful: I had to turn back. I would advise you not to go for a walk at night in a city you have not seen in daylight, especially if there is a blackout; and under no circumstances if you are on a secret mission and carrying a forged passport. At every street corner I bumped into a constable, and if it wasn't the police then it was the SA or a sailor. Seven times they aimed a full torch beam in my face and three times they asked for my passport. I was not lying when I said I had to leave it at the hotel reception for security purposes. In the end I had to ask a policeman to take me back to the hotel. Luckily no one asked my name because it had completely slipped my mind – all the more reason to head back and take a close look at the visitors' book. I was also curious about my en-suite apartment, the likes of which I had only seen in films, where they usually had three marble steps leading up to the bath and a 2m-high dressing-room mirror with plush fur carpets up to the ankles. Not that I was expecting such luxury. I wasn't in Miami Beach or Trouville, but in a small German port city in the middle of a war.

The reception was colder than when I left, by around 2½°C perhaps. The manservant who was also the porter spoke in a slightly aggrieved tone: 'Good evening, Herr Andersen.' Thank goodness, I knew what my name was again. 'We have moved your things into a different room. We would have liked to accommodate you but the council prescribes certain minimum room rates and we must comply. You are now in Room 21 instead of the apartment, also a very nice and comfortable room. Why did you take the trouble to telephone us when it was a matter of half an hour?'

I had telephoned? That was new to me. It must have been the *Geheime Macht*! It was an insult really to the hotel staff's intelligence. How on earth could I, as a complete stranger in a blacked-out city, have made this telephone call in a blacked-out telephone kiosk dealing with unfamiliar apparatus? All this so the *Geheime Macht* could save a few marks a day while I was risking my life for them. That's all the thanks I got. I exchanged the sadly unused apartment key for one with a bigger number which also had the disadvantage of being constructed in a way that made it impossible to put in one's pocket. A heavy chain was connected to a spiky ball, like a medium-sized magnetic sea mine – I could only hope it wasn't loaded.

I glanced again at the visitors' book which revealed my name really was Andersen – Wilhelm Andersen – and I was the first civilian guest since 3 September. Sea officers stayed frequently but were not required to sign in. The book had a printed reservation page for every day of the week, showing the numbers 1 to 21. These were all the rooms the hotel had. Until the start of the war the pages were full of Müllers, Meiers and Schulzes, but from then on only blank pages. Although this may seem to make no sense, the lift was not in use and I was too lazy to walk up the stairs and go to bed, even though I was very tired. Not that I was feeling adventurous either. The long journey meant that I had not changed my clothes for three days, nor had I washed and shaved. My stomach was feeling a little uneasy as a result of keeping up with the miserable Dane who used my travel allowance to continuously eat, drink and smoke.

The room servant who was also the porter looked at his watch, disappeared for a moment and returned wearing a cap with the words 'night porter'. With the cap he had also changed his character. He was no longer busily excited. He was now patronisingly smug. 'We switch off the lights in the hall at 10 p.m. Would you not like to retire upstairs to bed?'

I did indeed but the night was still young. Even though it was not possible to see into the hall from the stairs, there was a thin wall so that every sound could be heard. I had just reached the first floor when I noticed there was something going on downstairs. I stopped to listen. A taxi had pulled up; the door bell rang. Then loud steps hurried into the hall, accompanied by voices, a rumbling, the sound of a heavy suitcase being dragged across the linoleum and then the full gamut of female laughter. I could hear quite clearly what they were saying:

'I would rather have Room 20,' said the crystal-clear female voice with a southern German accent. 'One of my friends stayed there and had a very nice time.' I could hear how the chauffeur had to be persuaded to help carry up her luggage. Then the footsteps got nearer. It wouldn't have done to be discovered eavesdropping on the stairway so I hurried up the last steps and disappeared into my room.

Number 21 was the last one on the left. As I made my way with my torch, I had only just managed to open the door with the chained convict of a key when the nightly procession arrived in the hallway. In London, where I had been in a relatively peaceful environment, I would have told myself to stop playing Cowboys and Indians, but here, in these dangerous circumstances and on enemy territory, I felt I was right to behave with militant care. I sneaked inside quietly, pulling the door gently behind me, and lay on my stomach in the dark with my ears to the ground. The steps were getting very close to my room, the heavy steps of what must have been the chauffeur, the slightly lighter steps of the porter with the suitcase dragging between them. Then the light steps of the female, her springy step like Victoria leading her chariot, followed by four tiny light steps. Then I heard the door opposite me opening, and the suitcase was dragged in. The male voices departed and everything was silent. Slightly disappointed, I stood up to investigate my new realm and looked for the light switch with the glow of my torch, which was getting fainter by the minute. There wasn't much to see. It was narrow, dull and not especially comfortable. I was disappointed that I would never discover what the apartment looked like. The shoes were to be left outside the door, the rules of the house on the door instructed, so that was what

I did. I had already taken them off. When I opened the door ajar to put my very dusty shoes in the hallway, I could see the door opposite opening for a second. I had a brief glimpse of a woman's arm, long and white with flourishing curves. The arm deposited a pair of shoes, invisible as they were outside the beam of light. She disappeared behind the closed door and left a whiff of *Echt Kölnish Wasser* cologne.

I had little experience in matters of the heart but I knew this could be the beginning of an amorous adventure. In a hotel in a port city every pretty young lady, or those who thought they were, would be expected to lock up their doors, but the failure to do so appeared to signal: 'Hello there, come on in!'

What should I do? Was it now not up to me to make the next move? I had not shaved and was only half-dressed. Should I put my clothes back on and knock gently on the door? But then my reason and caution gained the upper hand. Perhaps the lady was tired from her long journey like me and forgot to lock the door? She would be scared witless and scream for help if a man opened her door in his nightshirt and an overcoat, or in whichever way I decided to present myself. Then there would be a huge commotion resulting in the police being called. I would be arrested and they would study my papers more closely than I wished, and my cover would be blown before I even got started. No. No adventures for me tonight!

I was much too excited to go straight to sleep. I unpacked my suitcase – I had already taken out my things for the night and found my flute. With my knees pulled up in my nightshirt and my overcoat, I began to play the *Leichte Kavallerie* (*Light Cavalry*) by Franz von Suppe, very quietly, so the lady opposite could not hear me. And just in case she heard me and took the sounds of the *Cavalry* for an invitation, I locked the door.

3

COUNTER-ESPIONAGE ON HOLIDAY

Early in the morning, after a comfortable sleep, I had it. I now realised what had been missing the night before. Here the films I had watched when I was younger helped me out. What I was lacking was a proper dressing gown! My travel kit did not even stretch to pyjamas, containing as it did only two nightshirts. It wouldn't do to throw my chances away by being insufficiently dressed for a chivalric adventure in a hotel at night. It was time to treat myself with the crisp new bills of Reichsmark.

The sink in my room had two taps and the words: *chaud*, *heiß*. Hot was written clearly and in three languages, regrettably, however, only cold water came out of both taps. So I went to look for a bathroom. Desperately longing for the object of the morning's important mission (a dressing gown), I made my way out of my room dressed in my nightshirt, trousers and bare feet. It was quite simply impossible to walk past the room opposite without stealing a glance inside – the door was ajar. The mistress had flown out and had left such a mess as I had not seen before. In the middle of the bed, the little Pekinese was panting for air. The bed was not mussed up in such a way that one would expect from a person with a light sleep and of an excitable nature. No, it was obvious that the lady and her pet had spent a good hour or so playing catch under the covers. I realised now that that was the noise that had woken me up. This is why the little Pekinese was now gasping for air and not able to do his normal duty of barking at a stranger as I passed the room in my bare feet. The communal bathroom was not difficult to find as it was on the same floor. The door was wide open, the splashing noises an indication of what was inside. But the anticipated shave was no easy feat. An array of washing lines covered in pants, stockings and shirts obscured the view of the bath from which hot steam was rising in thick clouds. Two white female legs could be seen through the curtain of ladies' underwear, one up to the middle of her calf, the other almost to the knee. These shapely legs undoubtedly belonged to the same lady I had seen glimpses of the night before. I recognised the pearly tone of her skin and noticed the well-formed shape of her calves. This lovely lady was making herself known to me in instalments; perhaps fate did not want to give too much away. I was, after all, still very young and impressionable. The girl could not have heard me amongst the splashes and sound of running water and intense concentration. She was singing to the tune *Fuchs du hast die Ganz gestohlen* with her own lyrics. It sounded something like 'I would do anything for a proper bar of soap'.

I felt the strong urge to go back to my room and bring her the large bar of soap that I had in my suitcase. But again, I held back. This time it was out of a sense of moral seemliness. The two naked legs did not give any indication of whether she was wearing any of the items of clothing that one might expect in a communal area. Perhaps this was the one day she had decided, in the resoluteness of her youth and beauty, to handwash all her clothes so as to take full advantage of the washing and drying capacity of the room. I decided not to risk it and went back to my room to have a cold shave.

It was quite late by the time I was ready to go out. The porter assured me that I would find what I was looking for at the department store Loewenstein & Kohn, but he was wrong. The shop was now called German–Aryan Mens' Fashion House and had been completely 'aryanised'. The dressing gown I was shown was red, gold and black and not quite what I was looking for. All the same, I thought, it was better to have an imperfect one, and it wasn't even my own money. After I had paid, he demanded a textile-rationing coupon which I didn't have, so it was unpacked and put back on the rail. Naturally I wanted my money back but he replied that it wasn't quite so simple. He had to get approval from the *Reichsbank* in Kiel as I was a foreigner and required authorisation for payments in Reichsmark. He wasn't sure if this situation represented an exception as he was, after all, a salesman and not an accountant. Thank goodness two sailors entered the shop who came to my defence. They held the shopkeeper long enough for me to retrieve my money from the till and run off. I was out of danger but felt the morning had been wasted. I went back to the hotel, and was looking forward to the peace and quiet but I was soon to be disappointed again.

The hotel had more visitors, although it was more of an inspection: an SA official from the regional management of the Nazi Party – a tall, rude man with a face like a wolf. The conversation he was having with the hotel owner was somewhat one-sided; he was swaggering and swearing, and when the old man dared to say anything in response, he shouted at him saying he should keep his mouth shut. As soon as the old man was silent for a while, he grabbed him by the collar and yelled: 'Why are you not saying anything, don't I deserve to be answered?' The old man tried to appease him by offering one schnapps after another but every glass seemed to add to his fury. The SA man did not even notice me. He looked straight through me with his bloodshot eyes. I pushed up a chair as if I was about to watch a circus act and listened carefully.

'I've been watching you,' the official continued. 'Don't feign innocence now. We all know what your wife was saying in the steam room, criticising the system. We have to stamp out the vermin that are protesting, all of them, get rid of them! Do you understand? We have to break the resistance, do you hear me? These brazen Czech students, even when they were lined up against the wall, they still proclaimed their paroles. If I had been in charge I would not allow this to happen, I would not tolerate such defiant behaviour. They would be humbly grateful for the merciful execution. One man was so grateful to me that of his own free will he made me his sole heir only fifteen minutes before he died. Only unfortunately he turned out to be plunged in debt. Keep your mouth shut, I wasn't asking your opinion. Where is your portrait of Hitler? All I can see is an oil painting of Venice, the Marcus Square and gondolas; away with this Jewish nonsense!'

With a wide stance he took out a heavy pistol and aimed it at the poor innocent print that was hanging high in the corner. He would have had a perfect shot if I had not just then brushed his elbow when I walked past. The bullet hit some pipework leading to the floor above which immediately started to leak slightly. I hoped it wasn't the wastewater from the toilet upstairs. The SA man stared at me in disbelief, slightly sobered by the incident.

'Herr Andersen from Denmark,' the hotelier introduced me. 'A gentleman from our neutral neighbours is on holiday here because he is sympathetic to our aims. I am sure he is very sorry to have bumped into you while you were preparing to shoot.'

'On the contrary,' I ventured in my convoluted German. 'It's our custom in Denmark when we are happy to interrupt the person just as they are about to shoot. It is easy to aim well when there is no interruption, but a true marksman will always hit their target even when they are disturbed! Come on, I'll show you, you try hitting this dear old man while I keep bumping into you. You will see you will not hit him.'

I wanted to be alone with the SA man; perhaps he would share some of his secrets in his state of drunkenness. I would not have taken such drastic measures otherwise, but it worked; the old man gathered his things and disappeared as quick as a shot, leaving behind half a bottle of Griotte. The SA man with pistol in hand stared at me stupidly in the middle of the hallway. I would have liked him to use up his munitions so as to be out of danger but I felt the hotel did not deserve it because it would be they who would have to call a plumber to fix the pipe. After half an hour the bottle was nearly empty and we were on first-name terms.

'*Prost, mein Junge*, to your health!' he said, with every glass he finished. We had taken off our jackets and I was wearing his cap. It was much too big. He had smoked nearly all of my cigarettes and was now showing me pictures of his girlfriends, the current and the two most recent. From my experience as a dentist, I knew that once the confessions start, for example when the anaesthetic kicks in, it usually goes on and on. I was trying very hard to pay attention even though the furniture in the hallway was starting to spin.

'Dear boy, have you heard the latest? Our secret weapon isn't the mines. I'll tell you what it really is.' I think it was my fate as a conspirator, just when I thought I was getting close, it all went up in smoke. 'Now you listen to me,' he said. 'I saw this at the drill ground, a type of ammunition that never needs to be replaced. The bullet hits the enemy and then comes back to the person shooting, slips back into the casing and lines up in the cartridge belt ready to be used again. If the bullet hits a Jew it goes through a rigorous process of disinfection. But don't tell anyone you heard it from me or else I'll end up in Buchenwald. Ha-ha.' He was so knocked out by his sense of humour that he fell and crashed under the marble table, his legs and arms askew. I finished the last glass of Griotte and slipped out of the hall. The stairs to the second floor were heaving up and down as I climbed. I had to hold on tightly to the banisters so as not to fall headfirst down.

The *Geheime Macht* was an unpleasant master. I was going through a similar experience as a friend of mine who had joined a foreign legion, *not* the Austrian. In the barracks he ended up the only person without a charge; all other officers and sergeants were his superiors. As there was no one else to rule over, they spent all day training, guiding and generally ordering him about. It was the same for me. The whole city was full of agents of the *Geheime Macht* who seemed to have nothing better to do than feed me instructions – by word of mouth, whispered secretly in the dark streets of the city, or by letters and furtive notes. And, as would later become clear, by drastically interfering in my private affairs. I had to ask myself, if the city was really so full of dissidents, why do they restrict their activities to secret radio stations and other similar simple feats? Why don't they just seize power instead? The instructions I received from my superiors were not consistent. One note said: 'walk straight, don't drag your feet. Don't keep turning around, you're arousing suspicion.' Ten minutes later another note arrived saying quite the contrary. 'Not so bold. You are an unassuming, foreign civilian, strongly impressed by the superior military force.' It was hard to do the right thing! And I felt I didn't deserve such criticism. I thought I was doing really well on the whole, apart from a few minor slip-ups. For example, there was the matter of the Danish national anthem in the coffee house. They were playing it in my honour as word had spread that a young man from Denmark who was favourably inclined was here on holiday. Of course I didn't recognise the tune and remained in my seat. Was I to stand to attendance at the sound of every piece of music that may have had relevance? I noticed the stares, but thought they were only out of sympathy for the neutral neighbour. By the time I had realised what was going on I was in no position to read any of the many notes I was receiving from all directions because I had become the object of everyone's attention.

Most of the instructions were in connection with my lovely, but still sadly unknown, neighbour. 'Do not take up contact with the lady in the room opposite.' This note had been deposited in my toothbrush yesterday, but I only discovered it the next morning because I only brush my teeth in the morning. Then on the breakfast menu: 'Lady in Room 21 most likely a spy from the other side.' The menu itself was less exciting: lentils with bacon, and bacon with lentils, that was the extent of my choice for the morning. There were further warnings not to engage, but all equally vague. It seemed a wasted opportunity for only a slight suspicion.

By now it was the third evening in the hotel and I still hadn't really spoken to her and only caught rare glimpses of her. Up until now we had made do with the briefest of nods of recognition, nothing more. One morning I had purchased two small bouquets of violets and left them in front of her door: one in each shoe – flowers were damned expensive in these parts. Later that day I found a gingerbread heart in my room, which much have been from her. It was very dry and lacked honey and spices, but on it was written *Ich liebe Dich*, I love you.

One shouldn't underestimate one's enemy, especially if they are German, a people of martial tendencies. I was prepared for everything: a furtive attack on the flank, for example, but that was not what she had in store for me. In the hotel all was still and dark and I was feeling my way down the corridor when I noticed a strange object moving in front of my door. I aimed my torch in its direction. There she was cowering on my doorstep, crouching down in a blue corduroy jacket with a deep v-neck. Her blonde hair was held back with a band and her smooth face was turned towards me. At first I didn't know where I had seen this face before, and then I remembered: it was the face, neck and arms I had seen on the poster in blacked-out London at the precise moment my fate had changed.

The girl was holding her dog with her left hand so he didn't roll off her lap. The other hand was held out towards me in an exaggerated manner of a beggar. In her clear, deep voice she implored: 'This poor old girl would be grateful for some comfort.'

Now would have been the right time for another warning from my colleagues, something like 'look into her eyes and you are lost' would not have gone amiss. Her eyes were like a mountain stream, forging its way through cliffs and down ravines. Eyes that grabbed, conquered and coerced. Those eyes were now looking at me and all I could do was throw caution to the wind as I was usurped by the rapids and carried away. I was ready to face whatever danger was heading my way, possessed as I was by the beatific sensation of a commander of a light cavalry facing batteries of enemy cannon: knowing the end was nigh but it would be a damned good fight all the same.

I knelt down and picked up the girl. She was incredibly heavy, much more so than I expected, and if she hadn't thrown her arms around my neck, we would have both toppled over. I am athletic, strong and perfectly capable of holding a girl in my arms who is bigger and stronger than I am, but if it had been the other way around, if she had been carrying me, then that would have looked more natural. The dog slid from her lap to the ground and snapped ungraciously at my trouser legs. For a moment we both didn't speak, for my part because I was gasping for air and she because she was trying to placate the dog. Then she began to stroke my arm saying, 'My, what lovely fabric this is!' In the hallway a floorboard creaked, a sure indication that someone was there. We both held our breath. She whispered to me, 'Someone is spying on us, come into my room. And bring your flute.' I lowered her on to the ground and she slipped into her room, pulling the dog in with her.

I couldn't find the flute straight away because I wasn't allowed to turn the light on before drawing the blinds. Just as I pulled the cord, I heard footsteps coming towards my room. The key that was in the door was turned and pulled out. The steps moved away; I was locked in.

After a while I received a note through the door: 'Where are you, why don't you come over?' I responded that I was locked in and shoved the note back under the door. After a few minutes the second note arrived: 'Be patient. I love you and will wait.' Initially I added, 'Be strong', but then I thought she might misinterpret this and be offended. She was strong, particularly around the hips, as I noticed when I picked her up. So I crossed the words out vehemently and wrote instead: 'Good night.' And that was the end of our correspondence.

It was a wonderful night, full of dreams of the girl. In the morning I woke up to the sound of another note being pushed through the door. My first thought was that it was from her and immediately rushed up to retrieve it. Sadly it was from the *Geheime Macht*. The word *Befehl* (order) was the heading and further instructions followed:

Report to Obermaschinenmaat G. Griesemann at daybreak: Old Sailor's Home, North Quay 27. Follow his orders unconditionally. Do not wear Danish badge. Permit is enclosed.

That was my contract – a grey paper sealed with official stamps and signatures. Fair enough – I would show them. I tried the door to my room; it was now open. Which one of my numerous superiors was responsible for playing the part of providence and censorship, I was not to find out. I got dressed with more haste than usual. As I got to the door of my neighbour's room I put two chocolates in her going-out shoes, one in each shoe. It was all I could offer in terms of a gift. I hoped she wouldn't put them on without checking first. I must have stood there a moment or two, contemplative and indecisive, when suddenly the door opened and a pair of strong arms pulled me into the room. Like a fawn in the clutches of a boa constrictor, I was helpless in her arms and found myself entwined in a long kiss. My room looked out on to the courtyard; her's had a view of the market. As it happened I could see very little past her rosy cheeks and well-formed ear but I had full view of the church's clock tower. Eight minutes into our kiss I was getting nervous on account of the urgency of the instructions in my pocket. There was so much I had to ask her before my departure. She showed no signs of letting me go on her own accord so I prised away my mouth and asked her, 'What is your name?'

'Christine.'

'Are you working for the German counter-espionage movement?'

'Yes, that's my occupation, but I'm currently not on duty. I'm on holiday here.'

'That's okay then.'

'Yes, my darling, everything is okay.'

Lovely as it was, I really could not justify a moment longer in her presence since it was long after daybreak. As I was walking down the stairs feeling light-hearted and uplifted, like after a full German breakfast, I remembered too late that I had meant to warn her about the liqueur pralines in her shoes.

4

THE NEW ROLE

The old sailors' home was no more than ten minutes away and was a rambling decrepit building with an old-fashioned gable roof. There was a sign over the door, decorated with a garland of pine twigs: 'A Warm Welcome to our Heroes!' A crowd of people surrounded the building in a boisterous and exuberant mood, which was a rare sight here as one usually sees only sullen faces. The SS guarded the inside of the building and municipal police were cordoning off the street side to keep away the curious masses.

It didn't take long to find out what was going on, but then this was Germany where everyone was desperate to share each other's business. A U-boat had returned which had apparently won a battle with a British fleet. The crew had arrived only an hour ago with their baggage, grey and dirty with three weeks' beard growth. They had sunk a battleship and two armoured cruisers. They were claiming it was two battleships and a whole flotilla of cruisers. The longer we stood there the more impressive the victory became. All this attention was not exactly beneficial to my task but I had my orders to follow. I made my way to the officer at the front and explained why I was there. He answered in the deepest North Sea bass tone, 'I'm sure you would like to meet one of our heroes but visitors are not allowed.'

It almost seemed he was one of the heroes himself. I showed him my permit but he only shook his head, unsatisfied. He pointed towards the SS Kommandant who shook his head even more, but at least admitted me into the antechamber where another SS man proceeded to frisk me in search of weapons. This was most unpleasant for me because I was incredibly ticklish. He found nothing of interest apart from a tobacco pipe which he promptly dismantled, expecting to find a machine gun inside. Visibly disappointed, he handed it back to me, leaving me to put it together again. He sent an orderly to fetch the sailor but in such a way that I understood nothing of what was going on. I had to concede that the SS had the right tactic when it came to conspirators. It seemed to work because the next I knew the Kommandant was reluctantly shrugging his shoulders and shouting to the orderly, 'Lead this gentleman to Obermaschinenmaat Griesemann!' The word 'gentleman' was pronounced with such contempt he may well have said 'individual' and it wouldn't have sounded any less derisive. I was led to the first floor, not like an esteemed visitor but more like a prisoner being led to the gallows.

Since receiving my order this morning I had been preparing myself to meet this Unterseebootobermaschinenmaat Gotthold Griesemann. I pictured him as a tall, strong, imposing, real German sailor with an open gaze and booming voice, my future friend and helper in my fight against Nazi rabble. My escort announced my presence: 'Your visitor, Herr Maschinenmaat,' and shoved me into a room consisting of a metal bed, metal oven, metal washstand and strangely pungent air.

'That will be it,' said the sergeant with a thin whiny voice as he waved the orderly away. Now alone, we looked at each other in mutual distrust and immediate instinctive dislike. This was my friend and helper? A measly little sea rat, not a seaman! The petty officer was not even ready for visitors. He was in ersatz cotton underwear next to the washstand looking into a mirror fragment in which you could barely see both nostrils at the same time, contemplating his three weeks' growth of dirty blonde beard. From neck to waist he dressed in a dazzling white long-sleeved bodice, evidently just thrown on. His long johns and thick socks were less dazzling and a sure indication of three weeks at sea. This was surely where the not quite fresh smell stemmed from. He carried on what he was doing and had a minute quantity of shaving soap skewered on his knife. He was deliberating how to use this precious relic in the service of this necessary shave without forfeiting the entire quantity. He began to soap his face without taking any further notice of me. As I began to break into questions, explanations and introductions, he waved me away and said abruptly: 'Give me your passport!'

In nervous haste and somewhat anxiously, he leafed through the passport with this left hand while scraping through the unruly growth of facial hair with his other. Artfully and with an unflatteringly cross-eyed expression, he alternately looked into the fragment of the mirror and then again at the passport. Then he looked at me, 'Why don't you take your clothes off? Come on, play up!'

Under normal circumstances it would have been quite pleasant to rid myself of coat and vest in a stuffy, overheated room. I obeyed but thought with clenched teeth, what does this bastard want from me? I was disgusted, but not frightened; confident that something he would say or do would shed light on the hitherto completely incomprehensible situation. I stared at him and that was the best thing I could have done. From under the beard stubble and soapsuds a familiar face emerged. It was the man whose photograph was stuck in my passport. If it hadn't been so hot, my brain might have worked more quickly, but as it was I could only slowly piece together the situation. It became clearer by the minute. I had been picked out only because I bore a striking resemblance to a petty officer in the German navy. He was part of the conspiracy and needed to leave the country with the help of the neutral passport that I was carrying: not a bad idea! With some palpable relief I slipped out of my trousers.

'We're swapping clothes?' I enquired naively.

I must have sounded as thick as a plank as he now mocked me: 'If you think it's enough to exchange business cards and buttonholes ...'

'And you will show me what to do in your place?' I responded, now somewhat intimidated.

'And what else – you stupid monkey face,' he replied frostily. 'Do you really think an illiterate frog like you with no brain could last in my position for more than five minutes? I'm not risking it. You will remain in bed until I'm gone. Here, take this powder. You'll get a fever, just enough so that they take you to hospital. There you will say nothing and no one will know you. They'll leave you alone for three days at least, enough time for me to escape over the border.'

That was all fair and well, but what was to happen to me when the fever had passed? No one seemed to have thought of that. We began exchanging our clothes. It wasn't easy to part with the lovely new suit that I was so proud of, in exchange for a uniform of unknown quality. Slowly I began to empty my pockets of my watch, money and everything else. But I misjudged my new partner. He not only saw my clothes as his, but also all that they contained. He slapped my wrist with the blunt end of the razor and hissed at me: 'Hands off! Take your thieving paws off my things!'

This was too much for me. I couldn't just sit back and put up with it. Without letting him see how much my hand was hurting, I stared fearfully at his razor as if there was a poisonous spider or scorpion sitting on it and screeched: 'For goodness sake, throw that thing away.'

I had judged him right; his nerves were shot. He threw the razor into the corner without thinking. It was my experience that one shouldn't attack anyone holding a knife. As soon as his hands were empty I punched him on the nose and started to sway. He was blind with rage and prepared his punch at my forehead. I had already worked out that he was no good at boxing and ducked his blow, so that he lost balance. With a sturdy kick I forced him into the opposite corner. Just then the door opened. A tall man in captain's uniform surveyed the scene benevolently. We both sprang to attention. It was hard to say who looked more guilty. But the captain was in a happy mood and not inclined to view a tussle between two half-undressed sailors with displeasure. 'Have fun boys, but behave!' he said with a twinkle and was gone again.

I regained composure more quickly than the sergeant, but then it wasn't my captain who had just interrupted us. I continued the fight. Capitalising on my advantage of having shoes, I jumped towards my sock-wearing adversary's stomach. I brought him to the ground. He gasped for air. It was my luck that at that point he asked for water. There was a glass of water by the sink, which albeit not fresh, would do for my purposes. I spotted the powder meant for me and quickly dissolved it in the glass, forcing him to drink it. He put up some resistance but I held his nose and poured it down his throat.

For research purposes I would love to have studied the effects of the drug but I wasn't sure if the circumstances allowed it. Although unconscious, I wasn't sure how long he would stay that way and whether his unconscious state was a result of the right dosage or the kick in the stomach.

At any rate he was now peaceful and for the time being I could do whatever I wanted with him. I helped him to get dressed: braces, tie and shoelaces were the most challenging. Then I put the passport in his pocket. At this stage I could have reversed the entire transaction as my partner was putting up no resistance. I could have pocketed the passport, taken back my clothes, put him back in his uniform and we would have each gone our separate ways. But I didn't want that. My adventure had begun and I had developed a taste for it. The role of a 'victorious hero' was one I was eager to relish. Besides, I was doubtful that the *Geheime Macht* would have let me get away with anything other than their plans. They had me well and truly under their control.

The current situation left little time for further contemplation: I had to act and fast. My victim was now slumped on the shabby seat of the only chair, wearing my fine English travel suit which was just slightly tight on him as he was a little bit bigger than I was. Every few minutes I had to shake him otherwise he would have fallen into a deep slumber. But time was precious and I, or he as the visitor, had been in the room far too long. I fed him some rum from his bottle. I had some fine cognac in my (now his) civilian clothes but I wasn't inclined to waste it. The rum did the trick and he was back on his feet and we hobbled down the stairs together.

As little as I was accustomed to wearing a uniform, I noticed straight away the benefits it entailed. That a civilian had arrived an hour ago stone cold sober and was now decidedly intoxicated, did not raise any eyebrows and was seen as perfectly natural. One sailor shouted to me: 'Parade at 11 o'clock, don't get too drunk!'

I could only wave back good-naturedly. He seemed to know me well but I knew neither his name nor what our relationship was. VIPs were arriving in a constant stream so it was not difficult to find an empty taxi. I pushed the bumbling passenger into his seat and instructed the driver to make the journey as smooth and slow as possible. The interlude with the sailor, who may have been my mate, had made me realise that I was ill prepared for my role. I made the most of the last precious minutes we had. I asked one question after the other, much faster than he could answer:

'Who's your best friend? Do you have family? Will anyone visit you, how does one salute a passing officer from a car, do you get an advance on your pay?' Whenever he threatened to slip into oblivion I started shaking him until he started to talk again. The question and answer game didn't yield very much. It all went so quickly I could only remember half of what he said. Although we were travelling at a snail's pace we were already approaching the hotel. Twenty metres away from the hotel I stopped the car and deposited my victim on the street. The porter was standing in the entrance. My patient approached him hoping for a bed for the night and some well-earned rest. I shouted from my hiding place: 'Watch out, he's had his fill!' I then asked the taxi driver to turn around and drive me back.

I didn't get very far. At the first junction we were stopped by a red light. As the taxi waited with its engine running I heard commotion and shouting from the direction of the hotel. As more and more people ran towards the hotel I couldn't help myself, despite it being close to eleven o'clock. I paid the driver, jumped out of the taxi and joined the crowd and the dramatic scene that was unfolding. The crowd was now so close to the entrance that I couldn't make out anything. I could not see beyond the heads of the people bigger than me. I was wary of getting so close to the building that I would be recognised, considering I was wearing neither a mask nor a false beard. I couldn't ask what was going on. The others seemed to know as little as I did.

Only once I had crawled through the legs of a bow-legged fisherman was I able to survey the scene properly.

The same civilian who had only been Wilhelm Andersen for less than an hour was now held by the shoulders between two SS men. The Kommandant was holding up the familiar Danish passport. People were shouting: 'Let him go!'

The Kommandant responded: 'Back off, mind your own business, anyone who doesn't will be arrested!'

The crowd consisted of workers, market women and a few members of the Hitler Youth who started jumping up and down delighted that something was finally happening, and also so they could see more easily. The porter stood distraught in the entrance of the hotel repeating the same thing over and over: 'The gentleman came highly recommended to us by the organisation of ethnic Germans', but no one paid any attention to him.

The scene was not yet complete. Christine, the woman I had previously kissed for eight minutes, came rushing down the steps fearing that her lover had come to harm and wanting to help. Elbowing her way past the crowd, the force caused the men to let go of their victim who, finding himself free, made his way towards the entrance of the hotel in search of the long-awaited bed for the night. He paid little heed to the words of the unknown woman who was calling to him to 'Run away! I'll help you. *Run*! I won't let them arrest you.'

But the leader of the SS patrol was in no mood for fun and games. With routine movement he disengaged the firing pin of the heavy pistol and aimed the barrel at the fugitive. The sound of two faint blasts was almost lost in the noise of the crowd that was rapidly dispersing. Cyclists mounted their bicycles, drivers of heavy-load vehicles started up their engines and drove off. Then the crowd gathered again; there was something else to see now. A soldier was approaching the scene towering amongst the masses. It seemed as if he was riding a horse, but no, he was only incredibly tall: a grey-haired Reichswehr Major. He was now confronting the SS Kommandant: 'Why don't you pick a different victim? A Czech, Pole or Jew maybe, but shooting down harmless German civilians will not go unpunished!'

The answer was cutting: 'Herr Major, I thank you for your advice but the Gestapo does not require it. We are expert at finding traitors in our midst whether they are in civilian clothes or wearing epaulettes.'

What impressive and bellicose personalities these Germans were. It would have been an ideal place to enact *Julius Caesar* or *Coriolanus*! The SS man gathered his patrol and withdrew. Others marched off with their faces set in soldier-like expressions, their backs straight. No one would have thought that a woman had nearly knocked them off their feet only moments ago. No one paid any further attention to the dead body. The poor little man was a sorry sight, lying in a dusty heap on the ground with a dark stain on his back that was gradually getting bigger.

At least I had been Wilhelm Andersen for a pleasant week as a neutral guest, with a suitcase full of lovely things and Reichsmark aplenty to spend at my leisure. I had dined well, spoken to pleasant people and kissed a beautiful woman. He, on the other hand, had hardly benefited: a few minutes in a taxi being bombarded with questions, then moments of being pushed and shoved around and finally shot down from behind. It was also a shame about all the nice clothes and other things, including my flute. It would all be ransacked and confiscated. In any case, it was time for me to make a move.

The square was now nearly empty and I was starting to look conspicuous and someone might recognise me. Christine was still standing by the entrance, looking tired and dishevelled. The porter was trying to placate her and move her back inside the hotel. She had at one point tried to throw herself at the dead body but was held back by a constable who said no one was allowed to touch the corpse before the police had examined it. She gave up resisting and was led sobbing inside. I made no attempt to reveal myself to her. It would have been an ugly form of suicide.

Apropos suicide, I remembered the parade at eleven o'clock; what was I still doing here? I quickly looked at the church tower and saw I had ten minutes to get there. My name was Gotthold Griesemann and I was a petty officer in the German navy. I had to get to the parade in time even if I had no idea what I was meant to do there. I had a task to fulfil and I was not giving up the fight. There was no taxi to be seen so I started to jog. After around 100 paces I wasn't sure anymore that I was heading in the right direction and stopped to ask civilians the way. I had forgotten that my cap showed the number of the victorious U-boat, and this proved to have its advantages. As petty officer of U-boat XY the crowd started to shout as they lifted me on to their shoulders. They wanted to carry me back in a slow celebratory procession, but I shouted, 'Faster, faster, I must get back', and finally they started to run with me on their shoulders like a drunken aeroplane. It was a good thing I wasn't very heavy.

All the windows in the tiny side streets were pulled open, gangs of children, a milk float and all the dogs in the city joined the party. One of the boys got hold of my right shoe for a moment and said, panting to his neighbour, 'Look at the quality of the shoes.' He was reading the well-known English label on the inside. It was my own shoe since we hadn't got round to swapping them. 'I bet they are looted,' the other one replied, also breathless. I was able to dangle my sock-clad foot back into the shoe they were holding towards me. That at least was only a 'minor accident'.

At two minutes to eleven my cavalcade set me down and the guard shouted out to me: 'Watch it, you'll get a dunking.' I didn't know what to answer. Was this how the guards normally spoke to petty officers or was he just displaying *Schadenfreude* at my unfortunate situation? Was this the norm?

The solution presented itself in an unusual form. A group of petty officers and seamen, all of them ready for the parade with the appropriate string belts and decorations, had been waiting for me at the top of the first flight of stairs. They all pounced on me. One of them swapped my cap, hung cords, straps and various attachments, belts were pulled, strings fastened and within thirty seconds I was bedecked and adorned like a Christmas tree.

'The *Schweinehund* doesn't deserve our assistance,' one of the helpers piped up as they carried out their finishing touches and led me outside into the courtyard. Various battalions of sailors in their finest military apparel were gathered in strict formations. We had free rein to converse and stand around as we wished, almost as though it was our birthday. At the same time various dignitaries at the other end of the courtyard were drawing our commander into polite conversation.

'When we look at one another,' one of the group commented. He was a skinny, tall man and like the others spoke like an intellectual. 'When we look at one another properly, it is almost as if we hardly recognise each other anymore.' He was running his hand over his chin as he said: 'Not only does washing and shaving become almost painful after a long absence, it seems to reveal unknown facial characteristics.'

'Certainly, it's like being amongst strangers,' came the grating voice of a large, fat man with watery eyes, his blonde hair closely shorn around his round head. He was called the Baron.

'Allow me to introduce myself,' he said. 'My name is Schmitt, Oswald von Schmitt. Very pleased to meet you. Hope you're enjoying the day.'

Nobody laughed. This wasn't unusual, I surmised, so he felt it necessary to arrange for further amusement, turning towards me.

'Hey, Griesemann,' he growled. 'You don't need to worry about anyone not recognising you, even with a clean shave. Now pay attention Gotthold,' he crowed with an affected commanding voice. 'Eyes to the right!'

Everyone stared at me expectantly. This was one of those moments where I was grateful for my razor-sharp intuition. They were expecting something from me – that much was clear. They were staring at my eyes, another clue. I had it! My predecessor, may he rest in peace, was cross-eyed! At the command, eyes to the right, I turned my head as ordered and in a painful squint I made one eye dance to the left while the other went as ordered to the right. The things one learns as a child can come in very useful as a grown-up. I was never any good at literary history or geography, but my two strengths were those that were taught secretly outside of regular lessons: squinting and wriggling my ears. My attempt at eyes to the right was a success. The laughter was raucous. The Baron slapped me so hard I was afraid he had broken my shoulder blade. I was about to explain the difference between appreciation and assault when our captain, nervously nestling against his weapon, shouted 'Attention!'

We scampered to our places. Professional soldiers had once confirmed to me, a parade is something terrible and can often leave more unpleasant memories than heavy fighting. It was even worse for me. Many years ago in a youth organisation I had learned a little bit of marching, saluting and how to hold a rifle, but this was something else. I didn't know any of the instructions and didn't even know the names of the men to my left and right. I clenched my teeth and copied everything the others were doing. I was doing all right I thought. I was concentrating so hard, I couldn't follow any of the speeches or who was overseeing us. It might have been good if I had made a bit more effort to discern what was going on. Then it wouldn't have been such a big surprise when they made the next announcement. I jumped out of my skin when the captain called out 'Obermaschinenmaat Griesemann'.

I automatically took three paces forward, clicked my heels and saluted. I must have seen it on a film. I was directly opposite our captain, although he towered over me because he was much taller. He fumbled amongst the cords and straps of my uniform, shook my hand and said: 'You deserve it comrade. My heartfelt congratulations. About turn!'

Three steps backwards and I was back in my row. On my uniform I was now carrying the Iron Cross First Class. After me another three sailors were decorated. They received the Iron Cross Second Class. Those who were honoured had to step forward and the other navy detachments marched past and left through the gate to the courtyard. The area emptied itself and the ceremony came to a natural end. We were dismissed and summoned for lunch. It wasn't very good and if this was a special day, I wasn't looking forward to normal days!

After the meal we were off duty. At least I could remember which room was mine. No one had bothered to tidy up. Everything was as we had left it in the morning. There was a coal fire burning which made the thin iron walls glow red. I was on the hunt for anything that might compromise me, so I could add it to the flames. There was what was left of the medicine in its package. It would have been enough for an analysis but I thought better of it. Then I started to look for the permit but remembered that the guards had taken it off us when we left. A packet of traveller's currency for Mr Wilhelm Andersen was of no use to me now and was, moreover, incriminating, so I threw it into the fire.

I got undressed, removed the English branding from my shoes (which sadly meant I had to cut a hole into the lining) and took stock. In one corner I could see my navy suitcase with my full new name. The lid was open. All that was in it was now mine but sadly the inheritance was somewhat lacking. It was a dubious trousseau comprising the following: threadbare undergarments; a few bottles of cheap liquor of poor quality; shoes I could not wear; a mouth organ; tobacco; a box filled with postcards; and finally, a fat portfolio of photographs depicting naked ladies, some so ugly I wondered if they were cut out of a medical textbook showing sufferers of scrofula. I felt a bit like an ermine waking up after a deep sleep to find I had metamorphosed into a skunk or something similar. I wasn't just thinking this because of the smutty photographs or the quality of the undergarments; there is no shame in being poor and tastes can differ. But the diary I found at the bottom of the trunk was meticulously kept and gave further insight into his dour and unsympathetic character. I planned to study this tome as well as I could, memorising as much as possible now and saving the work-related passages for later. For now I was interested in his, or should I say my, personal life. Just think of yourself in my situation: any moment the door could open and an unsavoury female could enter throwing herself at me who might turn out to be my mother, sister or even wife. I had to be prepared.

The diary was not only in chronological order, there were also pages devoted to specific subjects and statistics. I found the page devoted to his love life. His floozies had no surnames; they were called Lia, Mia, Lola, Mimi – simple names and easy to remember. Every name was followed by an entry of three or four numbers. I was confused. It could not be their age because some were well under 10 or even over 90. I also dismissed any purely physiological statistics – there were fractions and numbers such as 12a. What could it mean? After closely studying the calculations for a good measure of time I finally had it. The first numeral was the house number. There was no point looking for a street name as his 'girlfriends' were all found in the same type of back alley of a harbour. He was obviously capable of remembering the individual street names by heart. The second numeral was the room number. This was where I found '12a' and the like. The third rubric contained the remuneration value they were expecting, presumably proportional to their youth and beauty. It began with 5 marks and went no higher than 15.50. It took me some time to figure out the final category where there were numbers such as 5, 70 and accompanied by a plus or minus. I had to go back to the narrative part of the diary to work out what these meant. Minus was money advanced and plus signified money he had borrowed. He was not a noble character. Those ladies in the 10-mark category were often only paid 5, or if they were too energetic he even only paid 3 marks. Where there was no number to be found, no monetary transaction had taken place. The solution to this numerical mystery was insignificant to my future because I didn't maintain friendship with prostitutes. On the plus side, it had offered good mental training and invaluable insight into the character of the person I was meant to embody.

The petty officer entered the room (there was no knocking on doors in these quarters) and led me to the captain. I was happy to be interrupted as I was getting bored of studying the past of a stranger. Judging by his stripes he was of equal rank and by the way he treated me on my special day I got the feeling that I had often disappointed him in the past. I tried my luck: 'Will you lend me 2 marks?'

'No, you *Schweinehund*. You never pay me back,' was his answer. It appeared that my predecessor had burnt all his bridges with his colleagues so it was a good thing the captain had nothing against me. The building where the captain held office was a requisitioned school and he had taken over the library and equipment rooms. There was row after row of books, several coloured prints showing the battle of the Teutoburg Forest, a historic village and the coronation of Charles the Great. There was also a glass case with a stuffed penguin and an otter, obviously not on speaking terms because they each faced in different directions.

The captain was not alone. On the narrow side of the desk was an unattractive, no longer young, gentleman in SS uniform with horn-rimmed glasses and a shiny bald head. I couldn't discern his rank but could sense that he was a high official. He did not return my military greeting. My captain thanked me with particular warmth and offered me a seat on the sofa. I sat on the far corner ready to jump to attention if required.

'Griesemann,' the captain began. I sprang up.

'Stay seated,' he said smiling. 'This is your special day and you should be treated well.'

The Nazi was rummaging amongst the various objects on the desk, looking bored, until he found something that looked like a miniature bayonet and started cleaning his nails with it. He showed little interest in our conversation and yawned intermittently. 'Griesemann,' he started again, 'without any fault of your own, I am certain, you have been drawn into an ugly espionage affair. The Gestapo want me to send you to Berlin to be interrogated but I refused.

I need all my people, especially my trusted *Torpedomaat*, and I had heard that the Gestapo often don't return people they take. What was that, *Herr Polizei Vizepräsident*?'

The man could not answer because he was now busy cleaning his teeth with the mini-bayonet and was in the midst of a campaign with a bridge on one of his molars on the left. He just waved his fat hand at an angle of 110°, which seemed to mean 'lets forget about all that'. My heart was bursting with pride at the thought that my captain was protecting me against the almighty Gestapo. How many battleships must you have sunk to be able to talk fearlessly to these monsters?

'We have come to the agreement,' the captain said, 'that I will interrogate you myself with the kind assistance of *Herr Vizepräsident*. So be prepared. You have nothing to worry about but please promise that you will tell the truth. Let me proceed with an explanation of the situation.'

The Nazi who was pretending not to listen stared at me with his fish eyes as if to say, 'heaven help us'. The captain paused and leaned courteously towards the police official, giving him the opportunity to say something. He remained silent and gave a little wave again, thus permitting the questioning that was not to his taste to continue.

The captain continued: 'A suspect was stopped by the Gestapo and his papers were inspected. He was carrying a forged Danish passport that was linked to a dangerous group of political terrorists. The Gestapo were aware of the passport number and were watching his moves so we are certain there is no mistake. The suspect came to see you, gaining access with a forged permit. You were together for one hour and you were seen taking him to the front gate, perhaps even further. Now you tell me with all openness and honesty all you know. What do you know of the man, his cause, what did he ask you and what did he even want from you? Don't worry, you have nothing to fear. The Gestapo rendered him harmless. He was shot while attempting to flee.'

With these words the police functionary hammered his fist on the table so hard that the letter scales danced up and down and the globe turned itself by about a hand's width. I could now examine New Zealand more closely, which up to a minute ago remained invisible. The captain jumped. People who stay on a U-boat for weeks and weeks under water are left feeling jumpy with nerves. The Nazi policeman shouted: 'Sir, you are going too far with your openness. You're ruining my plans!'

'Never mind, *Herr Vizepräsident*,' said the captain, who had now regained composure and was smiling. 'Your notes are on the table. I can read your old-fashioned stenography. I was just reading your note: "The friend is in the next room and has confessed all." Let us leave the dead in peace and not confuse the living.'

The Nazi policeman's anger now intensified. Impatience and heightened concentration were evident on his forehead in the form of beads of perspiration. He demanded with forced politeness: 'Perhaps you would allow me now, Herr …', and here he checked his note, 'Griesemann, to ask you some questions?' He moved his head up and down with the result that the muscles in his neck expanded and contracted like the bellows of an accordion. Then he pulled a crumpled piece of paper out of his jacket pocket. It was on cheap lined paper, and he read out:

Dear Mother, it is awful here, the air is foul, the food terrible, all this only so that the bigwigs can afford a bigger castle for their actress girlfriends and a newer Mercedes for themselves …

He did not finish and started shouting at me: 'Did you write this?' At least I knew I had a mother.

'No,' I answered. 'I'm not envious of those in power. They are perfectly entitled to their actress girlfriends and their castles, and if you don't believe me, you can check my handwriting. Here, I'll give you a sample.' This could have been a grave error but luckily it gave me the opportunity to get up and cross the room. When I first entered the room he had been ostentatiously looking in the other direction, and with me sitting down he would not have been able to see my Iron Cross because it was hidden from view under the table. Now his eyes clocked it. Because it's a black and white band, and it is not the done soldierly thing to wash or chemically clean it, even he could tell that my decoration was brand new. This made him stand up. After pocketing the miniature bayonet he pointed at me with his fat, now halfway clean fingers. 'When was this fellow given the Iron Cross First Class?'

'A few hours ago,' the captain responded cheerfully. 'The man is responsible for the torpedo that has made world history for the German navy.'

The SS man was crushed. 'You decorated this person,' he repeated, 'and you probably did not realise he was a political suspect. We have been watching him for months. The web was closing and now this!'

'Military honours,' my captain retorted with pride, 'are not bestowed for political reliability.'

'That's all very well,' said the SS man, 'but we will not win a war with such sentimentalities.' He sat down again and I followed suit.

For a few minutes no one spoke and I could hear the school's clock ticking. Then he started again, now antagonised and lacking passion: 'You are already proven guilty. You did not even try to deny it and there is nothing for you to say because you have been under constant surveillance. I am unable to convict a newly decorated soldier, that would be a mistake and also distasteful. I'm not saying we have never executed a soldier with such an accolade, only normally there are at least a few years between decoration and justice. That means the army does not feel the lack of tact so strongly. I know you have committed treason but I do not feel I can put that into protocol. I would be grateful if you could help me to put together something credible I can account for. Your captain, whom I now understand better, has already tried to inform you and I will now finish the story with pleasure. I'm sure you know the facts better than we do but please do the honourable thing and explain to me the one point I am unable to understand. We know that the criminal came to visit you with a forged permit. When you were asked about the man, you said to let him through and that you were expecting him. He was with you for one hour. If he wanted to pick up something then surely he would have asked for someone else and then passed by your room so you could secretly hand it to him through a crack in the door. We know this method well but what can we prove? You sat together and discussed something quite complicated, that much we are certain of: a technical drawing and U-boat plans. Certainly your friend was a German sailor, the tattoos on the dead body leave no room for doubt. I'm not asking you what plans you received. You can even keep the money. I will not search your things. Just tell me one thing: where are the plans? Your friend is dead and there is no way you can compromise him. Just tell us what he did with the plans. The chauffeur you used to drive to the hotel is our agent, as is the porter of the hotel. While you were on the market there was always someone watching you. Three of our agents were keeping a very close watch. No one could see any sign of any papers being put aside, but yet, our searches have yielded nothing. We appeal to your honour as a German citizen, a member of the party and as a petty officer, help us to find the papers.'

This was starting to get on my nerves. If I had had the opportunity I would have quickly sketched a U-boat and its interior and smuggled it in. To my shame, however, I was no good at drawing and could neither draw one from the outside nor depict the inside plans. Just to prove this to myself I tried it at a later date and it always came out looking like a row of false teeth.

'*Herr Polizeirat*,' I said, as I felt the need to respond. 'I have nothing to do with this affair. When the officers asked me if I was expecting anyone, I felt flattered, as it was the first time anyone had ever come to see me, so of course I said I was expecting him. I don't have many friends, obviously. But then this drunken chap appeared and started talking rubbish. I felt a little sorry for him so I accompanied him back to his hotel. He could hardly walk straight. When I heard the shots I could see that the Gestapo was already there so I thought there was no point in me getting involved. Just a thought *Herr Polizeirat*: if you really think the man was a conspirator and was carrying secret papers, would it not have been possible for the exchange to have taken place with someone else? And that he stayed with me so long so as to divert attention and lay a false trail? You yourself mentioned that this was a common practice. Why don't you let me go through his things? As a sailor I may be better qualified to find these plans.' My thought here was to show willing and also to see if there might be an opportunity to get some of my things back.

So to my surprise the basket with Mr Andersen's things was brought to me because the captain approved of the idea. I could see immediately that there was not much that could be salvaged. All the clothes had been cut up and ripped so the lining could be checked; all other items, tobacco pipe and my treasured flute, hacked into little pieces, tubes of toothpaste emptied, cut open and rolled flat. I felt a little stab in the heart but I had to pretend that it was leaving me cold. The only intact item on this sad heap was the bottle of French cognac, the finest French make with a crown and three stars. We all saw it at the same time and the two others licked their lips. Even my captain who had the face of an ascetic was not entirely averse to alcohol.

'Perhaps it's written on the back of the label,' I added modestly. Both men grabbed the bottle at the same time, saying, 'Allow me' and 'May I?'

My captain's arms were longer and his fingers more nimble. He lifted up the bottle, held it against the light and said contemplatively, 'If we empty the bottle we should see more easily.' He lifted it to his lips and drank almost half. Here was further proof of the lack of abolishment of the class system. The leading classes stuck together and the poor ordinary man could see where that left him. My captain handed the half-empty bottle not to me but to the superintendent, and that was that, the rest of the bottle disappeared in one large gulp. If they only realised that it was my cognac and they didn't even offer me a small sip!

The SS superintendent looked at the inventory and modified the entry for one full bottle of cognac. He crossed out 'full' and wrote 'empty' over the top. Then he wiped his mouth, reasonably satisfied with the conciliatory result of the interrogation. He gave a short salute and left. My captain was squinting at me, his normally dry fiery eyes filled with moisture. The cognac was strong and his gulp had been hefty. 'Gotthold,' he said. Now we were on first name terms again. 'I think I know your secret. Even the smartest detective will not be able to solve a case if he does not have access to all the information. The life of a sailor is tough and of course no one has the right to condemn certain urges. One should forgive them even if one does not condone them, and often there are true and honourable emotions behind these actions.' And with these words he left the room.

I watched him leave, at the same time feeling a little disturbed as I had no idea what he was talking about. Then I had it: he was referring to the moment he had caught the real Griesemann and I cavorting around in our under-pants. No doubt he had come to the obvious conclusion, although I had the feeling that it was not as far-fetched as I had thought in these circles. I went a deep shade of red, as red as a tribune in Soviet Moscow on the first of May. If my mother had seen me – my real mother that is, not that one I had written the mutinous letter to – she would have been deeply ashamed of me.

★★★

It was wonderful to be walking down the streets at dusk. How easy my life would be from now on if only I did not have to return to the sailors' home and continue playing a role that I was not in the least prepared for. I told myself: have courage, my brave one – as I was changing my first name so often I tended to address myself in vague terms. There was less risk of making a mistake; have courage, I said again, the first days are bound to be difficult. But slowly the others will get used to your expressions and gestures. And by being in close proximity you will learn their nicknames, life stories and idiosyncrasies by heart. If the real Griesemann hadn't died and was to return in a year then he would now be the stranger instead, in danger of drawing attention to himself. I was easily comforted even though I was consoling myself and immediately walked more cheerfully through the darkness, albeit still deep in thought. What was it that made life so much more friendly and bearable since this morning? I found the answer: it was the uniform.

Walking around in civilian clothes in a port city at war, even if they were well made and elegant, was bound to be depressing. It was a bit like being on the promenade in Cannes wearing a suit and striped satin trousers amongst others wearing white flannel and pastel sweaters, surprised that people were eyeing you up and down in disgust, keeping a wide berth. As a sailor on a U-boat with an Iron Cross, I was finally dressed appropriately for this sea-faring environment. Dressed in the right way, people can be more inclined to approach you with a sense of goodwill and friendship. The shops were still open, so I went into a small cafe, sat down and ordered toast with ham and two soft-boiled eggs. The landlady and the few guests started to laugh raucously, much to my surprise. I wasn't making jokes, I just happened to be hungry. As a hotel guest I had been spared the harsh reality with the special food ration card I was allowed as a neutral leisure traveller. The catering had been more than adequate. I drowned my disappointment in a cup of lukewarm ersatz coffee. I felt a little better at the thought of all the lost money. It would have been of little use to me since there was not much I could have bought with it.

Only a few steps further on I discovered there were exceptions; it was possible to purchase musical instruments without coupons and I was able to buy a flute. The shop girl complained that no one came into the shop these days. The people of Kiel were obviously not in the mood for making music. She had the mournful look that young women have who spend half their life waiting for something, and although you could have called her pretty, she wasn't my type. For that reason my answer to 'how long will you be staying in this port for, sailor?' my reply was, 'I am sorry but I am unable to give details of the movements of the German navy to ordinary civilians'.

I was still in love with the beautiful Christine; it was only that morning that I had bid my fond farewell. She must now be mourning the death of her Wilhelm (was that my name this morning?) with her dog on her lap and tears in her eyes. It is remarkable how much can happen in a single day.

Deep in thought, I almost walked straight past the sailors' home; it would have been just my luck to get lost and spend the night in an air-raid shelter. I had no idea how to find something to eat. I didn't dare ask. On the ground floor smells were emanating from an open doorway. I entered the room; the area was dimly lit and full of sailors from a multitude of ships, none of whom I recognised. As I looked from one to the other, I took a plate, spoon and fork from the sideboard and stood in line for my dinner. It was certainly not where I belonged. All around me were sailors with no rank, not a single fellow petty officer, but I was so hungry that the voice of caution was left unheeded. In orderly fashion we marched past four dinner ladies, one after the other they each scooped up one ladle of *kraut*, one of fried potatoes, half a slice of *bratwurst* and a thick slice of wartime bread. I had been worrying how I was going to eat my dinner without a knife. In a flash, my concerns disappeared as quickly as the thin slice of meat did. I finished my meal, standing in a corner facing the wall so that I would not be disturbed, and made my way out of the room.

It was to my advantage that the Germans were not stingy with their signs and labels. It was easy for me to find my way. I studied the inscriptions of the diverse localities and found the petty officers' mess – that must be where I belonged. With some trepidation I pushed down on the iron door handle.

The mess room was a long, well-ventilated, clean room with whitewashed walls. A workbench stretched the entire length of the room and individual light bulbs cast a pleasant glow. Two large oil paintings of Hitler were hanging on the walls, one of which (I later found out) was meant for the officers' mess but was only here temporarily (by now three and a half years). The officers always found new excuses to prevent its removal because they were quite happy with their gloomy Tirpitz painting. At the table there were several petty officers, alone and in groups, reading, writing or in quiet conversation. One of them had opened his pocket watch and was adjusting it with a sharp knife. I quickly studied a few of the faces. Thankfully no one expressed any surprise at my entering and I spied a studious-looking fellow who was reading on his own at the end of the table. The Student invited me over with a slight raising of an eyebrow, so I pulled up a seat and joined him.

Initially I had thought the Student was a young man but up close and in this lighting I could see the grey strands in his receding hair. He appeared a little preoccupied but was nonetheless happy to see me. He checked no one was watching by looking around, but everyone was doing their own thing.

'How did it go?' he whispered. A mild panic engulfed me. A cryptic question deserved a cryptic answer.

I murmured back, 'Exactly as I had hoped.'

He sighed, 'Good news for us.'

I nodded, wishing there was any way I could find out which side he was on. Was he an accomplice or a spy for the Gestapo? I could sense that his attention was wavering and he resumed what he had been doing before I had interrupted him. He had a large pile of magazines that he was scanning through carefully in order of their publication. He was slow and methodical and appeared to be only interested in one or two pages. I looked over his shoulder. It wasn't the crossword or the letters to the editor; it was the book reviews he was after.

'Nothing, again,' he said, disappointed. It seemed appropriate that I knew what was not there so I acknowledged, 'How sad and unfair.' Anything to do with book reviews was unfair in my opinion. He added: 'I no longer expect reviews of my first book, especially as it wasn't actually published. You do remember it, don't you?'

'Not very well,' I lied, 'but I remember the subject was fascinating.'

He was happy to be able to discuss his work. 'You're a good man, Gotthold. I've always said it; I don't care what the others think about your character. Let me tell you ...

'My first book was called *German Men of Israelite Faith as Patrons of Hamburg's Naval Prestige*. A long title, I know. It was dedicated to Alfred Ballin and the publisher was certain that subscriptions of Jewish patriotic organisations would cover the cost of the first printing. Sadly, politics took over and the entire print run was pulped, apart from one single bound copy, salvaged and now in the hands of the Gestapo. They used the information to facilitate the "aryanisation" of the navy. But do you think I ever received any thanks or commission from them? No, I don't think so.'

My instincts warned me that he was about to launch into a summary of his entire literary repertoire, which was too much, especially after such a dire evening meal. To cut him short, and without wanting to offend, I enquired, pretending to be very tired: 'Remind me, what was the name of your last book again?'

'My latest book has the title *The Dissemination of Asian Epidemic Diseases by Jewish Bacillus Carriers*. The relevant Reichs officials have approved the manuscript and the authorities have authorised publication. However, the publisher will not go ahead with the printing since the subject has no immediate impact unless we experience an epidemic here in Germany.'

The Student was hoping that further negotiations with Moscow would lead to wartime activities in Iran or Turkestan which could lead to an outbreak of cholera or the plague in central Europe. In which case there was a good chance the book would be highly successful.

The Student was now getting excited, his Adam's apple bobbing up and down. 'They would only need to put one advert in the *Boersenblatt* trade magazine for 10,000 copies to be sold into shops all around the country. Wake up, you old devil! You haven't been listening, have you?'

He didn't seem too offended and led me upstairs to my room.

5

TIGHTROPE WALK IN THE DARK

Up until now everything had gone as smoothly as I could have hoped for. This meant that I was not mentally prepared for any adversity and quickly lost my composure when something finally went wrong. So, what had happened? The Student, having led me to the door of my room and bidden me farewell with a friendly poke in the ribs, proceeded to saunter off whistling the entrance march from *Aida* or the like. I suddenly felt the compelling need to gather myself and reflect on everything that had happened in the course of the day and how these events and people would form my life. I earmarked an hour for these musings and was going to devote the following:

– Five minutes to the real Griesemann, deceased. May his spirit rest in peace.

– Five minutes to my heroic new commander, my captain.

– Three minutes to the Iron Cross.

– Half a minute to the police vice-president.

– Two minutes to the Student and my other friends and colleagues.

The remaining 44½ minutes I planned to leave entirely free to fill with thoughts of the lovely Christine. I was very methodical and good at mental arithmetic and needed little time to work out this timetable; in fact, although it takes some time to relate these thoughts, it only took as long as the time it took to squeeze into the room.

Before I turned on the lights I was certain that I would not be able to manage any clear or contemplative thoughts because there was a snoring man in my room, and when there is snoring I am unable to think clearly. Who the devil was this and why was he asleep in my room? I switched on the light indignantly.

In the narrow space, which was already incredibly confined, they had managed to squeeze a second bunk, albeit the shortest one they could possibly find. When Bohemia was still a free and happy country, you could go to a guesthouse on a Sunday and order schnitzel. For the customer to be satisfied the meat had to spill over the edge of three sides of the plate. In a similar fashion my unbidden guest was sprawled out in his bed, his face covered by a blanket, his bare legs akimbo. On this day my powers of intellect and deduction had been used so often and intensely that I was slacking and therefore could muster only the simplest of observations. From his sailor top I could make out his rank. He had one stripe less than me and was, therefore, Maschinengefreiter. From the calm and deep frequency of his snore, I deduced that he was young, strong and healthy. I estimated his shoes to be size 44 (UK 9), and judging by the photograph of his parents in the tasteful metal frame by his bed he was unmarried and came from a well-to-do and pious family. I suppose the company could have been worse.

I had to pass over his bed to get to mine. It seemed easiest to step over his face as this was where the obstacle was flattest. After a few attempts I managed to synchronise my breathing with his snoring. I briefly wondered whether I should open the window but before the thought could manifest itself I fell asleep to the sound of the snores. When I woke up and opened my eyes it was late and there were more and more noises to be heard in the corridor. A pair of eyes was staring at me. The intruder, now only 1.5m away from my head, went from lying down to sitting up, only half standing to attention, and spluttered: 'Maschinengefreiter Dr Raimund Pachthofer reporting for duty.'

The first official encounter between a subordinate and their superior can determine the level of respect for the remainder of the relationship. I decided to be strict and admonished myself to show no weakness. My mouth was dry from having just woken up, adding to the sarcastic tone I was adopting: 'The next time I expect you to report for duty from the chamber pot, cigarette in mouth!'

This resulted in deep embarrassment. Turning puce, he leapt out of bed, looked for and finally found the only spot where his large feet could find a place, then repeated the action. I wasn't satisfied and made him strap on his bayonet over his pyjamas and put on his cap. I made him repeat it a fourth time because he had forgotten the Hitler salute.

I stretched to full height, savouring the moment and explained: 'The only times you are exempt from executing the Nazi salute is where the dimensions of the room forbid it or if you are in danger of knocking over delicate nautical instruments.' I then finally added 'at ease', and allowed him to remove his cap and bayonet and get back into bed.

I instinctively understood that the more forceful and bullying one appeared, the more likely you were to achieve submission. He thanked me profusely for the instruction and beamed with a sense of duty and subordination. Now I could afford to be more affable and I enquired after his personal details. He had a PhD and was a meteorologist. His most recent station had been a remote mountain outpost. When the war broke out he volunteered and was placed in the U-Boat Waffe, as he was used to the following: going up and down ladders; reading instruments; being constantly on the lookout; shaving infrequently; and surviving on tins for weeks on end.

'Herr Obermaschinenmaat,' he exclaimed, as his nostrils flared with excitement, 'you are the most experienced and respected petty officer of the German U-boat fleet. You cannot imagine what an honour it is for me to be trained by you.'

This was too much. I could hardly distinguish a torpedo tube from a cinema projector and I was meant to instruct someone? I was incensed but there was no need to fuel my anger with pretence. Sadly, I had not picked up the full range of navy swear words in my twenty-four hours of duty. But what of it? I was sure the man from the mountain provinces would not be able to tell the difference. Good acting was not achieved by imitation but by grasping the essence of the situation. Was Shakespeare himself there to have heard King Lear swearing or Caesar speaking to his wife?

I began my tirade: 'You sad little barometric worm. Do you really think I have the time and inclination to train you personally? Is this why I was decorated in the highest order? So that I can waste my precious talents in the manner of a primary school teacher? Oh no, I won't! I have a sailor's patent not a nursing diploma! You are more likely to see the German fleet rise from the bottom of the sea at Scapa Flow and start fighting again than hear me utter a single word of instruction. And even if our admiral himself gives me an order to do the same, I would throw my logbook on the floor and then he can sink the battleships on his own!'

The poor man sunk his head and was completely silent. Perhaps I had gone too far. Then I had an idea that could save me from this unfortunate situation. I continued: 'Of course, I realise how unfamiliar everything will be to start with and you will want to pose questions all of the time. Carry on, I don't mind, as long as you don't ask me. It is your duty to find out what you need to know. Don't hold back. I will even help you. If I think there is a situation where you should be asking more questions I will subtly kick your shins. You may want to put on an extra pair of knee-high socks.'

I thought to myself: if I manage to keep this chap with me all of the time, then I have an inconspicuous method of asking questions and finding out things that would otherwise have been impossible. In a nutshell, I may just about survive.

★★★

As it happened, it was a Sunday and no one was on duty that day. Lunch for the sergeants and my new recruit was served by the orderlies in clean aprons. Shiny cutlery was laid out and there was even a tablecloth. With my source of information close by, I felt relatively safe. For the time being everyone's sole concern was one thing: the post. I, for my part, had little interest in seeing what letters were waiting for my predecessor. I could only imagine the ladies from his diary chattering about their daily lives, demanding their money or sending photos. I was not looking forward to this. I have never enjoyed reading other people's letters, but here I had no choice. There was not a single moment where I was on my own, and if anyone saw me throwing the letters away without reading them I would no doubt arouse suspicion.

It wasn't as bad as I thought it was going to be. There were no letters from ladies with dubious addresses. He must have given them a false address. In fact, there was very little post for me. There was a postcard sent from Munich showing three women dressed up as *Münchener Kindl.*[1] The hood covered their foreheads so you could only see the tip of the nose, cheeks, mouth and chin. The voluminous cloak covered their figures up to the knees, at which point their bare legs stuck out which made them look more convincing. All three girls were from the serving classes. I could just make out a bruise on the instep of the one in the middle, likely to have been obtained from polishing the parquet too vigorously with a broom. This was assuming the girl was from an area where the polishing of parquet was not yet done mechanically. The postcard was accompanied by the words: 'Do you recognise me?' and I added, being the honest man that I was, 'No'.

There was also the latest chess magazine and a letter enclosing 5 marks for the correct answer to one of their challenges. Then there was a bill for tailoring services marked 'third reminder' and a few more unremarkable items. Then, to my surprise, there was a proper letter with female handwriting on violet paper. It was promisingly heavy but when I opened it nothing interesting fell out apart from some newspaper cuttings consisting of chess challenges and their solutions. I started to read the letter:

Dear Gotthold, I am sending you all the clippings I could find. I spent all day in the library collecting them. I fear I am making myself unpopular by cutting holes in the magazines, but there is another woman who collects the bridge and she is even worse. She tears out whole pages. They are calling me Jack the Ripper, whatever that means, I think it must be some kind of an insult.

My sister's bloke never writes to her either. He says he
is busy washing the deck, don't you dare use that as your
excuse. I know you are underwater most of the time,
With greetings and a kiss, your Jakobine.

P. S. I went to see Frau Schnuppelmatz. She says you are a
rascal. If you don't propose soon I will come and look for
you or write to your admiral to complain. Yours, the above.

This was obviously my bride-to-be. The letter was posted
in Wiesbaden before 3 September. I hoped that she was
now evacuated, preferably to a camp for civilians where no
letter writing was allowed.

As it was now raining heavily, the mess hall was getting
busier. I was getting used to the faces around me and feeling
more comfortable. In addition to the two paintings of
Hitler the mess hall had further ornaments: an aquarium
and terrarium in one corner that would have once been in
use. One was filled with earth and a few dried-out plants,
the other with water and some coral. They must have been
designated to hold treasures from foreign countries: exotic
fish and amphibians to amuse and instruct the comrades left
behind. Wartime activities had led to less exotic specimens
being brought back. Instead of fabled animals from the
Malayan Archipelago or the mouth of the River Amazon,
there were only ordinary central European frogs, lizards
and white fish. I could see the Baron pacing up and down,
on the prowl for a victim of his jokes. The ones who had
been there longer knew to keep well out of his way but
unfortunately he had already found me.

'Guess what happens if I break the lizard's tail off?'

'It'll grow back,' I answered, annoyed.

'If only it were that easy.' He burst into laughter. 'Why
shouldn't their tails be rationed too? First of all he needs a

ration card, then he can wait and see what happens … Ha, ha, ha.'

I ducked quickly as I was sure that the German sailors never missed their aim, but sadly there was nothing being thrown in the direction of the jester. They must be more tolerant than me.

For my part I would have been perfectly happy sitting on my own, leafing through my diary contemplating various facts that were emerging from my surroundings. For example, it was quite easy to differentiate those sailors who were based on a U-boat from those on other ships, such as destroyers or patrol ships. The latter had bronzed faces, the former an unhealthy green hue around their eyes and pale faces. Fortunately I did not stick out because I was just as pale – the air in London WC1 must be very similar to the air on a U-boat. I was sure no one from the *Geheime Macht* had thought of this small detail. If they had sent a young man from Brighton in my stead, his rosy cheeks would have given him away.

The post had given me no further information about the private details of my predecessor. If only there had been a letter from my newly acquired mother saying something like the following:

My dear son, I am sending you a photograph of our little house in XXXheim, which as you know cost us 2,000 marks and has 950 marks left on the mortgage. Your father Johann, the retired civil servant, celebrated his sixty-second birthday yesterday and he is well. By the way, he received no birthday message from you. I recently went through your papers and put them in chronological order. Your school leaver certificate from such and such a school in XXXmistdorf, a letter refusing a scholarship because you were caught stealing apples, etc., etc.

Although I could easily imagine such a letter giving all the relevant information about my previous life, it was alas not to be as these things only seemed to happen in novels. In real life you receive ridiculous postcards with barefoot, hooded figures, chess clippings and unjust recriminations. When I say unjust, I mean it only to the extent that I was not strictly responsible for my predecessor's sins.

I suddenly had a thought. It may be possible to look in the record office. They must hold some rudimentary information on the sailors, if only the basics such as date of birth, details of parents and other useful titbits. There was a slight risk of appearing suspicious but I hoped that my recent decoration was reason enough. Perhaps I could say, 'I want to check whether the Iron Cross First Class has been noted in my records'.

If I had been left to my own devices I may have come up with the perfect plan, which may have led to a more advantageous outcome. As it happened it was no surprise that in a group of people of different temperaments, the nervous and fidgety individuals cannot bear to see anyone content in their own company. It was to an extent my own fault as I had chosen my position badly by sitting down at one of the desks where the opposite seat was unoccupied. It was inevitable that I would be disturbed. Had I only chosen to sit with those writing letters, I might only have been jostled in the elbow or been asked to pass the ink pot.

The Student wandered in and came straight towards me and the empty seat opposite. I nodded and made a point of immersing myself in the act of reading my diary with elbows on the table and fingers in ears, but to no avail. The Student had brought a cigar case with bits of wood and glue with the intention of building some sort of wooden ladder for the frog in the terrarium so he could predict the weather. Our aneroid barometer was ultimately useless.

There is a superstition that a frog will climb up a ladder when the weather is fine. The Student had taken out his watch to see how long it would take and removed the frog so that he could acquaint himself with the ladder. But the Student was typically absent-minded and was not getting anywhere. He had the wrong tools and was then trying to feed flies to the watch. I was preparing to intervene if he went so far as to try to wind up the frog or tell the time from it. In the end he gave up. He brushed away the bits of wood and placed the frog on top of his toolkit, where it certainly did not belong, and he said in a whinging voice: 'It is so unbelievably boring, Gotthold. Please do something.'

I wasn't sure what he meant but extricated myself from the task by taking out my last clean handkerchief and wiping an imaginary bomb splinter out of the corner of my eye. I replied, 'Not now, can't you see I'm busy.'

I continued to watch him with great interest. He stood up, sighed and took the frog out of the box he was carrying it in, blew away the sawdust on its bright green skin and waltzed towards the corner where the two glass cases were. First he placed the poor frog carefully in position, then he pushed the glass cover away. The three lizards now darted around wildly while the frog was still in shock.

Behind the glass cases a control panel was now visible, with various buttons and a telephone handset. He started to turn the dials and the mouthpiece began to emit the sounds of glasses jingling and a stream of voices. I kept rubbing my eye, feigning lack of interest but I was searching for my source of information out the corner of my other eye. He was still next to me and staring at the apparatus open-mouthed. I kicked his shin with moderate strength to encourage him to ask some questions. This proved unnecessary since everyone stopped what they were doing to listen to the voice that was now clearly turning into our captain's. One stocky fellow took position at the door to keep a lookout …

'No, no, gentlemen! My dear people have no idea of the great pleasure that awaits them. We will announce it tomorrow morning, first thing. Thank you so much for everything and the honour you have bestowed upon me. I was warned countless times that I could not expect to achieve miracles with my people but I am pleased to say that I can indeed do so. Not only in the grand scheme of things but also in the little details. Let me explain, only yesterday I awarded the Iron Cross First Class to one of my petty officers who suffered from being terribly cross-eyed. As I was affixing the medal, oh wonder upon wonders, the man looked back at me with a straight gaze for the very first time in his life. That is what can happen – the force of mind over matter, but there is something else …'

It went no further. A red light came on over the door and we could hear a mild buzzing. Like a tiger, the Student leapt towards the control panel and turned it off, interrupting his superior mid-sentence. Everyone was very still and put their finger to their mouth. The Student and the Baron looked at each other and took their places at opposite ends of one of the tables. Both took a piece of paper out of their pockets and began to read in a clear voice over a large groove in the table. I had not noticed it before but it was a very large groove and the dimensions of the table were very unusual as the tabletop was very deep. The Student read out in an even tone:

'The climate in Germany is temperate, maritime on the North Sea coast, continental further inland. The average temperature is 7.9°C, in January 2.2°, in July 17.2°. The most pleasant weather can be found in the Rhine Valley from Speyer to Cologne, the worst in East Prussia.'

The Baron countered: 'Thank you, dear fellow, for the enlightening information. I would be most grateful if you could also advise me with regards to the average rainfall.'

There was another buzz and the little red light went out. Everyone went back to their seats. I kicked the young Raimund who had failed me so far. My kick this time had more force. What use was my source of information if he refused to ask any questions? With some trepidation he approached a grey-haired sailor who looked knowledgeable. 'Excuse me,' he said. 'I'm new here, what does this mean?'

'The great pleasure you mean?' he answered. 'I wouldn't hold my breath. We have been severely disappointed in the past. One day our captain called us and said he had a wonderful surprise for us and it turned out to be two British destroyers that we were meant to torpedo. The problem was they saw us first and dropped depth charges. We only just avoided being hit.'

The others agreed and added further comments, such as 'He's right, we don't want their surprises'. It looked like there was nothing more to be said about the incident with the mysterious voices, lights and buzzing noises. This led to an ever-increasing sensation of panic in me. The hairs on my head began to stand on end; the palms of my hands went cold and sweaty. I had to discard the cigarette I was enjoying after only a few puffs because it made me feel sick. If I couldn't get to the bottom of this, I wasn't going to carry on. I would rather desert the navy and blow up the entire depot of munitions than sit here like an idiot not knowing what was going on. I decided to make one last attempt and looked for my helper. He had moved his chair away from me inch by inch. When he saw I was trying to meet his gaze he lifted his legs and bent his knees. He was obviously not curious and had had enough of my attacks against his shins. For a moment I considered berating him to sit up properly. But then I thought better of it. We were off duty and in a sailors' home. Why shouldn't he relax and sit how he pleased? I tried a different tactic.

'A newcomer,' I began, 'must feel like a complete idiot. You are all as secretive as one another. Does no one want to give an explanation to the poor lad and put him out of his misery?'

The Baron took mercy. 'What did you not understand?' he asked the perplexed weatherman who began to stutter.

'If you please, sir, if it was the captain speaking, why did you interrupt him?'

The Baron laughed: 'Do you really think we need the Gestapo to find out that we can eavesdrop on our own officers, particularly when it is a device that we stole from their depot? As you can imagine we have some technical expertise here as one would expect on a U-boat. One of the electricians is very knowledgeable in all matters relating to surveillance devices. This is why we immediately spotted the listening unit hidden in our table. When we traced the wires we discovered they led to the officers' mess. It didn't take us long to wire up a connection for us to listen to what our superiors are talking about at meal times. Does that make sense?'

The poor sailor didn't know what to say and looked in my direction for guidance. I responded with a mock kick in the shins, encouraging him to keep up the questions.

'May I ask,' he enquired. 'What's the significance of the average temperature of 2.2° in January?' He was overdoing it a bit and asking the wrong questions too.

I helped out: 'The poor lad is not a weatherman! That's why he is a bit confused by the temperatures. Keep up the explanations. We were new recruits once.'

Of course, I risked hearing the answer I should explain it all myself and was prepared, should this be the case, to excuse myself with a coughing attack or nosebleed. But this was not necessary. The Baron was the kind of person who loved the sound of his own voice. He usually had problems finding listeners and was therefore happy to take on the role of the instructor, especially with half the room eavesdropping on their conversation.

'Listen, you rookie, we were tapping the officers' mess where they were preparing a surprise for us. The Gestapo tried to tap us. We recognised the signals that warn us when they switch on to us. The Gestapo expects to hear conversations and as long as the red light is on we comply by talking about mundane subjects. We have learned that there are few subjects that are truly mundane so we have to artificially create themes. We worked this through experiment. What does one normally talk about: food, holidays, work, clothes, plans for the future. If you say what everyone else thinks about these topics, it's virtually treason. We worked out that the only truly harmless subject is the weather. And that's the only thing that hasn't changed since the rise of the regime. This is why we talk about the weather whenever we know the Gestapo is listening. And just so they can see they are dealing with learned people, we have also taken a few pages out of an encyclopaedia and read these out for the benefit of the enemy when the red light is on. We are quite pleased with the results. We have a mole in the Gestapo quarters who has told us that since the installation of our device they've had two cases of nervous breakdowns – both people in the surveillance unit.'

For my part this was explanation enough and I thought it was time for the Baron to finish his speech. But he had only just got into his stride and was not going to stop now. There were only the three of us left now. I had already learned that if I was on my own with the Baron or the Student when no one else was around then I could speak my mind about the system.

'Another important detail,' he continued, 'is that it is much easier to tap telephones than to listen in on ordinary conversations. With a telephone it is very simple. The listener is informed by the red light that his subject is about to speak. He picks up the receiver and hears a click. Let us suppose the subject wants to ask a friend about the interesting story the station in Strasbourg has broadcast about negotiations in Sweden. As soon as he hears the click he says, "Good morning, I'm afraid I can't make it for coffee, heil Hitler!" and hangs up.

'It is much more difficult to set up surveillance units in private places or flats because civilians can't be trained to take their turn speaking for just their allotted five minutes. On the contrary, depending on the time of day, it's either completely silent or everybody talks at once. If you start in the city where people aren't used to being bugged you can still hear angry criticism of the regime, in which case the listener needs strong nerves. But gradually word is spreading that the Gestapo is listening in the dining room, the living room, the bedroom and the bathroom. Only nurseries are to my knowledge left untapped.

'It is from the middle classes that most of the listeners are recruited. Lacking courage the Gestapo no longer hears any criticism, quite the opposite; instead, discussions at home focus on complimenting the regime and saying how well everything is going. One bachelor I know of who lives alone, and has no one to lead these discussions with, has found the following solution: he kneels in front of the listening device and prays loudly, "Dear God, I, Comrade Schwämerlein, beseech you to protect from harm our dearly beloved Führer, to give him strength." He keeps to himself the final words "and enlighten his mind" as this could be construed as criticism and viewed as treason. He tries to include his own name in his prayers so that God (and the Gestapo) does not confuse his identity with someone else.'

The Baron might have gone on in the same vein for hours but I sent a signal to the Student with a discreet wink to pretend to be asleep, at which point the Baron abandoned his discourse and left the mess room in a huff.

NOTE
1 Munich child, the symbol on the coat of arms of the city, showing a small child in a black-hooded cloak.

6

IN THE DEEP

It dawned on me that I wasn't dreaming. In the tiny sleeping cubicle it was so dark that I could only guess what the shadows were rather than see their source. I could just make out a bent-over figure that was reaching out for me with long skinny arms. I would have gone for his throat if he hadn't aimed the torch at his face in time. I could make out the deeply lined but childish face of the Student, who had his finger to his lips. Almost imperceptibly he whispered, 'Are you ready?'

I didn't feel there was the option to say no and go back to sleep again. It also appeared that the sailor sharing my room was not to be involved. We tried not to disturb him but he wasn't sleeping as well as the night before. His slumber was punctuated with exclamations such as 'Rope!' and 'Climb when ready!' He was an active dreamer.

We both leaned over this restless sleeper. The Student whispered, 'I wonder what he's dreaming about.' His inquisitive nature became apparent. I studied the easing and tensing of his shoulder muscles, the way he gripped the blanket with his fists and the athletic rising and falling of his chest, and came to the following conclusion: 'He's dreaming of a difficult climbing expedition and desperately trying to get a pick in the rock face whilst his feet are losing grip.'

'We had better hope he doesn't fall off the cliff.' I promised to do my best. I took the towel that was hanging from my bed to dry, started waving it in the air over his head and made a few guttural screeching noises to imitate the wing beating and shrieking of a jackdaw leaving the tower. Hearing these accustomed sounds, the sleeper found foot again and became calm; his breathing now regular. Since he had his arms under his neck and his knees raised, it was not possible for me to climb over his bed. If I couldn't go over him I would try to go under him. I made myself even skinnier and flatter than I was by nature. The Student grabbed me by the neck and pulled me under the camp bed and out into the corridor. I thought back to how protective I was of my underpants three days ago and here I was wiping the floor with them!

After the complete darkness of the room, the intermittent lights of the corridor seemed unnecessarily bright by comparison. I studied my mate. He was wearing working trousers, a roll-neck jumper and had some boat shoes in his hand. I went back into the room to get similar apparel and finished getting ready as I walked down the corridor. Four times I was about to ask where we were going but I stopped myself in time. The whole manner of this nightly excursion seemed to be based on meticulous planning and if I showed ignorance I would compromise my role. I let the Student go ahead and we crept like mice down the stairs into the courtyard. There we sat down and put our shoes on. It was a moonless autumn night; the clouds rushed above us in the courtyard almost as if they felt put to shame by the geometric regularity of the spotlights shining upon them. My comrade gave a deep whistle through the gap in his front teeth. From the darkness of the courtyard, a long and wide shadow came towards us. It was a navy sentry with a gun on his shoulder.

'Is everything okay, Anton?' the Student whispered. 'I've put the light on in the barn and it is all in place apart from the one window.'

We looked up. The row of windows was blacked out. In some we could even make out the reflection of the spotlights. Only in one of the windows could the light behind it be seen. Then there was a clanking, the gap in the window widened and a glowing spark flew out in an arc on to the courtyard only a few steps away from us. I could still see the sparks. I bent down and lifted the butt end of the cigar as the Student aimed his torch on it. With there being a cork mouthpiece he decided it could only be the captain. No one else smoked this brand.

'There is no need for you to play detective,' said the sentry, grabbing the cigar butt and disposing of it in a makeshift ashtray. 'This morning the old man set up an office up there. It looks like something is bothering him. I've already brought him up two ashtrays. These must already be full or else he wouldn't throw them out the window. You mark my words; he won't go to sleep tonight. He'll smoke all his cigarettes and then go out on an inspection; you can look forward to that.'

I had no idea what was planned but it appeared I was the leader, since the other two were looking at me expectantly. If I had now said, 'Guys, if we look at it like this, we may as well abandon the whole thing,' then the Student and I could have gone back to sleep. The sentry, of course, would still have been on duty. But once I had started with something I wanted to finish it, and I was curious. The bed was small and uncomfortable anyway and my roommate noisy.

I said nothing and we continued the discussions about whether our captain was now in bed or on his restless wanderings. The Student felt it necessary to drum some safety precautions into the sentry.

'Anton,' he said, 'if the captain comes down into the courtyard ready to go out, then you must warn us. I don't care how but we need to be able to hear it within a mile's distance. You could ring the church bells, set the tower on fire or start a shooting match.'

I thought this joke was a bit silly and I don't think I was alone in this. The sentry smiled grimly as if to say, 'Don't you worry. If I need to warn you, you'll know about it.'

We crept through the courtyard with our backs pressed to the walls, past the kitchen, wash houses, utility rooms and storage units. Everything was properly signposted on enamel signs and locked up for the night. My companion headed for one of the doors with no signage, left slightly ajar with a faint light emanating from within. As we proceeded inside we were hit by the homely smell of stables. There was only one animal, a fat brown horse with chains rattling. It was dear Ursel, whose task it was to get provisions from the bakery. She was an old mare and could sense she was no longer needed in the age of machines. She led a reclusive life and had certainly not reckoned on having visitors at this time of night.

'Can you push this thing aside?' the Student asked.

I could tell that he wasn't used to dealing with animals. I called its name and went into its stand, forcing it into the corner. It was a friendly thing and put up no resistance. The Student followed me tentatively and began to move aside some of the straw from the spot where the horse had been standing.

A trap door became visible, no more than 2 square feet inside, just big enough to let through two skinny sailors. There was a metal ring in the middle of the door and with a gentle pull it opened. Cold, dank air escaped from the opening. The Student rested his elbows on the floor and dangled his spindly legs into the black, empty hole. His feet took hold and slowly his upper body was enveloped by the darkness. I could hear him going down some steps. Once he had reached the bottom he switched on his torch and then it was my turn to follow.

From an athletic point of view it posed no real challenge. I had no problem gripping the top rung of the wooden ladder with my feet and mastered the descent easily. I was reluctant, however, to leave the warm comfort of the stable and the reassuring proximity of the friendly animal for the dark, cold existence in the underworld. I made sure I closed the trap door above me since I felt the animal had the right to a stable floor without a dangerous hole to fall into. I was not entirely happy with this situation. What if we needed to open the door and the creature was fast asleep over it? I could hardly move aside a full-grown horse while perched on a rickety ladder. There was hope that the horse preferred to lie on the soft straw rather than on the bare floorboards. There was no time to think through the consequences. I had to concentrate on my task of following the Student and the faint glow of his torch down the dark corridor. There was a slight danger of slipping on the wet muddy floor and bumping my head against the metal pipes.

I tried to assess the situation: we were in a disused sewer and, judging by the cables above us, only a few metres under the surface of the road above us. I wasn't sure what our aim was, but I felt certain it was not going to be buried treasure; somehow my companion didn't appear to be the type to be attracted to treasures. In fact, he seemed in no way generous, judging by the number of times he had scrounged a cigarette off me, if that was anything to go by.

The subterranean route seemed endless. One turning to the right was left unexplored as the smell indicated this could be the main sewer, which I also surmised from the sound of trickling water. I decided to put an end to things soon. A bad smell was one thing that was very difficult to get rid of, especially when there was no soap to be had. In the end no one would believe I was a decorated sergeant; everyone would think I was a sewer cleaner or the like, especially when it was dark.

At last my companion stood still and put away his torch. He fingered a grate that was obstructing the path. Did that mean we were imprisoned? Even this he removed with professional ease and we had the comforting strong whiff of fresh air, salt water and tar, and machine oil. The darkness was not quite as dense. Here and there I could make out some faint lights. The sounds were of an outdoor kind and there was no doubt we were nearing the outside world. The iron grill only appeared to be set in cement. On moving the right stones it could be opened like a door on hinges.

We crept out taking deep breaths, stepping over the bank on to a stone platform that seemed immense. A fresh sea breeze was gathering the clouds in the north. The rear end of the Great Bear was now just visible, not only as comfort and solace for those who believed in the might of the stars and their course, or whatever role they might play in the reign of dictators, but for the faint light they cast on two sailors who had grazed their elbows on walls in the darkness.

Men over the age of 40 often have to catch their breath after they have spent half an hour crawling over obstacles in the dark. This was the case with my companion, giving me the opportunity to further take in my surroundings. The platform was punctuated every twenty steps or so by low pillars of wide circumference. Behind us there was a wall with menacing spikes around 18ft high. There must have been a city behind it because we heard the sounds of a busy street: cars, a tramway and some horns beeping. Straight ahead of us in the distance the searchlights were of different colours, creating patterns in the darkness of the horizon. I knew that Kiel was not a city with a film studio or a theme park so these sharp spikes had to be something different. And because these formations were bobbing in the complete darkness of the sea, their steel cables groaning in such a way that even a landlubber like me could work out that we were in a wartime harbour. It was only in the first few seconds of our coming out of the tunnel that it seemed like an abandoned wasteland. In actual fact there was a hub of determined activity. Each light or spark was carefully concealed. Every blow of the hammer was as faint as possible. I could now make out cranes swinging in ghostly silence. It was so still, one could hear the echo of the wall of the quay as a sentry walked along in his parade-like gait. Twelve steps in one direction, halt, about turn and the same again.

My leader and companion had now caught his breath and we resumed our journey with renewed vigour. Where the platform ended we took some stony steps down on to a different path which followed the quay wall for a short while. The cold wind blew straight through my work trousers and I was cold. With further displeasure I found that the inky black mass that was gurgling at the plank at our feet was the sea, an element that I felt no sympathy towards, nor did I trust it. The Student, who was distinctly nervous upon leaving the tunnel, ducked and flayed his limbs as if in fear of an unknown predator. Then he regained his composure and innate calmness. He even put his hands in his pocket and was quietly whistling a tune which sounded a bit like the Torero March from *Carmen*. He started a conversation: 'Do we have any tools, Gotthold?'

'No, we haven't,' I replied.

'That doesn't matter, Gotthold. Do you remember those manoeuvres in '37 – the things you managed to do with nail scissors and a 50 pfennig coin? We all know you're a swine, but in technical matters no one comes close.'

I decided to be humble. Whatever I may have done with or without a pair of scissors, my reputation could only suffer henceforth. It was better to lower expectations. 'Adalbert,' I said, for this was the Student's true name, so called when the others were not teasing him. 'You do realise that everyone can have a bad day and I'm not always at the height of my technical prowess.' I thought to myself, *Let's wait and see.*

The plank went off at a right angle from the wall of the quay and was getting more and more slippery as it was being increasingly engulfed by the mass of water. I wondered what we were doing. Were we going to walk all the way to England? What would I do if a seagull grabbed me by the collar and led me into the water, realising that I didn't belong here? Would it not be easier to turn back time to the point when the kind Ursel greeted me with such warmth in the stables? I could have whispered in her ear, 'Dearest, let's flee somewhere where the ground is firm and arable, where there are rooks instead of evil seagulls, where the air smells of burned potato shrubs, not of tar and machine oil.' But I left it at the thought; I wasn't really going to flee.

I concentrated all my efforts on following my sauntering companion along the slippery plank. In the semi-darkness I could now see a narrow surface protruding, like a sluice surrounded by a narrow enclosure. We stepped onto ribbed steel plates that had excellent grip. I was about to comment that the situation was improving but I was wrong. The Student pushed open a hatch somewhat clumsily on something that looked a bit like a chimney. The next thing I knew he was climbing inside. It was as slippery as if the devil himself had smeared the sides with soft soap. With the smoothness of a letter being posted through a slot, he disappeared with a slight rumbling into the depths. It could not have been very deep after all because I could hear a grunt of pain and shortly afterwards a faint glow appeared. I stepped carefully onto an iron stepladder hoping to avoid an unpleasant landing and admonished my friend.

'One would think by the way you are carrying on that you have never set foot on a U-boat before,' I said to him, watching him rub the sore points on his bones, which due to his physique were not well cushioned. I could easily guess where we were. On every bucket and every box I could make out the significant numbers that had only recently started to play such a role in my life: U-XY. This prison of iron ramps, pipes and iron sheets was the home of the person whose life I was now leading, and it was likely to be (and I shuddered at the thought) my home for the foreseeable future, if not even my grave.

'Are you going into the torpedo room and I'll go to the diesel machines?' my friend enquired, slowly regaining strength after his exertions. That was all I needed, being left to my own devices in this dreadful place.

'No, my friend. You're staying here with me! If you get hurt again, I don't even have a cloth to pack your broken bones in.'

Then I made myself a promise: enough of tapping in the dark, literally and otherwise. If I don't find out what's happening here within the next ten minutes, I will ask the Student straight out. I didn't care what he thought of me, but it didn't come to that. My friend no longer wanted to lead the way but left it to me to go ahead. I thought, *Not much can happen, it's not a big ship and the direction should be obvious, not like on Piccadilly Circus or Etoile where there are seven or eight directions that can be taken.* But I couldn't have been more wrong. I was inside a U-boat and still had no idea what it looked like inside. It was pitch-black. First I went to the left to pull aside a slide door and crawled into a very small compartment. There was a wooden floor as well as what appeared to be a wooden ceiling. I pulled on a piece of rope and immediately let go again as it began to run through my hands very quickly giving me rough hands, which was something I couldn't bear. Then my stomach lurched and I went crashing down several levels.

'Are you at the bottom?' a frightened voice enquired from three levels above.

'That's right,' I replied. 'You can come down now. I can't see anything without a torch.' As I heard the Student making his way down step by step, I resolutely and unwaveringly vowed that if the plan was to go to sea in this device, then I would sooner die the death of a traitor at the wall of the barracks or be executed in the whitewashed surroundings of a state prison. Being on a U-boat was bound to be unpleasant enough with everyone in their rightful place and a commander who knew what he was doing, but with a skeleton crew on the wide-open sea, or even underneath, that was a way of ending my life that I was not prepared to accept. Thankfully the conversation turned to going home rather than going out to sea.

The Student limped towards me; his previous fall must have been quite bad. 'You're a funny man, Gotthold. You'll break your neck one day with your dare-devilry. Why on earth did you have to take the munitions lift? You didn't know whether the harbour engineer had taken out any of the parts to fix or replace. What would I have done if you had crashed and left me to fend for myself?' His words were almost endearing but didn't remain so for long. 'Any idea what the time is?' he asked, since his watch had shattered in the fall and I had no pockets in my work trousers. 'We must get back before someone else takes over from Anton, then we really will be in trouble.' Those were the magic words. Then we both said at the same time, 'Let's get to work!'

Sadly I still had no idea what the work entailed but I was content again. If work was required of me and I was given the right tools, I was happy to tackle anything, even if it meant planting a bed of seeds.

My mate was now ahead of me, leading the way unsteadily with the faint light of his torch towards the torpedo room. Slowly I began to revise my preconceived opinion of U-boats. Once you were used to the atmosphere it was all quite neutral and factual, a bit like being in a power station where the master builder has had to employ space-saving devices. The room had an off-putting name: TORPEDOANSTOSSRAUM, but from appearances could just as well have been a little bakery or suchlike, only that the two large openings housed torpedoes rather than loaves of bread.

As the torch cast its faint glow towards the wall I could make out the round dials sunk into the wall, and next to these handles there were bolts and massive steering wheels. This is where my friend had ended up. I couldn't quite see what he was turning. I could just detect that he was trying to aim the light of the torch at one of the dials which was now twitching furiously. Judging by the unnatural position of my companion's head I presumed he had either lost or forgotten to take his glasses or they had broken at some point along the journey. In short, they weren't there and his naked eye was incapable of making out the reading of the flickering dial with the insufficient lighting available.

Feeling that I ought to be doing something, I grabbed the nearest handle and turned it to the left. As quick as I could, I turned it back to its original position because there was now an ear-splitting screech from the area above us. The light of the torch was now aimed squarely at my face and the Student remarked in a voice that sounded like he had lost his belief in God.

'You rotten piece of carrion! If the devil sniffed your soul he would recoil and reject you. You would rather let us both die than pass the opportunity of frightening a friend.'

An icy silence ensued. The Student carried on trying to read the dial but appeared to have lost all faith in life and his surroundings. My heart was softening. In the kind of situation we were in, where each of us was reliant upon the other, it seemed foolish to bear grudges even if the insults he had bestowed on me weighed heavy. I crept up towards my friend and he said, with no further introduction or apology, 'Here, read this. I must have something in my eye. I'm having trouble focusing.'

'342,' I read out, but only a few seconds later I could see my reading was wrong. It was in fact 542 but I didn't want to correct myself for fear of losing face.

'342,' he repeated as his mood swung from subdued to joyful ecstasy. 'What do you know!' he exclaimed. 'I was right! Did I not point out during the last attack that something wasn't right and we were losing pressure? How long do you think it will take to rectify? Do you think it will take fourteen days? That would really save us some efforts.'

'At least fourteen days,' I responded with great conviction. What on earth was going to take fourteen days I hadn't the foggiest idea but my friend's enthusiasm about the change in plans was infectious. Our 'work' was now no longer necessary and we could go back. I soon realised that our efforts were, in a judicial sense, tantamount to sabotage. That I was let off the hook so easily without having to resort to dynamite or even a screwdriver could only be seen as a great success.

As we headed back over the slippery planks, I prepared to console myself that the excursion had been hard work but most instructive. We had just reached the end of the walkway, stepping onto the drier stone steps and thinking how well I would be able to sleep after a brisk walk with lots of fresh sea air, when suddenly all hell broke loose.

The night air reverberated with a single shrill tone. It was the unmistakable sound of an air-raid warning that we all knew and feared. We took each other's hand and ran up the remaining steps. The maritime harbour had turned into a madhouse. All those not directly involved in air defence were confronted with a mass that were keen to prove their merits otherwise. Dozens of those in their lookout positions had been waiting eagerly for this historic moment to bark commands and control the masses. Voices shouted from the darkness: 'Lights out! This way to the air-raid shelter! Down with you! Take cover! What are you doing just standing there, clear the passages!'

'Run, Gotthold!' the Student ordered.

I threw my arms around the shoulders of my limping comrade and said, 'I won't leave you now in your hour of need.'

He pushed me away. 'Are you being thick? Don't you realise that Anton has instigated this? Why did I not foresee that the unlucky soul would sound the warning sirens? The mains go through the courtyard; he must have put a nail through the wires to create a short circuit and warn us. If only he had let us be then the captain might have found us and we might have had the excuse that we were just checking everything was in order.'

That was typical of the Student. Instead of positive action he dwelled and moaned about the past and things we could no longer change. He should have pulled himself together and tried to disguise his limp. One young man in Hitler Youth uniform, who was holding watch on the harbour, had discovered us as he was surveying the walls of the quay with his torch. He shouted: 'An injured party, this way!' He was the first to discover someone wounded and was not about to let go of this triumph. The boy was already envisaging a decoration – a Knight's Cross of goodness knows which order. There was nothing we could do.

'It's late! At least you get the hell out of here. If they ask, say we haven't seen each other since last night.'

That was all I heard him say. From all sides the emergency units were approaching, carrying stretchers. 'This is our wounded man,' the first unit called out, 'and we saw him first!'

'Out of our way!' the second unit responded. 'This is our patch, you have the north-eastern side of the harbour. Let us through or we will report you.'

I wasn't able to see how it ended. *Why don't you all start fighting each other?* I thought to myself, *Then at least units 3 and 4 can make full use of their stretchers*. I fled as quickly as I could.

7

DANGEROUS GAME

One good thing that came out of the alarm was that the way back proved far easier than the way out. All gates were wide open – three cars could have fit through. I walked as slowly as I could towards one of the gates sealing off the harbour, but it appeared that in this situation no one was allowed out on their own.

I was pulled aside by someone very big and strong, aiming a torch at my face such that I couldn't see him. I was pushed into a row of four, being formed by the dockworkers. He was instructing the adjutants: 'We only have a six-minute march to the shelter, so one minute to go until we close the exits. We have been informed by a secure source within the regime that the alarm is sounded exactly 12½ minutes before the air raids. This leaves us exactly one minute to group ourselves in the correct formations.'

It was typically German how he trusted the official source; such a shame that he would be let down in this instance. I waited the full one minute, marched with them for a few hundred metres and then broke away from the formation. It was a good thing they were not armed. They might have shot at me in the darkness. It was now two o'clock in the morning. There were very few people on the streets, apart from the armies of air-raid wardens.

Their number made my chances of escape slim; I was sure to be picked up and brought to shelter. I did not think that wandering aimlessly into the darkness would bear success either. I would probably encounter patrols, and then the question was what was going to be more resilient, my nasal bone or the many lamp posts I was likely to walk into? On the other side of the road the air-raid wardens were rounding up a group of people that had been in a nightclub, so they could be herded towards the nearest shelter. I could hear a female voice, deep and clear as a bell, inspiring confidence: 'How romantic. We're being led into a shelter. And when the enemy has given up, we can come back and continue where we left off. Don't you think the wine will keep flowing, so cheer up old boy!' The voice stirred me deeply. It could only be Christine.

I crossed the street and bumped straight into her. The impact of the collision was softened by the curves of her bosom. She recognised me too as I clutched her hands and whispered, 'Christ!' I put my arms around her hips and pulled her away from the group. Trembling with joy, she was having trouble orienting herself because she had only just come out of the brightly lit premises into the darkness.

'Christa, Christa,' an annoyed elderly voice cried. 'We have lost our dear Christine. Let's have some light everyone. Help me find her. If the girl is no longer with us, then I won't be the one footing the bill and paying for the wine.'

The air-raid warden told him to be still and extinguish all lights. An angry grumbling ensued but we were already disappearing out of their earshot. 'I am no longer at the hotel,' she reported. 'I have my own place not far from here. I'm so glad I haven't told anyone where I live; they are fine people but not really friends of mine, mere acquaintances. There's no need to be jealous. But I thought you were dead. I saw with my own eyes your dead body lying in the street, surrounded by blood. I cried so much you wicked man. Why didn't you come and find me? You look different. Your lovely clothes are all gone and you sound different. What have they done to you? Don't you love me anymore?'

There were so many questions. I was only gradually able to explain. I needed her to lead the way since I had no idea where we were going.

'It was only a graze,' I lied. 'If it hadn't hit an artery in my back, there wouldn't have been any blood. As it was I lost a lot of blood and became unconscious. It was only once I was in the hospital morgue that I regained consciousness. They let me go because there appeared to be a bit of a mix-up. The wound was only small and had closed completely and according to the nurse you can hardly see anything. Of course, I'm unable to check because I can't see my back. But my money and all my clothes are gone. When I return home I will be left with a bitter feeling when I think of German hospitality. Of course I bear you no grudges.'

It is one of those facts that late at night, when a lady says that she lives only a few blocks away it is usually at least a mile. At last we reached one of the last buildings of the dark, completely silent suburbs. The house was at the very end of where the fields of potatoes and carrots were starting. She led me over a small fence and we strolled along a gravel path and a neglected flowerbed to the rear entrance. 'Stay here my love. I'll go up on my own. My neighbours are so curious. If someone wakes up and sees me leading a man home, I would die of shame. She knelt in front of me, undid my shoelaces and took off my shoes. They were wet and dirty and the soles were worn but she held them to her breast like a bouquet of flowers, then hid them under her suit jacket. Then she stroked my bare feet. 'You poor thing, you're all wet and cold!' She left a damp kiss on my nose and disappeared into the darkness. The sound of a door closing echoed into the night. I was puzzled. Why was she leaving me outside with no shoes on my feet? After a few minutes one of the windows opened and the beam of a torch illuminated the wall near where I was standing. A large wooden trellis led up to her window. I climbed it easily. Just as she was pulling me inside the window, the all-clear signal was given.

As I was trembling, wet and cold, she draped a red dressing gown over my shoulders. 'My poor darling,' she said. 'I have nothing to offer you, not even coffee. I went to get some this morning but they didn't have any left, not even the dreadful ersatz mixture.'

'Don't worry, my darling,' I replied. 'At this time of night I am not used to eating or drinking anything anyway.'

Then there was a little awkward pause. Despite our obvious love for each other, we were essentially strangers and I felt that I was by no means master of the situation. I sat on a green upholstered bench with the little Pekinese staring at me from a chair opposite. I was sure he was raising his eyebrows. I was a little embarrassed and turned around so my back was facing the dog, but to no avail. The little creature trotted around the bench and took up his previous position. 'What does the little doggy want, my sweetheart?'

'Oh darling, he's only wondering why we are still up. We should be in bed at this time of night,' she replied, and turned a bright shade of red that could be seen all the way down the V-neck of her top. She had already removed her jacket. And while I battled with my clammy and now slightly shrunken jumper she was getting undressed with the sure and confident moves of a truly beautiful woman.

Before I set off on my journey into this evil country, where so many unfair things were taking place, I swore to do one good deed a day by way of compensation. I was not yet able to put this into practice. When I thought about it,

I had spent more time teasing or even deceiving my people. Now, to put the little doggie's mind at ease, going to bed was my first truly noble deed. The fair lady spoke:

'My dear heart, if you are angry with me you must forgive me. There is no need to be jealous. I was certain that you were dead and when someone has died there is no point in considering their feelings. None of the people I've been with are my lover but I cannot stay in my cold room all day and night with only the dog for company. As soon as I recognised you I distanced myself immediately and came with you, didn't I? Now if you really don't have anything to wear for your journey home, then I can give you a nice warm shawl and my brother's old overcoat; a shame though, that they will both be a little large on you. You can also have my golf shoes, although they may also be a little large, but if you stick some tissues in the pointy bits then they should do. They are in a male style and I don't get around to playing much golf these days. I haven't told you yet because I didn't want to spoil our evening together, but I will be working again tomorrow and won't be able to see you until my next holiday. When I'm on duty I'm not allowed to see any other men, but I guess you have to leave anyway. No, don't get upset, darling. I won't cheat on you. When I am keeping watch on someone it does sometimes happen that we become intimate but have no fear, it is not out of love but purely because the situation demands it. It doesn't mean anything. I do really love you, even if you are quite poor now. I'm even giving you my lovely golf shoes. I firmly believe that they will never produce shoes that are so solid again, even when the war is over. I am no ordinary girl. My friends have always said that I have a heart of gold. Come, feel my heart. How it is pounding only because you are here. We must sleep now, you are going away, and I must report to the Gestapo at twelve o'clock … I know who I will be spying on next and shouldn't really tell you but I don't want to keep anything from you. Listen closely, it is a petty officer in the navy and I hate petty officers, especially sailors. They're so common and always spit on the carpet. If I had the choice and won the lottery I would only sleep with civilians. The Gestapo knows the man is a traitor but they're unable to prove anything and have to be careful because he's highly decorated. Strange, because he is such an unremarkable man. He squints and has liaisons with common prostitutes … Ouch! What are doing, you're hurting me!'

So as not to shout out loud, I was digging my nails into my flesh, but in the darkness I had made a mistake and dug into her flesh. I apologised, 'My darling, I did not want to hurt you, but I was reminded of when they shot at me and stole my things. My hands started to cramp up involuntarily …'

Was there no way out of this? I thought hard and then asked, 'What if they tell you to follow someone but you are unable to get to them and indeed, you are not their type because they prefer the garishly made-up drunken old hags? What if he does not react to you? Will you then get a different assignment and they put someone else on to him?'

'You have no idea, darling,' she responded, obviously hurt in her professional pride. 'There's no such thing as not getting close or getting no reaction. They choose us well and there is no danger of failing to get a reaction. First of all I'll go to the baths of the old sailors' home. I know he goes there for a bath each morning and I have no doubt that he'll be attracted to me. Although I'm beautiful, and I know it, even men with ordinary common tastes are attracted to me. And once I have gained their trust they tell me everything. And if there is anything they neglect to tell me I will then find out by looking through the bins or reading their letters.

But don't you worry, there's no reason to be jealous. I have already told you that I am only doing my job, my heart remains completely uninvolved. If it wasn't I wouldn't have such a history of success: in thirty-seven cases there is not a single failure.'

I didn't know what to say to that so I pretended to be asleep.

8

ARREST

'Maschinenmaat Griesemann,' the captain said with his arms behind his back and chin resting despondently on his chest, 'you're a swine! Nothing but a common swine. If ever there was any one of God's creatures who deserved comparison with the even-toed ungulate, who spends most of his time wallowing in the muck, then it must be you. Take your eyes off that clock there which, if you had bothered to look at one while you were in your lover's den, you may not have been late for duty. I guess there are men, or sorry pigs, whom we cannot treat with goodwill and respectability, but who deserve a kick in their grunting swine face. Look how you are standing! You can hardly stay awake and up straight, you bucket of vice. Do you know what you missed today?'

I did know but I was too tired to care. I had almost missed the opportunity to meet the Führer face to face, which should have been the fulfilment of my utmost desires but I didn't feel it was so. A delegation of our crew, including all those decorated, had been invited to Berchtesgaden – one of the greatest honours that could be bestowed upon a German sailor or soldier. And for this visit we had to decide on something we all wanted that would be paid for by the treasury, provided that it complied with the soldierly discipline of the Reich. For my part, I had no other wish than to be a thousand miles away, preferably on a South Sea island where I could sleep a little longer – and avoid meeting Christine in the baths tomorrow morning where she would be handing me a threadbare towel with the steely smile of a professional and in the service of my most dangerous enemy. I hadn't had any breakfast that morning. I was dragged in here as soon as I turned up, dead tired at ten o'clock in the morning. I had left my gifts behind. What was I to do with a pair of ladies' golf shoes? Surely they would not be appropriate for wearing in the German navy, and even less for such an important stately visit? I was no longer listening to the captain's sermon, but as he ended I was awakened from my thoughts.

'Herr Kapitän,' I began. 'I know that I do not deserve your kindness. My flesh is weak and I easily succumb to temptation. Please lock me up and only let me out once we are marching to the station for the visit to Berchtesgaden. I know then I will not be able to do any more mischief, and if I am still allowed to make a wish, then I will come up with something that can be fulfilled in prison.'

The captain appeared moved by my speech. I could read in his face that he was thinking, what if there is a hidden agenda in this newly found humility? I was only trying to avoid Christine. I had no experience of naval prisons but I was sure there was little chance of fair maidens gaining access to me. The captain took several long strides through the room, his chin was now raised and his arms folded across his chest.

'My dear chap,' he responded, 'it seems that uncharacteristic feelings have taken over your conscience. Admissions of guilt and a need for punishment – those are quite new for you. I had no intention of locking you up. I was only going to give you a firm warning. I'm not sure if I have already done so?'

It just went to show that there was no point in taking any of his scolding seriously. In the same way that absent-minded people forget whether they have just brushed their teeth or taken medicine, he could obviously not remember what he had just said.

'You wanted to kick my swine face,' I responded helpfully, but also with due contrition.

'Fine, fine,' he said. 'But really, you must pull yourself together. If you think being locked up is good for the soul then I won't hesitate. Everyone is allowed to enjoy their life, but duty is duty. There's no excuse for failing us. You know what happens when you fail to take your duty seriously! Just remember the torpedoing of the *Minna von Barnhelm*? You yourself were on the second periscope and are one of the few that know all about it.' Immersed in thoughts of an event that was buried deep in his conscious, he paced up and down the room and stopped in front of me. 'Gotthold, a question for your honour and conscience, was it really kept secret?'

With one eye on the clock I knew it was half-past eleven; only half an hour to go until lunchtime. Cheered by this thought I could answer with full confidence: 'I swear on my honour, Herr Kapitän!'

★★★

So I wasn't thrown in the usual prison after all. The captain seemed to fear that the Gestapo might get their hands on me if I went there. That they were already closing in on me in the form of Christine was something I was unwilling to disclose because it would reveal too much of my true identity. Instead I went to another prison on the first floor. Two rooms away from the captain's makeshift office there was a room with bars across the window. In the early days, when even married sailors were permitted to live in the home, one of the helmsmen had added the bars as a measure to prevent further accidents after one of his lively children had fallen out the window. The room was currently empty and had been adapted as a temporary prison and was identifiable as such by a nicely handwritten sign. It was meant for solitary confinement yet offered greater comfort than the room I had been sharing recently. The door was locked and the key always in the pocket of the duty sergeant. There was no one guarding the door. I had been shown how to open the door without a key, with a deft lift and a push in case of an emergency, like an air raid or fire.

The food I was given was the same as the others and I was allowed to receive post and smoke cigarettes. The only inconvenience was that for all the journeys that had hitherto been easy, I now needed an armed escort. I slept through the first twelve hours and was beginning to think this was going to be quite pleasant. Then they started to allow me visitors and I was no longer left in peace.

It was the evening of my first day, whilst I was not yet allowed any visitors, when together with my evening soup I received a letter delivered by the orderly with a grin. It bore a Danish stamp and was written in the handwriting of a 9- to 11-year-old. I spooned my bean soup but was quickly bored by its blandness and focused my attention on the cryptic letter:

Dear kind Uncle Gotthold,
How is the kind old man … have you sent me anything unfortunately not received? Dead perhaps? Sincerely I do truly hope now that he is alive. Did my uncle not die? I confess that I don't know or expect to receive another letter.
From your loyal nephew, Leo.

My initial reaction was what a stupid letter! I don't even have a nephew, at least not according to the diaries I had studied. Then I thought – could this be from the Leo I had met in London? The one who put me on this mission? It was a bit strange that I had not heard anything recently. I remembered the code he had given me: the first word of a sentence was of meaning, then the following two had to be ignored to pick up the next relevant one, and so on.

> Dear Gotthold,
> The man sent, unfortunately dead. I hope he did not confess. Don't expect another, your Leo.[1]

Of course, it all made sense now and explained why the letter sounded so childish. I also now understood why the *Geheime Macht* had given up on me. They really believed that the anonymous fellow with the will to change the world was dead, and the slimy Griesemann lived on. Fair enough, there would be no replacement. I didn't think I could stomach another change of identity; one was enough for me.

After the terrible tiredness had abated, I tried to make sense of what it meant for me to be invited to meet the Führer. I really should have felt honoured but I didn't feel any reason to celebrate. People in Germany had nothing decent to eat and their money wasn't worth anything. All they had was their Führer. Keeping watch on this prized asset were tens of thousands of young men. These capable young men had no other task than to protect and to shield him. I'm sure they wouldn't let anyone suspicious close to him, especially not if the contact was close and without supervision. I had put myself under suspicion, not because they knew who I really was but because of the nature of the person they thought I was. This was not helped by getting into trouble all the time, and now being penalised for it, and for having a beautiful and unscrupulous person who has never failed a mission lying in wait.

I sighed and wondered where she was. The baths had the same entrance as the laundry rooms, leading off the ground floor of the courtyard just opposite my window. Had I been accidentally peering out the window while she was on the lookout for me? No, I couldn't have. I had been in bed all day. And, I further calculated, the baths were only open until eleven o'clock. If she had to meet with the Gestapo at noon, then she would never be able to make it here before tomorrow, even if everything was arranged in time. I had to be on my guard tomorrow: the girl was not to be underestimated and was by far my superior in terms of wit and craftiness.

The grinning orderly returned to take my tray. His grin seemed even more malicious as he picked up the bowl with the untouched cold bean soup. I now recognised him as the same person I had spoken to on my first outing in uniform, carried on shoulders by the youngsters gleefully predicting that I would be dunked. Surely I was his superior? Didn't I have the right to shout at him and make him stand to attention? The next time I would be sure to study all the relevant rule and guide books before commencing such an adventure; then I would only have myself to blame. Who knew the rules for the navy? What rights did I have now that I was the imprisoned and he was my custodian? Could he answer by taunting me that I was no longer his superior as long as I was a prisoner? I decided not to try my luck and let it be. The man was still standing there with his dirty thumb resting in the cold soup. He had something else to say.

'What do you want?' I asked a little rudely.

'The captain wants me to let you know that if you have any specific requirements or wishes, whether for your breakfast or any other occasion, then you should let me know and he will see what he can do.'

'Fine,' I said. 'Please convey my thanks to him. If at all possible I would like some porridge and a whole coconut. You may want to write that down otherwise your tiny brain may not cope. Anything else?'

He sneered even more. 'Yes, Herr Maat. Someone spoke to the captain about the baths. I am supposed to tell you that you have permission to use the baths every morning and the officer on duty will accompany you there and back.'

'Thank you but I decline the kind offer. I have no intention of having a bath or shower. By the way, can you swim?' He looked at me stupidly and nodded.

'Thank goodness. At least that means there is no danger of you drowning in my bean soup.' His entire hand was immersed in the bowl but he showed no understanding of my joke. Only when I hissed, 'Get out!' did he understand and leave the room.

I was a sergeant and member of the navy in combat, decorated and imprisoned for the mishap of being slovenly and not reporting for duty. I didn't think this gave them the right to force me into a shower like a political refugee. I was also sure they wouldn't allow me female visitors. That was not the done thing. Even in ancient Rome or the Middle Ages there were certain rules and regulations when it came to prisoners, even under the darkest regime. I didn't think she would be able to follow me to Berchtesgaden, before which I was unlikely to leave my prison. After that we would probably re-embark, and that made it a little more difficult for her. I lay down in bed and fell asleep to these reassuring thoughts.

The next morning I was brought a bowl of porridge and the requested coconut. I was sure they were not easy to get hold of and not cheap. In a few months' time they would be even scarcer. It must have been knocking around Europe for some time with hardly any coconut milk left inside but I was not that bothered. I removed the bast fibre and made thin strips which I dunked into the porridge and formed a set of sideburns, long thick eyebrows shaped into a mono-brow and some longer bits at the back of my neck that now fell messily on to the sailor's collar. Then I stuck the headrest under my shirt. It looked like a real hunchback but gave me the appearance of being more narrow-shouldered than I was. Thus disguised I approached the window, taking care to be only partially visible and in profile.

I was right. Christine was in the courtyard in a fetching white apron, with a bonnet covering her blonde curls. It was still early and a chilly morning at that. Not a single sailor had felt the urge to visit the shower rooms yet. This meant she could focus all her energy on spying on my window. Luckily I had the Griesemann squint down to perfection, enabling me to show only my face in profile, at the same time keeping a watch on her and her surveillance tactics.

Of course, she was immediately aware of my presence and began to display the full catalogue of her charms. As if entranced by the fresh morning air, she spread her arms towards the heavens above and burst out a cheer of exultation. I was not sure who this was meant to impress: the two hungry seagulls encircling the courtyard or the white tailcoat shirt hanging on the line, billowing in the morning wind between two chimneys? Her apron straps slipped a little and her top tightened around her upper body. Then she bent down to pull up her stockings, silk and of the finest quality, surely by now unavailable to normal girls. They must have come via the Gestapo arsenal. Bare legs on someone with skin like Christine's would have been beguiling enough, but without stockings there would have been no reason to show her legs in such a way. I had to stand back from my vantage point because all the windows were filling with spectators. The heads of tousle-haired sailors appeared everywhere. They were only just awake but in good spirits, hardly believing their eyes. My disguise was only for Christine's benefit and not meant to be made public. As I was expecting visitors shortly, I had to quickly remove the telltale signs.

★★★

Sailors on leave do not tend to play charades or other games where you need to guess what the other is thinking. That is something I learned over the last few days. However, should there have been such a game, such as 'Guess what I am thinking about now', then it would not be difficult to guess what the obvious thing on everyone's mind was: the new fräulein who worked in the baths and her fine bosom. Nobody talked of anything else. Even those mates I only knew vaguely were coming to see me, saying: 'Hey you, she's been asking after you' or 'Listen, Griesemann, the pretty new girl is wondering why you don't come down to the shower rooms, you know the captain has allowed it!' The entire torpedo crew was being used to achieve her goals.

The Baron was particularly fiery and sang her praise: 'Oh pray, remove this fair bosom – I will not be willing to go out and die a hero's death if she remains here to tempt us. Gotthold, you're an idiot. I hear you sit there and crack coconuts while the fairest woman in the world is crying her eyes out for you. Should I put a word in with the captain? I know he thinks highly of me. It seems to me unjust to imprison someone while the Iron Cross is still warm on his breast. Gotthold, you are missing the opportunity of your lifetime!'

'Thank you, Oswald!' I responded haughtily. 'But I'll not beg for mercy and won't send others out to defend my cause. This bosom you are all raving about, and the fair lady attached to it, does nothing for me. You can stop trying to whet my appetite. I have seen her from behind and she possesses the broad hips and gait of a common working-class broad. I no longer have a taste for such womenfolk. With my distinction I now belong to the elite of the nation and I deserve better. If you know of a captain's or privy councillor's daughter, then you can count on my interest, insofar as the lady has sufficient beauty and intelligence. Stop looking at me like that. I'm serious. My newly discovered sense of class forbids any such dalliances as you propose.'

My lack of interest and dismissive manner was, of course, feigned. In reality I was quite flattered to be pursued by such a proud beauty, even if her interest was purely professional and her soul not in it. With all the visitors and unsolicited advice I was receiving, I was still feeling a little lonely and isolated. I can honestly say my exclamation of pleasure was unfeigned when at last my old friend the Student entered the room in the evening, limping of course. We threw everyone out of the room. He sat on my bed and stretched out his injured leg. As both of us wanted to tell our side of the story first, we had to toss a coin. Because neither of us had any money on us, we had to find an alternative. The Student tore a button off his trousers, from where the lack of a button would not cause any problems. He started to philosophise: 'How slowly are we gaining a new principle of power – or how long do trouser buttons last?'

Mendl & Rabinowitz was imprinted around the edge of one side only, surely not an Aryan company, and these were of military stock! He tossed, he won, pocketed the button and began his tale:

'Stretcher number two won the battle. They pushed me into an ambulance, which was waiting for me with its engine running. From the harbour we sped off in the pitch-black night towards the hospital as if I was fighting for my life. The driver, a member of the voluntary Automobile Corps, must have been hoping for some kind of special mention in the news by being the first person to bring a wounded person to the hospital. They had telephoned ahead, which was fortuitous, as the ambulance was going so fast the sirens may have broken the sound barrier and gone silent. They were prepared to operate straight away. The head physician was waiting for me, a well-known *Ober-Nazi*. He had gathered all his staff and was wearing his surgeon's uniform of coat, mask and rubber gloves. Two strong helpers held me down while they unstrapped me. My first instinct was to run for my life but sadly that wasn't possible. They put me on a trolley and took me to the top floor. The glass roof of the operating theatre was covered with a black curtain, giving it an eerie effect, like a chapel ready for the body of a general to be laid out. I was feeling more and more uncomfortable with all of this. Thank goodness they didn't put me under general anaesthetic and start cutting into me straight away. The head physician was on the phone waiting to be connected. My thought was that he may have been struggling due to the fact that all the telephone operators were in the air-raid shelter. He was not holding the telephone himself because he had already washed his hands; one of the nurses was holding it for him. Apart from these two there was also an assistant, an anaesthetist and two attendants. They removed all my clothes and covered me with an ice-cold linen sheet, from head to toe like a dead body. I was glad that it was taking so long to get a telephone connection. I think this may well have saved my life. Now he was in the room next to me and I could hear every single word.

'"Is this the office of the *Kieler Morgenpost*? This is head physician Gründemeier from the *Kriegsreservespital*, the wartime reserve hospital. Yes, of course. I am speaking personally. What! It is not possible to send a reporter to this location? Don't you understand this hospital is one of the most prominent buildings in the city and is sure to be the main target of our enemies? Perhaps I should add, if you are not already aware, that the operating theatre is on the top floor under a glass roof, G-L-A-S-S, I said, that's correct. And in this most dangerous position I am about to operate with an unfaltering hand on a poor wounded individual, a sailor if you must know. I see we have different views when it comes to how much publicity this feat deserves. Should I add that I am a member of the party, the head of the surgeons, perhaps my opinion does count after all, especially when it comes to appointing the chief of the local division of a German national paper. Fine, Fine. I am not threatening you, but if you are sorry, maybe it would be best to send someone you can spare. Tell them to bring a camera; no lights are necessary, we have the strong operating lights. I will not start before they get here."

'The nurse put down the receiver and the surgeon said: "Katherine, please wipe my brow. I have developed a sweat. My goodness, it takes some effort before these people see any sense." I wanted to say: "Please sir, my leg hardly hurts anymore", but the second assistant made a threatening move as if to say, "shut up or we'll give you some gas".

'"I wonder if we should ring up a second newpaper," the doctor said to Katherine, "perhaps the *Ostseebote*?" but before this could go anywhere there was another signal – the all-clear. His face turned ash-grey and he murmured, "typical". He was so angry that he didn't even let the nurse help him remove his coat and gloves. Already with his hat on, he pointed at me and called out to the first assistant:

"This man has a dislocation of his second knee joint, probably a torn ligament. You may want to x-ray him. I do not think an operation is necessary; the best option would be to cast it in plaster. If the reporter turns up, just send him away." Without saying another word he left the room, slamming the door behind him.

'The second assistant, the one who had previously threatened to anaesthetise me, followed closely behind. The first assistant, who had been the nicest up to now and was wearing the smallest swastika, approached me and asked where it hurt. Then he lifted my leg and stretched it in all directions before instructing the nurse that it was only a sprain. "You'll need to bandage the knee but do it so that he is still able to move it. You may want to rub in some alcoholic liniment first." Then he got changed, carefully and methodically, said goodbye and left.

'I was looking forward to receiving attention from the kind nurse, but it was not to be. "If he really thinks I'm going to go to the locked cabinet and fetch a bandage, seeing as it's three o'clock in the morning, just for a sailor with a sprained knee, he must be joking. We ran out of liniment months ago – I could have used some myself for my sore shoulder. I am off now to see how our head is doing. I'll try to cheer him up; otherwise he may go and do something stupid which we'll have to sort out. And then I'm off to bed" – here she yawned – "otherwise I will look like a ghost tomorrow."

'I was left alone with the attendants who were giving me back my trousers, saying, "count yourself lucky, you got away lightly". I then had to limp down the stairs on my own. As you know, it is not far from here and the place was still in chaos following the sirens. I was let in without problems. Anyway, now it's your turn!'

This was a bit of a challenge. Just like with the captain, it was impossible for me to talk about my experience with Christine without giving away too much about myself and the secrets I was keeping. I didn't think it right to lie outright so I had to edit my experiences and shorten the story somewhat:

'As I was on my way to the sailors' home I met this wonderful person. She took me back to her place in her love and kindness. As you know, I had no money on me. I stayed all night and overslept so that I was late for duty.'

'Out of love and kindness,' he repeated, full of acrimony. 'But then of course, you're about twenty years younger than I am.'

'When I came back here at ten o'clock in the morning,' I continued, 'they took me straight to the captain, and I had to explain myself. We had a long chat and he came up with this penalty. And here I am!'

'A long chat with the captain,' he asked suspiciously, 'and what exactly did you talk about?'

'The *Minna von Barnhelm*,' I said, innocently.

His friendly face turned puce with rage and he barked at me angrily: 'Have you forgotten our oath? If any of those in the know dare to give anything away, even in fleeting conversation, then the others have the right to dispose of them. By poison, without warning, if necessary. So be on your guard!'

I was very hurt and said, 'I made no mention of this ship, Adalbert. You can believe me. You were asking me what the captain spoke of and I was only answering your question.' Not that I feared that the Student, this good harmless fellow, was really going to secretly poison me, but I did worry a little. I wondered if all those in the know received a small amount of poison, only enough to finish someone off without his or her knowledge. Only yesterday, didn't

I discover a mint in my pocket which tasted a little strange when I thought about it? These dark and completely unnecessary thoughts were soon abandoned as my friend rested his sharp chin on his bony hand.

'Yes, the *Minna von Barnhelm*. You were on the second periscope. There was a large British flag painted on the side of the ship and an English name, I cannot remember which. If the idiot of a signalman hadn't dallied and spent ten minutes reading the dispatch from the command of the flotilla, then we would have known that it was not a British cargo vessel. If an entire ship or even a single passenger had managed to get away that would have been a disaster for the captain. As it stands, no one has the faintest idea how the *Minna von Barnhelm* mysteriously disappeared.'

At least I now knew what had happened. I didn't feel I had to poison the Student for talking about the event; after all, I hadn't taken any oath myself. With the last words of the Student still ringing in the air, the door opened and my previous roommate Raimund Pachthofer entered the room. I don't know why he thought that being an ex-roommate gave him the right to barge in without knocking. He must have just heard the last few snippets and said, 'The *Minna von Barnhelm*? Hey, that was the ship that disappeared without a trace. Any idea what really happened?'

The private was used to being kicked in the shins for not asking any questions and must have been surprised and not a little puzzled that he was now being snubbed and thrown out of the room for an innocent query.

NOTE
1 The translation of the letter has been slightly altered here to accommodate the code.

9

THE NIGHTMARE

The previous night I had managed to fall asleep with no problem. Tonight, after all the visits, it was proving difficult to find peace and quiet. I tossed and turned, uncomfortable, and with an agonising feeling as though my head was in a steam heater, my feet in a refrigerator, a piano on my breast and a crystal chandelier under the sheet. Even in a nightmare I showed my newly acquired expensive tastes. Where in my previous life would I have encountered posh items such as a chandelier, piano or fridge? My lips felt so chapped, I was sure I could have lit a match on them if I had felt inclined to practise such tricks.

My breath was rasping and laboured. My nose, up until recently a fairly benevolent organ, trustworthy in carrying out its duty, was equally useless in its two purposes: breathing and smelling. It was reduced to a painful red instrument of hellfire. At last I fell into a semi-conscious state, hovering between sleep and waking. I tortured myself with harmful musings. Last night I fell asleep calmed by the thoughts that my fair and dangerous adversary would not be able to follow me all the way to Berchtesgaden. Tonight the voices were taunting me. Did I really think she would be so easily put off? If she had the task of following me, would she not find her way whether it be through oceans and deserts? She would have no trouble making her way to a peaceful health resort … one that could be reached by train, especially if the Gestapo was footing the bill and easing her passage. It was difficult to foresee what role she would play and how she would disguise herself, but the diversity of the German people offered many options and the Gestapo would have the means to provide anything she required. I would have to prepare to bump into her at every step of the way. There was no escape – *So jagen sie ohn' ermatten*, they hunt him without tiring, as the poet had put it.[1]

Stop! I said to my iron bed … it had begun to roll away and was circling around the room. *Not so quick, you are making me dizzy. Please come back to the ground and don't take the corners so quickly!* But the bed showed no mercy. *If you insist on this movement please don't go in circles but move in a straight line.* This was the extent of my technical knowledge. The speed at which the bed was going around corners defied all sense of centrifugal force. The sensation was so unnatural that it could only be a dream. *But please dear bed; refrain from any further tricks such as bucking or trying to throw me off. I'm already feeling very nauseous.* I felt that even in a dream I deserved consideration. The bed obliged and forged straight ahead but it was no longer a bed … it was a compartment in a first-class luxury train that was hurtling through the darkness. A streamliner made of black glass and metal with radio sets in each compartment.

'*Achtung, Achtung!*' the speaker toned. 'All Germans take note, it is now twenty-one hours and fifteen minutes, Germany, stay awake! Think of Germany's magnitude, think of Germany's hardship. Do not fall asleep before the Reichs-Sleep-Chamber official gives permission to do so. The Führer is also still awake. ACHTUNG, ACHTUNG, stay awake!'

My head was hurting and I wasn't sure how I could make myself stay awake. I stared at the emergency brake, the only square item in the compartment. All others were streamlined and so smooth they didn't register. The brake was biting its handle: '*Bitte sehen sie mich nicht an. Ne regardez moi pas, s'il vous plaît. Si prego di non veder*' … 'Do not look at me' in three languages. It was a train that used to travel from Vienna via Tarvis, Udine and Ventimiglia to Cannes and the emergency brake was accustomed to communicating in three languages on its journey. 'Please do not look at me,' the emergency brake repeated. 'The collisions I always have to face as a result, such a pain, I'm so nervous. I feel hypnotised by their gaze and lead me to commit suicide' … The brake kept saying everything in three languages. A man walked down the corridor and opened all the compartments. It was the attendant in his brown uniform. He bore a strong resemblance to my captain. 'Good evening, sir, madam,' he called out to each occupant of the compartments. 'Please refrain from hypnotising the emergency brake.' I waited until he had disappeared from view, then shouted: 'How dare you tell me what to do. I am the passenger and you are the attendant whose duty it is to serve me.' In defiance I kept staring at the emergency brake. It is a technical item and I must fight against it; all such items are my enemies. Then the brake responded with a screeching voice: '*Mein Gott, mon dieu, dio mio*, I can no longer bear it,' and it activated itself. A terrible jolt went through the train and we came to a standstill …

A deep male voice said, 'Pull back the drapes, nurse, let the patient watch the enemy fighter planes. Now that we are standing still we can start the operation.'

The compartment was full of men in white coats with long grey beards that gently undulated in the breeze as they spoke to each other. 'It is a hopeless case of *Femiphobia acutis*,' said the eldest. 'Sister, do the necessary.'

Christine was with me in the compartment, dressed exactly as I had last seen her in a sleeveless pinafore.

Only the bonnet was different. She was now wearing the coquettish cap of the nurse's uniform. She curtsied and said, 'Heil Hitler! Herr Maat, show me your tongue. Your tongue is white. You must have swallowed pieces of paper. Just a minute, Herr Maat.' She bent over to retrieve the first-class spittoon which was kept in the corner of the room; her apron was tightening around her like a barrage balloon causing the seams to stretch and threatening to burst. She held the spittoon under my chin. 'The bits of paper, please sir. The Gestapo will be able to piece it together again ...'

★★★

'If he is feverishly ranting and raving, we cannot leave him here on his own. This at least we owe the captain. Who knows what he might reveal.'

I opened my eyes, blinking heavily as it was now as light as day in my room. My friends the Student and the Baron were seated next to me on the bed. It still felt as though there was a piano on my breast but it was no longer a grand piano, only a little pianola. I was still finding it difficult to breathe. 'What is happening to me?' I asked my friends.

Both answered in unison: 'Don't call in sick under any circumstances.'

I felt little inclination to do so after all I had discovered about the hospitals there. 'This must be my reward for being an exemplary soldier,' I complained. 'Yesterday I went straight to see the captain even though my feet were ice-cold and still wet. I had to stand to attention for at least ten minutes and that must have finished me off. At home I used to be told off for coming back wet and dirty, and the first thing I always had to do was take off my shoes. If I had been able to hop around a bit or jump from one foot to the other while listening to the captain's lecture, I may not have been hit so hard. I can only say that the captain has only himself to blame if he loses one of his best petty officers as a result. And what about you two? Are you just going to hang around and watch me die?'

'He is having a go at us so he must be feeling better,' the Baron said in a friendly manner. 'Don't get too close, Adalbert. Influenza is very catching. We were just debating whether it would be necessary to cut off your tongue if the harbour commando realised how ill you were and transferred you to the infirmary. We were thinking a few deep cuts might have been sufficient.' I was feeling sick.

'Is that the way to treat an ill person,' the skinny Student said to his corpulent friend. 'You forget what can happen! Ah … thank goodness, here come our saviours!'

Heavy steps could be heard outside the door and two sailors appeared, carrying an oxygen siphon from the U-boat.

'How did you manage to smuggle that out?' I asked, my voice still faint but full of admiration.

'We told the sentry that it was a devil of a machine and that we had to demonstrate its workings to the officers,' the Baron said. With that the sentry stepped aside and let them pass. Then he took it off them and, opening the valve, passed the refreshing blast of air to me and said, 'Take deep breaths and don't forget: every quarter of an hour is worth more than two bottles of champagne. Enjoy!'

The sailors wandered off and I was hoping for some clarification with only the three of us in the room, but it was not to be.

There was a sharp knock on the door. Without thinking I called out, 'Come in!' I was very surprised to see a male civilian at the door, bowing elegantly in the doorway.

'Don't disturb us! Can't you see we are busy attending a dying man,' said the Baron. At the same time the Student called out, 'We're in the middle of a secret instruction, no visitors allowed!' Unfortunately there had been no time to co-ordinate their responses, so both lacked the necessary impact.

'Excuse me, what did you say?' the stranger asked. He didn't understand because both had spoken at once. This was good because their messages were mixed and would have confused him no end. The gentleman was tall and broad, had a complexion of milk and blood, rosy, wonderfully smooth cheeks, flashing dark blue eyes and a blonde handlebar moustache. Despite having a bit of a belly, one could say with full conviction that he was a truly attractive man and in the prime of his life. He was dressed impeccably in a silk-lined, pale brown overcoat of the softest material which he was wearing unbuttoned over a charcoal-grey jacket of rough English cloth, striped trousers and patent leather shoes. Pale gaiters, a pearl on his silk cravat, and a solitaire on his slightly chubby fingers added further distinction. His rosy, freshly washed neck contrasted against the snowy-white collar of his shirt. His teeth flashed like chalk cliffs. The man smelt of Russian cologne and all that was good and expensive. His clothes and looks gave him an air of confidence, which made his momentary discomfort all the more comical.

'Do I have the honour of being in the company of the petty officers from the torpedo room?' he asked, looking from one man to the next, surveying the room containing the siphon and the man on the bed with a sore red nose. He must have been trying to piece together some sense from the snippets of information he had gleaned from the other two men. My mates remained silent to avoid further confusion so it was up to me to take control of the situation.

'Yes, we are petty officers,' I clarified to the intruder, 'but as you can see, we are busy. If you have brought tokens of appreciation, please leave them on the table. You may throw my clothes on the floor as there's nothing fragile in my pockets.' It appeared that he hadn't come bearing gifts.

'My honoured sirs,' he continued, in a flattering tone, 'pray give ten minutes of your precious time so that I may explain myself and you won't regret it.'

As the others didn't say anything I responded graciously, 'Go ahead. We are all ears.' I deposited the siphon on the floor, being accustomed to operating a similar apparatus in my employment as a dental technician.

The tall attractive man prepared to shed hat and coat and sit down but we didn't encourage him. He was left standing awkwardly in the middle of the room and began talking, not quite at ease. 'Dear sirs, between you, your military awards prove without doubt that you possess fine fighting spirit and exemplary patriotism. I do not need to assure you that my intention is not to question your loyalty. But there is change in the air. No one can foresee the future and those who are smart will look at alternatives to the current climate.'

The Baron was the first to lose his patience. 'I don't know what you're suggesting but you can stop there. You have brought no tokens of appreciation, and we're not interested in what you have to say. We value our time on leave and don't want to waste a moment of it. Besides, any minute one of our officers could come in on an inspection.'

'I do not fear your officers,' said the civilian. 'On the contrary, I invite them to join us so that they may see what I have to offer and you can witness the respect in which I am held by the command of the navy. Only last week I wrote a cheque to cover the fitting out of two U-boats, and that was without any ulterior motive; out of pure patriotism. If this fact was not well known then I would never have been able to visit you here personally. Your officer-in-command offered to show me around and introduce me, but I had my personal reasons for not doing so because I wanted to talk to you without supervision.' He was finally getting to the point.

'In the '20s I had an intimate relationship with the National Liberal Party and I was very supportive of the party members. I could afford it because I am a factory owner in the tinned food and canned drinks business. But even then I had a higher aim and was weighing up my options carefully, coming to the right conclusion at the time. I supported our Führer in the early days when he still knew all the names of the other members of his party. I must say that this money was a very good investment. I have not regretted it for one minute. But now gentlemen, I have it from a good source that you three are members of the opposition, intellectual leaders of the growing resistance to the current system. Please count on my support, but I will not leave the NSDAP, the Nazi Party, at this stage. You know only too well how impossible this would be because you yourselves are esteemed members of the party. I would like you to realise, dear sirs, that I wish you all good luck and success in your endeavours, and please remember that I was one of the few who showed the foresight to seek you out. I count on you to remember this conversation; have I made myself clear enough?'

'We understand you fully,' I responded, as the others were as silent as carps. 'We are three educated men, even if we don't look like it in our current outfit. I myself have the gift of poetic language. To sum up, you wish to support and revere the dawn of a new beginning.'

He repeated the phrase. 'Well put,' he said, obviously moved by the words. 'Our beloved Führer or Bismarck himself would not have been able to express it in finer words. Yes, gentlemen, that is indeed my intention. Make me your supporter and benefactor. Every idealist movement needs cash' – and here he took out his cheque book – 'and

I am not one who puts things off, especially when it comes to paying out money. What shall I put on the cheque to enable me to become a member and sponsor?'

Before any of my friends could say a word I stepped in quickly. 'This is something we will need to discuss privately.' I pulled the heads of my mates close together, regardless of the danger that one of them might catch my strain of influenza. It was one of those cases where one had to throw caution to the wind. We could not talk out loud with him present but I was also reluctant to let him out into the hallway. He might have a run-in with the sentries or change his mind about the donation. In my pocket there was a folded piece of brown paper and the end of a pencil. I said to the others: 'Write down what you think is a fair amount so that we can come to an agreement.' The Student was the first to get the pencil and wrote 25 marks. Without batting an eyelid I passed the paper on to the Baron who wrote down 400 marks. Then it was my turn and both watched me over my shoulder.

I wrote down 36,500 marks, then corrected myself and changed one of the digits, making it 36,**6**00 marks. I wasn't sure what we were going to do with all the money but it seemed to make sense to have a sum that was easily divisible by three.

My friends were too shocked to protest. I said to the fizzy drinks tycoon: 'We have agreed on the sum of 36,600.' As his face grew longer, I added: 'You are under no obligation of course. If your circumstances do not allow it, then we can forget everything that was discussed in these four walls.'

'No, no, don't be so rash. Do you think I'm a small child? I'm a factory owner and in charge of more than 12,000 workers!' He seemed mildly offended and started scribbling away in his cheque book. 'One more thing: I would be very grateful if you did not go to the bank and cash it straight away. A sum like this would be a little unusual and could lead to unwelcome attention which we all want to avoid. It would be best if you went to the cashier at my factory. I will arrange for enough money to be available for you in the morning. They are used to me requesting such sums as I often require them for loans.' He seemed proud of this fact. 'Here is your cheque,' he passed it to me since I had been the one conducting the negotiations. 'No, please don't bother writing a receipt. I don't have a safe on the moon and I don't know anywhere on this planet safe enough for such an item. I only ask that you remember me once you are in power. Very kind of you, dear gentlemen, to offer me a seat now but I was just about to go. I am pleased that we understood each other so well. Farewell and all the best. Do you have a special salute or slogan yet? ... No? Well for the time being, heil Hitler and God bless.'

Once he had left the room we didn't open the window, as all the pleasant smells that surrounded him would have disappeared within minutes. Since I was still recuperating, the windows remained closed and the smells of expensive hair pomade, expensive soap and expensive cologne lingered in my room for at least an hour.

Note
1 From *The Cranes of Ibycus*, a ballad written by Friedrich Schiller.

10

DIVISION OF THE LOOT

If there had been a clock in the room we all would have been able to hear it ticking, we were all three so very quiet. I turned the cheque around in my hand and studied the date, the signature and the fantastic sum. Then I passed the slip of paper to the Student, saying, 'Here you go. You look after it!' The Student gave it to the Baron: 'No, you take it. I don't have a briefcase and my pockets are full of holes.'

Many a young man from a humble background like me has become rich and powerful. That was nothing new. But the new thing was to become rich and powerful without being aware of it and having put no effort into it. Perhaps I, who was lying feverish and shivering on a simple straw bed, was destined for greatness and did not know it. Perhaps there were already hundreds or even thousands of fearless soldiers who saw in me their new leader, the organiser of a second, more ground-breaking revolution? In the old days many great men were led away from their ploughs while fate bestowed on them a crown and sceptre. Was my background as dental technician not just as worthy as a farmer's in a muddy field? But as always when I was painting too rosy a picture of the future, doubts and reservations began to take hold. If I really was this revolutionary sailor, this born-again Spartacus, then where were the clues in the diaries of my predecessor? Where were his hidden funds without which one shouldn't enter into a revolution?

The Student broke the silence first. 'Do you think they have a psychiatrist in the navy commando? I think I may have lost my mind!' He put his hands on his head.

The Baron interjected, 'That's so typical of you, looking for help in the wrong faculty. We don't need a doctor. We need a lawyer. Someone who can tell us what needs to be done with the money. What do you think, Gotthold?'

I made as if I was about to answer and tried to sit up straight but then let myself fall back as if lacking strength. With a faint movement of my hand I gestured that I was too weak to answer. As I was going through these motions I noted with satisfaction that I was indeed finally feeling a little better.

The Student answered on my behalf: 'I don't think Gotthold will come up with any explanation. I have a much more urgent question: How did this man find us? Do you think he knows of our connection to Leo?'

The Baron answered with some irritation, 'The *Geheime Macht* is a fairly secret and private operation with purely practical aims. Nothing to do with this dawn of a new beginning that so captured the man's imagination. But if you really think we should act like crazy people then we may as well send Leo the money so he can spend it all in the expensive nightclubs of London. That good-for-nothing doesn't deserve it. He promised to get us all out of here and now it's autumn and we're still sitting here waiting.'

He was right, I thought: Leo was useless and I also didn't think we should send him the money. I was very doubtful that the *Reichsbank* in Kiel would allow a transfer of that kind of sum in any case. But the fact that all three of us were still waiting to be helped was not quite true in the sense they thought. However, this was something I could not explain to them or to elucidate further.

'Mates!' the Baron exclaimed, after some time considering the situation. 'I think I know what has been going on. Psst! Come here! Come a little closer.' He checked under the bedspread to see if there was a hidden microphone or bug. 'Last night U-boat XYZ arrived from the Baltic. I was speaking to Anton who happened to overhear that their petty officers in the torpedo room really are connected to ...' His voice became so low that I could no longer understand anything. I did, however, have a good idea of whom they were referring to.

'And you think that the man with the super-clean neck just got us mixed up?' the Student asked, almost holding his breath.

'Do you have any other explanation?' the Baron retorted.

It seemed plausible to me, but sadly it had also put an end to my dreams of becoming a revolutionary with thousands of followers. At least I still had two mates and a few sailors on my side, although Anton was not showing due respect of late. I was disappointed, very disappointed. I was not destined to play the role of a hero such as Francis Drake or Klaus Störtebecker. Even if my plan did come to fruition my name wouldn't make it onto the billboards. It was possible that I might get a small mention at the very end, thanks to a friendly unnamed consultant or such like. I drew a breath and asked the Baron: 'Getting back to question number one – what do you think of our situation in your capacity as a legally trained person?'

He sat down comfortably, stretched his legs and began to expatiate. 'It is very likely that the money isn't meant for us but the petty officers on our sister ship, the U-XX. It is probably a case of the beneficiary being mixed up; an error in persona so to speak. If it had been a simple donation then we would have been committed to returning the money or passing it on to the correct party. As this was not a donation as such, but a gift that necessitates a service in return, then *do ut des* – I give that you may give, as one would say in Latin. The case is further complicated by the fact that we, or should I say you, set out the sum to be paid thereby acting as a director without authority. This also poses the question of whether we are indirectly obligated to the donator and have committed ourselves to a service in return? This is further complicated by the fact that the expected service was linked to a condition. You heard with your own ears how our odoriferous patron said *if*, meaning, only in the case that we (or rather, the other U-boat) should come to power. This leaves us with the following conundrum: If we give the money to the swine on the other boat, are we not thereby harming our benefactor? He is an amateur in all matters pertaining to the military and would not understand the ignominy of being the sponsor and donor to a U-boat that constantly misses its aim.'

Since we weren't legal experts, most of what he was saying went straight over our heads, but we fully understood the implications of his final argument. We came to a unanimous decision. We would keep the cheque and the Baron would cash it first thing in the morning. He was the only one of us who would not be in danger of being arrested and executed only because he was carrying a large amount of cash on him. My fever had receded, my fantasies had stopped and therefore my friends had no further cause to keep watch over me and left me alone.

11

THE GIFT

I was feeling fine, albeit a little wobbly. I'm sure I would have been able to recuperate more quickly if I had been able to sit by the window in the sunlight and fresh air. Christine, however, kept a steady watch in the courtyard, only leaving at four o'clock in the afternoon, after which the weather turned cold and foggy. I kept the coconut fibres under my bed just in case, in the firm knowledge that no one would sweep under the bed and get rid of them by mistake. Unfortunately it was difficult for me to appear by the window in disguise because the others in the home knew me too well. My mates were back on duty during the day. As a prisoner I remained exempt. The trip to Berchtesgaden, and with it the end of my incarceration, was approaching rapidly. My friends could only come to see me on their time off and when they had nothing better to do. This evening was one of those times.

'We were able to eavesdrop on the officers again,' the Student said. 'The local organisation *Kraft durch Freude* will be carrying out the ceremony. There was some argument about who would have been the most suited. They will be arriving tomorrow morning and have reserved one of the offices. They are still waiting for the president and his deputy – both long-standing members of the party. Do remember to have a shave tomorrow morning, Gotthold. You know that you are also to be granted a request. The captain has agreed that despite your solitary confinement, you will be granted an audience with the panel.'

The Student tended always to dwell on the negative. 'Now that we have all this money and have no idea what to do with it, we also have a request that will be granted.' He coughed. Now that he was able to buy as many cigarettes as he wanted and could smoke one after the other, his health was suffering rapidly.

'I beg to differ,' the Baron offered. He tended to see things in a more positive light. 'With money alone there is not much we can achieve in the current climate. Food is rationed: they have put a stop on importing pineapples and goose liver, clothes are rationed too and fine fabrics are nowhere to be had. We cannot even buy a vehicle. Just think of the fantastic cars we would normally have been able to buy with the money we have. Alas, there is little petrol to be had and no tyres. And books are forbidden. In the theatres and cinemas we are presented with utter dross. We can't travel to the Riviera because it's forbidden. I currently see no imminent need to consult medical specialists or lawyers. All in all, I have no idea how we are going to spend the money. But when it's the party's turn to dish out rewards, they who are not bound by the restrictions, just imagine what we would be able to do. An omelette made of three whole eggs, eaten in one go to start with, then roast pork with cabbage salad!'

'Will that be your request?' the Student interrupted, and licked his lips.

'I'm not sure. I'll have to consult my conscience,' the Baron laughed and pounded on his large belly. 'But I have to fight against this, poor neglected white lump of flesh, whose wishes do tend to be granted. Gotthold, what will you ask for?'

My answer was simple. I put my finger to my mouth and replied, 'That's my big secret!'

'We all know what Gotthold's greatest desire is,' the Student remarked. 'He has been fantasising about it for hours. Even the captain is aware: a game of chess with one of the greats, with a little bit of a head start and a large audience. Am I right?'

I just nodded and said, 'How can I keep a secret from you?'

'So what shall we do with all the money?' the Student repeated.

We had already discussed various options. Should we give it to our old captain? He always looked so miserable and did not seem to have much money. So many people congratulated him that most of his salary was spent on the telegrams sent in return. I do think the captain would rather fry his own galoshes and eat them for breakfast than accept anything from us. There were many things we could invest in on the boat, more defences for example. But we didn't want to support the arms industry because all three of us were committed pacifists.

'Why haven't we discussed spending our money on women?' the Student asked. Women were his greatest weakness; that at his age not one lady had deigned to love him just as he was, was an insult to the core of his being. 'We are all aware that even the most beautiful women have a price. Why haven't we expended any efforts yet? Is it out of consideration for Gotthold because he is currently imprisoned? I would think that that is not necessary. Am I right, Gotthold? You don't mind, do you?'

'Not at all,' I answered. 'You know me. I'm not one to begrudge someone anything. I may have been in days past but now that I have been awarded the cross, I have let go of this bad trait. If Adalbert fancies women, why not go out and have some fun and get the best our money can buy.

I don't mind being left out. Don't worry about being fair and taking it from your own share. I don't see how we can spend the entire amount anyway.'

'If we were in Monte Carlo,' the Student enthused, 'I would know exactly what to do. I have seen this in a film and thought at the time that if I ever had lots of money I would do exactly the same. The actor Hans Albers walks into a casino, hands in his pockets and his head held high. From all directions coquettish women slink towards him. He chooses the most beautiful one, takes a 100-franc note, rolls it up, and throws it across the table towards her. Out of the corner of his mouth he growls: "Hey babe, catch! This is for you!" And all evening the beauty does not move from your side. You buy her a diamond brooch, a sports car maybe, and then she moves in with you. But try something like that in Kiel! The first problem is that we aren't allowed any female visitors here. Secondly, I don't know any woman in Kiel that you would (captain's wives and ladies excepted) spend more than 10 marks on, even if you were loaded. Of course, there is one exception.' Both looked at each other and nodded in agreement.

'You're thinking of the tart in the baths who hands out the towels,' I interjected. 'The one you were trying to pair me off with a few days ago.' My friends were filled with indignation.

'Gotthold, how can you say such a thing? You only saw her from behind, and on a bad day when you were not feeling very well. You must have been suffering from a fever already. Never has a more beautiful girl handed out and picked up towels in the baths. And she remains as unapproachable as a queen.'

Of course, when she is on duty she is not allowed to start anything with another man. She explained this to me in some detail. But this was something I could not share with my mates.

'For my part,' I said, 'I am strictly not interested in this woman. But please do try your luck. You have unlimited funds at your disposal. But what will you do? Will you throw bundles of banknotes at her when she is handing out towels? You can't buy her a sports car. There's no petrol so she would not be able to use it anyway.'

'What about a diamond brooch?' Since my success with naming the amount that was to go on the cheque, I had turned into an oracle of all knowledge. Nothing was decided without my approval.

'It's not so much about what you get for her,' I said, 'it is more about how you present it to her. I would recommend the following: remain anonymous at the start. This has the advantage that you are unlikely to be met with a rebuff. If she really is as you describe, she might throw the gift back in your face and exclaim: "You can keep your gifts. I don't want them" or something along those lines. Therefore, remain anonymous and wait for the opportunity to reveal your identity by alluding discreetly to the token of appreciation. This is still no guarantee of success, but it greatly increases your chances. Do you know where she lives?'

'We have been making enquiries,' said the Student. 'She's living with eleven other working women in converted municipal offices a little out of town. I would not dare send anything valuable to this address and we can't send anything that she has to sign for because that would reveal the sender. No, I don't see any other way of presenting her with a gift other than face to face, here or at her house.'

'You have no imagination,' I berated my friends. 'Do you know which route she takes home?'

'I have been watching her for days,' the Baron admitted. 'Normally when she finishes around lunchtime she dawdles and finds things to do in the courtyard, staring at the windows. It's normally gone 4 p.m. before she gets changed and leaves the premises. Then she goes straight to a cake shop and drinks an *Ersatzkaffee*. She takes her time going home, always going down the same streets, not looking to the left or right and without turning round. She normally walks so quickly that I have a hard time keeping up with her. She always stops to buy the evening paper at the same spot. The first time she also threw some change at a beggar sitting near the viaduct but he is no longer there. He must have been drafted for military service. I only followed her three times, no more.'

'Think hard,' I said. 'When she reaches the viaduct, it must already be quite dark?'

'Yes, that's right,' the Baron admitted, 'but it is getting lighter every day.'

'I can see only one option,' I explained. 'Both of you must wait for her there. Wear facemasks because she might have a torch. Oswald, you are the stronger one. You grab her from behind and cover her mouth so she can't scream. And you, Adalbert, pin the brooch to her breast. Be very careful not to prick her skin with your shaky hands. If she really is as full-blooded as you describe her to be you may get blood on your shirt and you could get arrested for attempted murder. You needn't worry too much about being arrested – even with facemasks it would be difficult to classify your attempt as assault. Once the brooch is in place, let her go and she will run off into the darkness. Once she realises nothing is stolen, she will notice the gift and stop screaming. Do be careful, she is as strong as a pack of polar bears.'

As soon as the words left my mouth I knew this was a mistake. Even if you are so careful when lying, there is always the danger of making a slip and causing suspicion. The Baron raised his eyebrows. He looked at me closely. 'There you have it,' he said. 'Gotthold, I knew it! Pretending in all innocence that you want nothing to do with this woman, a common working-class broad, you called her and you had higher aspirations. Admit it, you hypocritical swine!' His voice was getting louder and louder. 'Where and when did you secretly meet with her to know how strong she is?'

My first instinct was to pretend to be offended by the accusations and invent a pack of lies about how I had seen her from the window lifting two of the Colonia vats with ease. These vats are in the courtyard, used to transport waste, and are so heavy that it normally takes two sailors to lift them because one on his own would be risking a severe injury to his back. There are exact rules about this: the two men have to grab each other by the shoulder. But I found it difficult to lie to my friends and remained quiet, relying on the Student to defend me, and he promptly obliged.

The Student had been taking careful notes, 'under the viaduct: black facemasks', he kept repeating. Then he sprang to my aid: 'Oswald,' he said, 'your jealousy and argumentativeness will be our ruin. Even if Gotthold really had met the girl in secret, and now denies it, what of it? Maybe he is saying it out of chivalry? Meaning that he is trying to protect the reputation of a lady? Gotthold has been unselfish in providing us with a tactic. You must admit, neither of us would have come up with a similar simple and practical plan involving a masked raid. Now you are making him angry and we've not even decided what exactly to get as a gift. We will need Gotthold's help, as we would not be able to think of anything suitable on our own.'

The Baron looked at me. 'Well, what do you suggest, you crafty old bastard?'

I had a flash of insight. 'Listen, just opposite the shop selling musical instruments there is a small jeweller's. These days he doesn't have much on display but I have seen a few things that will do nicely. One of them is a small dog studded with tiny diamonds, the other a clock face with hands but without movement, only for decoration. If you bring these items to me I will fashion a first-class ladies' brooch. It will be highly original and she will, if she has any taste at all, be very pleased.'

The dog was a little Pekinese and I was planning to set the hands of the clock to two since that had been the time of night I was with her. I was sure she would pick up the hint if she had only the smallest amount of female intuition. She would then know that her beloved Wilhelm Andersen was thinking of her and she would think of me in return; full of affection, as this was something she was permitted to do even on duty. I had no intention of deceiving my friends and gaining any form of material advantage from the present I was preparing. The soldering would be easy. I was used to a similar technique from making dentures in the past. I was looking forward to the work and the anticipation of Christine's warm feelings towards her Wilhelm. With no material gain forthcoming, I was happy to revel in the expectation of romantic feelings.

12

KRAFT DURCH FREUDE

The next morning I waited in my provisional cell, fully clothed and clean-shaven. Even my shoes were polished to perfection. The sentry refused to let me out before the captain had signed the necessary paperwork proving that my arrest was temporarily suspended and he was not yet in his office. I knew that the *Kraft durch Freude* panel was already in full throes on the floor below and I tormented myself with the thought of missing out on my slice of paradise due to bureaucratic formalities. Finally the door opened and I leapt down the stairs, taking three steps at a time. Perhaps I had not missed much; there can't have been many inside. My friends the Baron and the Student were standing outside the offices, apparently arguing.

'What is an absolute national disgrace?' I enquired of the Baron. I had only managed to catch his last words.

'They didn't send any reporters, Gotthold,' he informed me promptly. 'My friend, you look like a piece of cheese that has been in the open for three days. It is a good thing you are here now. You can help me to persuade Adalbert. The one time I demand a favour from a friend and all I get is hesitance and refusal.'

'What does he want you to do?' I asked the Student.

'No, you had better let me explain,' the Baron

interrupted. 'Listen. Adalbert has to wish for something a little piquant or sensational so that all the reporters flock over. I desperately need one present when the panel asks me for my wish. Here, this is what I will ask for.' He took up his pose, relishing the opportunity of a dress rehearsal.

'Heil Hitler, fellow members of the party. All my life I have had one wish only: to fight for Germany's naval prestige against the British arch-enemy. This wish has already been granted, so I have no further desires. Hey? What do you think?'

He was expecting applause, I think. 'I can understand,' I said, 'that you have no real desires because we already have all the money we need. But why you find it necessary to proclaim such fatuous nonsense is beyond me. Everyone knows that you enjoy playing golf, smoke navy cuts and normally rave about England.'

'You don't understand,' the Baron complained. 'I only want my declaration to make it into the papers and, provided that the party bigwigs read newspapers, I'll catch their attention and they will realise: "Oh, here is someone who is so good at lying. He is wasting his talents on a U-boat and should be working for the Propaganda Ministry."'

The Student took pity. 'If it really means that much to you I will help you. What is the sensational thing that I should wish for?'

The Baron thought long and hard. 'Why don't you wish for a lady of the night?' he finally said. 'Whether they will be able to grant you your wish or not is irrelevant, but in either case it will cause a stir. Women are your weakness after all.'

The Student grinned sheepishly. 'Let's go inside.'

We pushed down the handle gently and entered the room. There was a long table arranged in such a way that it divided the room into two halves. The area behind the table was the officials' area, housing the panel, which consisted of a bald, middle-aged man with short legs wearing pince-nez and an imposing lady with white streaks in her otherwise black hair, wound in thick plaits around her head. She had one of those enormous swastikas on her silk blouse, normally only worn by those unfortunate enough to possess slightly hooked noses or those failed in other ways to look like northern Europeans. I learned from my mates that they were married and were the owners of the largest pharmacy on the marketplace. He was the president, she the vice-president of the local KDF organisation. Next to them there was an impressive array of presents under a Christmas tree: books, catalogues and boxes carefully packed up so that we could not make out any details.

The Student forged ahead and approached the makeshift counter. The female commissioner gave him her full attention and the sweetest smile: 'Someone has to make a start. Please do go ahead. What is it that you wish for? Something pleasing to the eye maybe? Or some delicacy?'

The Student answered: 'I thank you kindly, my lady commissioner, but I desire something for the heart!'

'*Liebe ist eine Himmelsmacht.* Love is a heavenly power,' she sang with a pleasant voice and good pitch. 'I have thought of such wishes and have not come unprepared. See here, we have a lovely photo album bound with proper ersatz-leather with the pleasing title *Anmut huldigt der Tapferkeit* – Grace pays homage to bravery. We will insert pictures of the prettiest women in this city. Personally I think you shouldn't have only young women represented since I firmly believe that a female's traits improve with age, gaining beauty and dignity, but I will not insist, not for you sailors. You can have a nice album of beautiful young ladies; don't worry, our photographer is not prudish. There are some risqué pictures of fine young women with wreaths of flowers in their hair and substantial décolletage, a gauze veil, artfully draped around their shoulders. In my day, when I was young, young ladies would have never allowed such pictures to leave their hands, but nowadays young people are more free.' With this she sighed, much happier too. 'We will get every young lady to write an inscription under each image. I have some templates just in case the young things are unable to think of anything appropriate. With this album you will have a wonderful memento; something to last you a lifetime and to provide a warm feeling every time you take it in your hands.'

The Student said, 'Thank you very much, my lady commissioner, but I was thinking of something a little different. I don't mean to appear rude but in this instance I would much prefer to talk to your husband. My wish is a little bit of a gentleman's thing.'

She lifted her monocle to her eyes and looked at her husband who had remained silent throughout, and said: 'Theobald, this is a case for you. A sailor with similar instincts to you, you will get on better with him than I. Please take over.' The lady beckoned me towards her but I pushed one of the others forwards. I was not sure I would be able to talk to her and hear the end of the Student's story, and I was desperate to hear how it would pan out. Anton the sailor, whose turn it was, quickly declared: 'I would like a venison roast with cream sauce and berry compote with fried potatoes.' He was very loud and I moved away so that I could more easily follow the Student's conversation with the male commissioner.

The Student was aware of the fact that the others were trying to listen in and tried to speak very quietly into the man's ear – something he was bound to be used to as the owner of a pharmacy. The pharmacist listened intently with a professional mien. Then all of a sudden he must have realised that he was not at work but in fact representing the

Führer and the party. He proclaimed loudly for all of us to hear: 'I see, you would like sensual pleasure!'

Everyone laughed. The Student's patience was wearing thin and he confirmed, 'That's right. I'm so glad we finally understand each other.'

'Fine,' the commissioner said, regaining his professional composure. 'Not a problem.' He took the telephone receiver out of his wife's ear, thereby interrupting her order of venison, and dialled a number.

'Who are you calling, Theobald?' she enquired, but he was not answering.

The respondent could be heard saying, 'Vice Squad, how can I help?' which led to further grinning in the circle. The female commissioner blushed and her colour intensified by the minute. She no longer knew where to look. 'Excuse me,' the man said, 'is there another line I can use?' and waited to be connected. His wife had given up trying to order the meal via the telephone and had handwritten the order on a slip of paper, detailing the weight of the roast and the provenance of the order, then gave the paper to the orderly.

Her husband had returned in the meantime, waddling in on his short legs, grinning at the Student. 'Everything is being organised for the fulfilment of your wishes: the female is on her way and Office No 14 is being prepared for it.' We all knew that this room contained a large sofa and we were all devilishly pleased for the Student. He, however, was embarrassed by the whole thing and wished he was miles away.

The lady addressed Anton again with her sweet smile, 'Would you like your berry compote with or without sugar?'

Her husband was already occupied with the next in line, a sensible request finally and one who was satisfied with two tickets to the cinema. Two tickets, rather insensibly after all, for every day of the week and to include two viewings in a row. It took a while to reach an agreement and then they were interrupted by the telephone. There is a 'lady' at the gate who says she has been ordered, the watchman said, is it okay to let her in? The commissioner replied: 'Of course, of course. Will one of the sentries lead her in, please?'

The Student cleared his throat nervously and shifted from one foot to the other. I would have liked to have lent him support but I didn't know how I could help. 'Would you like your venison larded?' the lady pharmacist asked Anton, after a long whispered conversation with an emissary from the kitchen.

I made my way towards the door as I was reluctant to see my friend suffering. Here I had the fright of my life as a truly horrific creature was about to enter the room accompanied by one of the sentries. She was tall, dark, very skinny with sharp knees, a long sharp nose and an unattractively lop-sided mouth that was crudely painted a deep shade of crimson. The rest of her make-up looked like she had applied it in too much of a hurry, running down the stairs without a mirror perhaps. Behind her a companion stood – a thin man in civilian clothes with a pad and paper in his unkempt hands.

'Here is your lady, sailor boy,' the commissioner shouted leeringly across the room. Rather than going to meet her, the Student made his way towards the counter and began to argue with the pharmacist. At the same time, his wife enquired further of Anton: 'Would you like a beaten egg in the sauce or perhaps a spoonful or two of rum instead?'

The Student was speaking so loudly that I could understand every single word from my position at the door.

'You owe us equal treatment,' he reasoned. 'I can't believe that for a simple meal, every small detail is approved, but no one asked me about my taste in women. As it happens

I only like chubby blonde women with lots of dimples. This one here is dark-haired and bony.'

'I'm sorry, sailor,' the commissioner responded coolly. 'How was I to guess your specific wishes in regards to the amount of fat on a woman or her hair colour? Unfortunately it is a little late now. In a kitchen it is always possible to make last-minute changes, add a little salt here or there for example, but you have ordered a woman for specific purpose, and here she is. Did you think you were a minotaur and deserved a virgin sacrifice? Oh, pardon me, I'm not sure if you understand my reference; you may not even know what a minotaur is?'

Now this was a true insult to the Student. We all knew that in his youth he had declined an academic post in ancient Greek history and culture, and this common pharmacist was trying to teach him a lesson, whose field of expertise was such that Greek sources were only looked at when searching for an exotic name to give to the latest miracle cream or newly patented hygienic rinser.

I was standing so close to the object of the debate that I felt obliged to speak to her. 'Excuse me,' I said. 'I am conducting research for the Office of Statistics and would like to ask you: how much is the party paying you for work this morning?'

She smiled her most seductive crooked smile, showing off her neglected teeth, and said, 'Fifteen marks is what I am paid but the man from the paper has promised another twenty marks if I share my experiences with him. Pardon me,' she burped loudly. All in all she seemed to be suffering a little from lack of sleep and being out and about at this time in the morning. She turned around and faced the newspaper man. 'You always write about how the Jewish people tampered with food in the previous war, but what about what the landlords put into *gluehwein* these days? No one seems to take any notice.'

We were being interrupted. Now the Student made his way through the crowd, resolutely took the girl's hand and led her to Room 14. The whole mob followed with shouts of glee, only pausing once they had reached the door to the room. After only a few seconds alone in her company the Student emerged with an imprint of lipstick on his cheek, but dignified and transformed. He informed the superior who had come waddling out of his office with mock military posture, 'I have pleasured my senses and declare myself herewith rewarded and strengthened.'

The reporter carefully took notes. The others wandered back into the commissioner's office and the Student's name was struck from the list as done. Sailor Anton was just finishing off his venison sauce and looked satisfied.

Now it was the Baron's turn. He said to me, 'Make sure the reporter is listening' and moved forward. The reporter was about to leave and I held his sleeve.

'Listen,' I said. 'You must hear this man's epoch-making patriotic statement. You will not regret it. It deserves to be printed in bold in your paper.'

He resisted. 'Please, you must let me go. I have ten minutes before my deadline. I will lose my job if I miss it.'

The Baron had already finished his three sentences. The man from the press had hardly listened as he was thinking of his deadline and how to escape my clutches. But my dear friend was unlucky in other respects. After his little speech the entire room erupted in laughter and ruined the effect. Once a prankster, always a prankster; even if you are holding a funeral speech people expect you to be joking. As there was nothing else I could do, I let the reporter leave.

Now it was my turn. The lady waved at me. 'Now, my dear boy, don't be shy. Come a little closer. I don't bite. On the contrary, I will help you choose a lovely reward.'

'What about a brand new rubber dummy,' the Baron whispered helpfully, ever the joker. I looked dreadful, pale and drawn as a result of my illness and arrest. The woman thought I was much younger than I really was. Young people who look a little ill and helpless always have good prospects with women of her type. I was not given the opportunity to make my choice. As soon as I had reached the desk the people in the room began to shout: 'Check mate, seize the king!' My unlucky predecessor must have made no secret of his innermost desire to play a game of chess.

'Aha! You would like to play a game of chess,' the male commissioner interjected and pulled out the catalogue of a toy manufacturer. No one else had chosen anything from it yet but he had brought it just in case. 'What would you like? We have a set made of fake ivory here or one made of fake milkstone. And these sets here made of cardboard or paper are also very practical and can give much pleasure in their assembling, even if they are cheap to make.'

They really were treating me like a baby. No one was letting me – the main person in this dialogue – say a word on my own. Everyone was shouting: 'He doesn't want a chess set – he wants to play a game of chess!'

'With a master!' another one said. 'He wants to beat the world champion!'

The official asked for silence. 'If I understand correctly, Herr Unteroffizier, you would like to play a game of chess with a master. Although this is a sensible and honourable wish, I am not sure how feasible it is in the current climate, but hold on a minute.'

The man was a magician. He managed to pull out a registry of members of the local chess club. He scanned the names: 'Elias, struck off; Witkovski, struck off. Aha, here is one I know personally but ... hmm, hmm.' He leaned over towards me. 'I know a man who is a truly recognised player and once one of the internationals. A nice man, very learned, only …' Then he asked me straight out: 'Do you mind, the man is a bit of a half-breed: out of his four grandparents, one of his grandmothers is not 100 per cent. He had been removed from the board of directors of the chess club but is still allowed to carry on as a normal member. He is meant to be one of the cleverest and most dazzling players around.'

I nearly answered, 'that's ridiculous, why would I mind', but I remembered Leo's words. You can get away with most things: bigamy, perjury, incest, forgery, but the one thing people will not forgive is religious tolerance or indeed philo-Semitism. My answer was a little frosty: 'If the man can play, then why not. Perhaps you could urge him to hold back when it comes to social situations. We wouldn't want him to fraternise too much or have to shake his hands.'

The efficient commissioner already had the telephone in one hand: 'Hello, hello. Good morning, my dear Dr Kronhelm. Or should I say good afternoon. Yes, I too regret that we have not seen each other for so long. But you know how it is: business worries and activities for the party. We sacrifice most of our days. Now, don't be silly, no one is criticising you! Having said that, I do have the perfect opportunity for you to do something for the Fatherland. We have a young sailor here. One of the U-boat XY crew. You must have heard of the rewards we are giving out. The young man would like to play chess with a master and I immediately thought of you. Now, now, that's enough now. It's not as if I'm bestowing an honorary citizenship! Yes, he is aware. I have just told him. No, he is fine with it. I will fill you in before the game. Yes, why don't you make your way over? No, don't be ridiculous. There is no need for you to bring your decorations from the previous war. Nobody is in the least bit interested. Now, now, you should be glad you are not young enough to fight in this war. You know where to find us. The home is on the north side of the quay. I'm expecting you!'

He put the telephone down and wiped the sweat from his brow. 'I estimate that the man will be here in fifteen minutes. You have a chess board and chess pieces in the mess hall, is that right? I thought so. Everything is in order then. A game of chess can take hours, I have been informed. But that is okay, we are in the middle of a war. If you are entering a battle you cannot always say when you will finish. It is a matter of grinning and bearing it. But I don't want you to think that my duties are without dangers, on the contrary!' None of us felt like arguing with him.

I was feeling quite peckish by now, and the rewards were starting to repeat themselves, so I took the opportunity to have some lunch. I felt a little anxious about the impending game of chess. How was I meant to play it? My predecessor had wished for this opportunity all of his life. And I was not keen at all. At best I was a mediocre player, good enough to know how the pieces moved from square to square and even how to set them up at the beginning. I was also dreading my opponent. After what I had heard on the telephone he seemed to be a bitter man with a tendency to be overly effusive. I also hated the silly business about his not being of pure blood and the role I had to play in this comedy. I could not stop myself; I was secretly hoping for a Jew in a traditional cloak with a Russian-Jewish name, long beard and side-curls. With such a partner I would know where I was from the first moment. He would look right through me with his beady eyes and help me survive this difficult situation. Perhaps he would also tell me the latest joke that was making the rounds. I was not so sure about this partner with a diluted bloodline of 1 to 2.5.

'You're still not eating. You need to get your strength back!' the Student said reproachfully in passing. I was eating my soup listlessly with my mind elsewhere and it had gone cold in the meantime. I was due to go back into the hall because my partner had now arrived. His face worn and grey, features regular and striking, he looked a little like Goethe or Gerhard Hauptmann. His lips were engaged in a constant mumble. I could not help but imagine he was saying, 'I am only three-quarters; I am only three-quarters' to remind himself.

When the sentry brought him in the official moved towards him, shook the listless hand he was offered and whispered something in his ear. The man with the elegant brow nodded earnestly and greeted me, bowing slightly, his arms pressed firmly against his side. I nodded coolly. He said, 'This is my first happy day in a long while. This is also the first little thing that I am able to do for my country during this war ...'

'All right, that's great,' I interrupted. 'I would be grateful if we could start now if that is okay with you.'

We took our seats opposite one another in the middle of the room where the improvised games table had been set up. The spectators had surrounded us in a close circle and were reverently watching the master as he took a white and a black piece in his hands and offered me his closed fists. I refused to leave the decision in the hands of fate and demanded black. I had no trouble setting up the board, remembering the order reasonably well, and I was also able to follow my opponent's actions. He nodded as if to say we were ready to proceed. One of the spectators shouted, '*Achtung, Los!* – Watch it, here goes!' and the master made his first move.

At this I protested. 'I would like to make the first move,' I said.

The master looked at me despairingly. 'But how could you, you chose black.'

On this occasion I thought it best to concede. 'Okay fine. Have your own way, but I must say I find it a little strange that you will not allow me the first move as this game is in my honour.'

My friends mumbled discontentedly. The master was not making himself popular by showing himself to be an unyielding pedant so early on in the game. He chose to open the game with a very simple tactic of moving a pawn two forward. I replicated the move, smiled satisfied and leaned back in my chair. This was the sign the audience was waiting for. 'Bravo, Bravo! Give it to him!' they shouted in their support. I thought it was a bit early for applause but it went down very well and my mood improved no end.

The chess master looked pained and a little nervous. 'I'm not used to playing in such an environment.' Now was a good opportunity to have a go at him.

'Whatever happened to doing your bit for the Father-land?' I queried. 'Did you intend to measure the atmosphere first? Do you think that this is what we sailors would do in a naval battle?' The applause and mutterings grew louder. They appreciated my ready wit and the master apologised grudgingly.

The game progressed quickly. Only six or seven moves later he claimed check! His knight (mine were still in their base) was threatening both my king and queen. I thought long and hard about how to counter his attack, but the more I thought, the less my perspectives grew. If I saved the king, the knight would take my queen, my king would be in danger again and I would not even be in a position to punish the impudent knight for his cheeky move. I did not think the man was capable of such perfidious actions having such a noble brow.

'Queen in check! King in check!' My opponent was saying.

The spectators gathered around the table. They weren't holding their breath. On the contrary, there was much audible wheezing and sniffling. It was up to me to save the reputation of the entire fleet. I finally had the answer. I always thought it was a little unfair that the king could only move one square forward or to the side – no better than a pawn really. I corrected this. Why shouldn't the king move at least as far as a knight? I leapt forward with the king, took his knight and jumped back straight away because I didn't feel he was safe in his new position. Then I leant back and smiled victoriously, while the audience applauded wildly. Not one of them knew the rules of chess.

'You are not allowed to make that move! Take it back!' my opponent threatened me, his brow furrowed.

'I wouldn't dream of it. I won't take it back! Do you think I didn't witness the planning of your treacherous attack?' He went very pale and did not move. 'You must continue.' He shook his head.

Now the audience grew unruly: 'You must play on. We won't put up with it!'

It was getting so noisy that the commissioner, who was dealing with the last two sailors and trying to persuade them to accept cinema tickets to save time, looked over and gave us a disapproving look. The master conceded but changed his tactic. He placed piece after piece so that I could easily capture it and, after each gain, booming applause was heard. Words of encouragement and acclaim were raining down on me: 'Hey mate, give it to him! Blitzkrieg it is indeed, ho, ho, torpedo him down to the ground!'

When I finally took his king, he was only protected by a few solitary pawns. The other pieces had already fallen in battle. I was preparing to capture the final pawns when he stopped me from doing so by getting up and wiping all the remaining pieces off the board. He bowed.

I remembered and understood: this was not out of malice. Once the king is dead, the game is lost. Although the master had his arms behind his back, I managed to grab his hand and shake it vigorously. I hoped that this action would not be interpreted as a sign of my philo-Semitism. What a funny little man; that he had been degraded and ostracised by a perceived fault in his grandmother's ancestry was something he had resigned himself to, but to play a game of chess with special rules was something he was unable to bear. I was not able to reap the benefit of my mates' applause after my clear victory.

This episode paled into insignificance next to the occurrences that were about to take place. Doors were opened wide, commands shouted. Everyone began to run around aimlessly. We were given the instructions to board the trains to Berchtesgaden.

13

HEALTH RESORT, HEADQUARTERS

This was meant to be a health resort? Normally you would find a good number of benches, a spa, a picturesque promenade and a benign attitude towards visitors. We were guests here, esteemed guests, invited by our Führer and yet we were treated with military brevity. If I had to honestly write down my impressions of the atmosphere I would have likened it to General Headquarters. Even the reception was typically military in its courtesy.

The nice man from the *Leibstandarte* was somewhere between *Ehrenkavalier* and Grand Inquisitor. 'Where would you like to put up?' he asked me, but spoke so quickly that I didn't understand him straight away. 'A single room? I can offer a small room on the fourth floor. Or with your comrades? In that case, I would be able to offer you a bedroom with a view of the mountains.' Without thinking I went for the single room because I wanted to collect my thoughts and reconsider my situation. I quickly regretted it as I feared being on my own and the inevitable descent into negative thoughts. But it was too late to change my mind. He had already crossed my name off the list and allocated a room on the fourth floor with a small window facing the courtyard.

It was already late afternoon, damp and grey outside and rain threatened at any moment. There was no view of the mountains. Despite the hotel's grandness I found my tiny room depressing. It was nicely furnished with a chest, wash cabinets made of pale wood and a comfortable spring mattress. There were two paintings: a hunting scene on one wall and a stag resting in a clearing on the other. The bedside rug was made of goatskin. The air was a little clammy. It seemed that the room hadn't been used for a while. Dead flies had gathered on the windowsill and the light pull. Although I was a little cold from lack of heating, I pulled back the floral curtains and opened the window. All I could see was the dreary grey brick wall opposite. There was a bit of daylight left enabling me to see a little more. There was also a rain gutter painted dark green. I lay down on the bed, half-clothed, regarding the gutter and began my negative musings …

I had set out on an adventure, in the worst of seasons, hoping to help all mankind and bring peace back to earth. But this was not to be! Maybe if I had been a true genius such as da Vinci or Copernicus. As an ordinary person I must lack the deep and heartfelt connection to humanity. I was unable to see the whole picture, seeing instead a mass of individual beings, similar to meal worms, each occupied with their own little worm interests. These do not form a collective mass. On the contrary, one might desire the sunshine, the other yearn for rain. Even if I brought peace to all, I would not be able to help each and every one of them. Let us consider, for example, a Herr van der Stixt in Nether-Neutralia, who has just purchased 100 boxes of tinned sardines with his friends. If the war ends the price of these will plummet and he will lose all his money. Signorina Nina Baldi from South-Neutralia, near the coast, is not so keen for the war to end either. That would mean she would see her husband again, an officer in the *Bersaglieri* unit at the border, and could not see her Carlo every day. Humankind does not form a coherent unit or family, but rather is a concept in natural history and as such does not benefit from such sacrifices.

In only a few days from today I would be required to help solve the great historical problems we were facing and I was unable to concentrate because I was stuck in this room without a view. The only highlight was the constant sight of the gutter. But then my heart skipped a beat. The gutter, the only noteworthy object in my otherwise bleak outlook, suddenly made a noticeable movement downwards. I stared aghast as it jerked again, moved further down and disappeared slowly out of my view, like a snake creeping into a hole. I was reminded of the terrible story of King Belshazzar, who experienced the writing on the wall of his palace by a disembodied hand. What terrible warning I was receiving! Here I was thinking, 'I have nothing to rest my eyes upon but this rain gutter' and, at that moment, the gutter disappeared. I didn't want to delve further into the potential symbolic meaning of this. All I knew was that I no longer wanted to be alone. I needed company, laughter, friends with whom I could discuss trivial things, otherwise I would go mad. I was at least half-dressed, albeit without shoes and with my shirt unbuttoned. I quickly ran my fingers through my hair, which was looking a bit wild by now, and ran down the stairs all the way from the fourth floor to the lobby, hoping to find my comrades and their reassuring words.

The lobby was an elegant room with a wood-panelled ceiling, bucolic scenes on the walls and comfortable seating arrangements. Disappointingly, it was almost completely empty and quite dark. In the corner, however, I could see a solitary hotel guest writing with great concentration and speed at one of the desks, surrounded by a soft green glow and obscured by his cigarette smoke. He was wearing a navy officer's uniform and next to him the ashtray was overflowing. He turned his head and I recognised the captain. I was ready to disappear quickly so as not to bother him, but he beckoned me. I stopped in front of him, stood to attention and saluted, but unfortunately, being without shoes, my heels didn't click.

'How are you, Griesemann?' he enquired in a friendly manner, but didn't wait for my response. He had just finished writing the letter and was doing the address in large letters. 'Griesemann, you couldn't do me a favour, could you? Next to reception you will find my overcoat on top of my two suitcases. If you reach into my right-hand inside pocket you should find my wallet. In my wallet you should find some stamps. Get me one that will be enough for a letter within Germany, will you? I do not feel like going myself because the people from the hotel management will probably be up and about and want to discuss things with me. Nice as they are, they have no understanding that I am not in the mood to get involved in any kind of discussion. Or even better, if anyone is around, you may as well bring my coat, else you might be suspected of pick-pocketing if they see you with your hands on my wallet.'

I turned around and made my way to the entrance. I could see the two suitcases with the initials of the captain on them and a navy overcoat spread across them. Absolutely no one was around. All was quiet and almost completely dark. I found the wallet straight away and opened it. There was nothing inside apart from business cards, membership cards, a note for a furniture depot and a single stamp. I didn't know why, but without thinking I grabbed inside my trouser pockets, took out the cash I was carrying, smoothed the notes and deposited them deep inside the wallet before returning it to the silk lining of the officer's overcoat. Each of us had taken 1,000 marks spending money out of the funds. I knew I had not spent very much and although I did not bother to count, I was sure that there were at least 950 marks there. Then I turned around carefully to check if anyone had seen me. I lightly stuck the stamp onto the thumb of my right hand and sauntered back to the captain.

'The envelope please!' I said. I did not think it right that he should lick a stamp that had been stuck on my thumb so I did the necessary. The envelope was already sealed and addressed to a lady called Katherine. She had the same surname as our captain.

'Thank you, Griesemann,' the captain said. 'You are a kind and obliging young man.' Then he spied my bare chest. 'Good gracious, where on earth is your fine mermaid; she has disappeared! That's what you get when you do not put a preservation order on such works of art!'

'The tattooist was a swindler, captain,' I said, without hesitating. 'He must have used temporary colours; the image faded more and more every time I washed and now there is hardly anything left.'

'How strange, that's the first time I have heard such a thing,' the captain said, shaking his head. I could sense that his thoughts were already elsewhere in the meantime. As he had started to speak of personal matters (I was sure that a tattoo of a mermaid on one's breast constituted as something personal), I thought it would not be impertinent to ask the captain something personal in return. 'I could not help but notice that your suitcase was packed. Does that mean you are leaving us?'

'Yes, dear boy,' he said in a friendly manner. 'I will be taking the evening train. A driver is coming for me shortly. You are wondering about my audience with the Führer? Do not worry; that has been arranged differently. But you will not be left out. Your turn will come tomorrow or the day after. I am not happy about leaving you, so please behave and do not get up to any mischief. Here you go,' he reached deep inside his pocket and gave me a 10-mark note. 'Have a drink on me, but take care – don't get too drunk. The Gestapo is watching you, Griesemann! You have always been my problem child, so do watch yourself and God bless!' He gave me his hand. I had to avert my eyes in a squint, as my eyes had filled with tears. It was very rare for the captain to offer his hand and it could only mean something very serious. I did not hesitate to pocket the 10 marks, even though he was obviously not rich, but I had just given him ninety-five times the amount, although he would not know who the generous donator had been.

The captain was already on his feet, letter in hand, and was taking large strides towards his luggage on the other side of the lobby. I was left alone in front of the now empty desk, trying in vain to contain my emotion, the wrinkled 10-mark note in my hand. One of the cigarette butts had escaped from the overflowing ashtray and was burning a hole in the priceless material of the desk. I played voluntary fire marshal and extinguished the fire. On the blotting paper underlay I could clearly see the imprint of the captain's bold handwriting. I thought it was a bit of a waste that the paper was otherwise pristine and was sure to be thrown away when the Gestapo did its nightly rounds after the lobby had been cleaned. *Fine*, I thought, I would do them a favour and remove it for them. Then I slowly walked up the stairs, my earlier warning of a potential nemesis half-forgotten.

★★★

My friends in their lovely balcony room must still be awake, I thought. Without doubt they would be delighted to see me, especially as I had been a little isolated in recent days. All the while, these two always seemed to be huddled together, whispering. I entered and retracted in panic. It seemed as if the terrible prophecies were being fulfilled. *We are definitely cursed*, was my initial thought.

The Baron appeared to have hanged himself from the window frame, while the Student was kneeling on the floor amongst nails and screws, and in his inimitable manner was playing with the tools seemingly oblivious to the Baron's plight. Why was he not cutting him down and helping him? What was going on? *A double catastrophe*, I thought, *suicide and madness*.

I ran towards the window, 'Stop!'

The Baron warned, 'I'll kill anyone with my bare hands who dares to interrupt me!' He was alive but obviously insane. The light inside the room had not yet been switched on, but it was not completely dark either so I was able to make out more and more details. The Baron was not hanging by his neck – his arms were lifted over his head grabbing a thick wire-rope hanging from the ceiling; his back was facing the room. Now I could also tell that his feet were resting firmly on the ground.

'Come here, Gotthold,' the Student said. 'Since you're here we will let you in on our secret. Our beloved is back!' Our beloved – wasn't that the name of a symphony?

'And who is the "beloved" and what does she have to do with the fact that you have both lost your minds?'

'Don't be so stupid,' he said. 'The girl we gave the brooch to obviously.'

I sat myself down quickly. 'She is here? But where?'

'In the room above us,' the Student replied.

At the same time the Baron turned around and said, 'She has turned out the lights. I can't see anything anymore.' He pulled the item that I had taken to be a wire-rope towards him into the room. It was a dark green pipe that seemed to be breaking up into small fragments as little round mirrors were spilling on to the precious rug. My ability to show surprise was already used up; even if Easter bunnies had started to come out of the pipes I would not have batted an eyelid. Gradually, however, my feelings were evolving into a powerful rage. I recognised the rain gutter from outside my window and the terror I had felt when it disappeared.

'What do you think you are doing?' I said angrily.

The Baron answered, ready for an argument, 'Calm down! Although we purchased the mirrors to make the periscope out of communal funds, we will account for every single pfennig of what we spent.'

Only now did the penny drop. They had fashioned a periscope out of the rain gutter and mirrors so they could spy on the fair Christine in her room. I was outraged. Not only for her dignity but also because I now knew that they had removed the gutter, and as a result I felt silly about my overreaction to the symbolism of its loss.

I offered: 'It is not about the money. You have my full authorisation, but it is unfair and immoral to spy into a lady's bedroom. She was probably getting undressed and ready for bed. No self-respecting person should be spying on a woman doing something she would not be prepared to do on a stage.'

'What do you know about the things you can see on a stage these days?' the Baron sneered. 'If you don't stop moralising, I won't tell you what I was able to see.'

I had leant over to pick up one of the mirrors when the blotting paper fell out of my sleeve.

'What have you got there?' the Student pried.

'Oh, nothing,' I replied. 'I wanted to write a few letters later so I went to get some blotting paper from the lobby.'

'Can you give me half of it?' the Student asked me. 'I was thinking of writing a letter too and don't have any blotting paper either.'

'If we cut it in half it is no use to either of us. Besides, you normally write with an ink pencil. You just can't bear the thought of anyone having something you don't have.'

'And you are the stingiest person I have ever met,' was his answer. 'We thought that you might have changed after your decoration, but no. You are as mean as ever and can't even share a piece of blotting paper!'

The atmosphere was becoming increasingly icy and fraught. The Baron had been annoyed with me for a while because Christine had taken a shine to me, and now he assumed I was angry because he had been spying on the girl through a periscope. The Student had a bad conscience as he was spending our money without consulting me first. And I was angry mainly for one reason: they had removed my rain gutter which had terrified me into thinking my end was nigh. We gave each other hostile looks. 'Is there a reason for your visit?' the Baron enquired. 'Or are you just here to say unpleasant things and curry favour with us?'

'No,' I replied. 'You're right with the latter. Although I always relish your company I have quite simply spent all my money and need more cash.'

'Help yourself.' The Baron and I opened the drawer containing a cigar box with the cash. I took out ten 100-mark notes. The bundle was dwindling rapidly. When we first got the cash we had trouble closing the box.

I pointed out, 'One should not give one's money to people who have the habit of ripping down rain gutters. If it starts to rain, and it's looking likely if you ask me, there will be no drainage and the house could be severely damaged. It may even collapse as a result. I am not an expert but I doubt very much that it is possible to rebuild the hotel for 30,000 marks, or whatever is left of the money we have. How did you remove the gutter anyway? Did you unscrew it or cut it down?'

I leaned over again to inspect it and for the second time the blotting paper escaped. The Baron put his big foot on it and said, 'This blotting paper obviously does not want to end its days as a pristine piece of blotting paper in the services of a small-minded and resentful individual. The paper stays here and you were on your way out anyway. You may as well take the detour via the lobby and get another sheet!'

I knew that he was only trying to aggravate me but my patience was at breaking point. I jumped up and slapped him round the face. Even though he was twice my size, and twice as strong, he was sluggishly slow to retaliate due to his weight. He lunged out at me but I used my proven tactic of evasion and ducked. His punch hit thin air. The Student tried to come between us and a bit of a riot ensued. The hotel we were staying in was not suited to engaging in rough conflict between friends. The hallway was being patrolled and our little scuffle had only just begun when our dear *Ehrenkavalier* from earlier was at the door.

'At last, about time!' he said. 'I was beginning to give up any hope that you guests might get up to something. You all seemed as tame as lambs and that could well have cost me my job. My role is to intervene in such cases. Not in the manner of a policeman – anyone could do that – but rather in a mild, diplomatic fashion as only someone of my standing could. I am impressed with you three. You have my respect. Not only have you begun to demolish the building and started to kill each other, but also by the looks of it, you have just robbed a bank!' My 1,000 marks in large notes were still lying on the table. I quickly pocketed the money.

'If you look out the window, lieutenant, you might still be able to see the reason for our distress,' was my quick-witted response. He quickly made his way towards the window.

In the meantime, I whispered to my friends: 'Get rid of the blotting paper for our captain's sake!'

The Baron was quick. 'Well,' he said, 'if our dear inspectors are watching us so closely, then we must oblige by being as obedient as small children.' He picked up some of the chairs that had toppled over, straightened the tablecloth and picked up the piece of blotting paper, spread it out on the table and discreetly covered it with any other papers he could find.

The *Leibstandarte* man had come back from the window. 'Nothing of importance out there,' he reported dutifully.

'Oh dear, that means she has left,' I said with regret. 'A very beautiful lady was sending us air-kisses from the street and that caused an argument between the three of us. Oh, and the money is my inheritance.'

'All fine and dandy,' he said. 'I would be grateful if you could leave the rain gutter in the corridor. We are very quick; it should not take more than twenty to thirty seconds before everything is in its proper place. Are you carrying any dynamite? If you are you may as well hand it over. Explosives are one of the few things we do not tolerate. If you can think of any further mischief for tonight, please do let me know – I will see if I can be of service again.'

He looked around in a friendly manner. 'My friends, I can fully understand your boredom. Sailors are used to being entertained. Have you been to the Königssee? One of the seven natural wonders of the world in my opinion. You must go and see it.' He was looking at me now. 'With your authorisation to visit the Führer, you will be able to travel there and back free of charge. Well, what about it? When are you going on your outing?'

'Sure! Certainly! Thank you very much, as soon as possible!' I responded.

The Baron looked amicably at our *maître de plaisir* and picked up his monocle to take a closer look. 'Do you mind my asking, but are you from Mannheim?'

'I certainly am,' the gentleman responded. 'From the moment I first saw you I have been wondering if you are not Oswald. Well, I'm very pleased to see you my old schoolfellow!' They shook each other's hands vigorously. Then the usual followed: What is A doing these days and how is B. Whatever happened to C? They did not keep at it too long as they were both men with taste. I was still worried about the blotting paper and would have preferred it if the other man left the room sooner rather than later.

'Are you still the Great Discontented?' the inspector was asking my friend.

'Right you are, Edgar. As you can imagine, more than ever. But everyone has to do their bit as a soldier. But how did you get where you are now? You used to be a follower of the Gracchi brothers, liked Ulrich von Hutten and other reformers and idealists.'

'Listen,' the man responded, 'if your friends think in a similar fashion to you,' here the Baron nodded, 'then let me tell you the story of who I am and how I got here. So …' He smoothed his hand over his face like a hypnotist.

'It is true. I once had ideals, and they were set fairly high. But I am not alone in this world and I do not want to bring shame to my mother. She was always saying "Isn't Edgar a splendid lad?" I wanted to remain splendid, meaning I would please my mother by having a career, getting promoted and bringing money home so that she needn't worry. Our nation isn't a club where you can resign if you no longer like how it is run. Enough philosophy, it is all going a little bit too far.' He smoothed his face again. 'Right, we are on duty again. Have a good evening, comrades. Don't kill anyone tonight. Remember to put the gutter in the hallway and don't forget to plan your trip to the Königssee!' He waved his goodbye and disappeared.

'What about our captain?' my friends asked simultaneously.

'He is going back tonight, and the last thing he did was to write a letter to his wife or mother,' I replied.

'You know he is unmarried,' the Student corrected me pedantically.

I continued, taking no notice. 'Anyway, he blotted the letter with this piece of paper here, which means we should be able to read every single word he has written ...' I picked up the biggest mirror I could find. My intentions were obvious – I didn't need to explain further.

The first lines were smudged. The first word we could decipher was 'sobered'. We first thought he was telling his mother that he was no longer drinking but then the next thing we could make out was 'ideals', so the word must have been used in relation to these.

The ideals I have been adhering to all of my life have been sullied. After talking face to face with the men who run this sorry Reich, I am convinced that I am not fighting for the people but rather for gamblers and pirates. I do not want to live any longer, dear mother. If I die in battle, do not for one minute think that it was for Hitler. Farewell, please forgive me. May the grace of God ...

The writing stopped abruptly.

'... be with him,' the Student completed and crossed himself. He was the most God-fearing of the three of us.

'It is astounding,' I said, 'to learn that a man one has loved and revered is ready to end his life.'

'Even more unsettling,' the Baron added, 'is when this man happens to be the captain of the ship you are boarding in the near future.' I hadn't thought of this aspect but he was right. All the same, at least we were sitting together like old friends again.

'What were we discussing last?' I asked. 'That's right. Oswald, you were about to tell us what you had spied through the periscope. I don't even know how your adventure went. Did you manage to pin the brooch on to the girl?' Both grinned at the happy memories.

'Of course,' the Baron proudly regaled. 'It was not difficult to pin her down. She hardly resisted and only screamed once she was set free. She shouted something after us but we could not understand what she was saying. Adalbert wanted to stop and ask what she meant but I pulled him away. I think the police had already arrived. Sadly, there was little time to make the most of the situation by dropping the appropriate hints. Only just as we were about to leave we had the opportunity when we bumped into her at the gate. I put two fingers in the air, and Adalbert barked like a little lapdog, woof, woof. I think she understood. She said, "let me through, you silly monkeys" and she laughed. I think the proof of the pudding is that she followed us here. She will become our U–boat mascot and join us on our travels.'

'And what is she doing in her room?' I asked.

'She was wearing traditional peasant costume,' the Baron replied. 'But she had already removed the apron and the scarf of the dirndl. Then she did something strange. Sitting on a stool, she was grasping her umbrella, a small collapsible one. Rigidly upright, she stretched, bending her upper body forwards and backwards.'

'As if she was practising her rowing?' the Student asked, as he was one accustomed to exercise.

'Yes, like rowing practice.'

'What is the nearest body of water,' I enquired of the Baron.

'Probably the water from the taps,' he answered. 'But if you mean where one can actually row, then the Königssee would be the nearest option.'

There was a knock on the door and the hotel porter demanded the rain gutter. We had forgotten to place it in the hallway. My friends had also neglected to get rid of the compromising bit of blotting paper showing the letter to the captain's mother, but luckily they remembered in time to remove it the next morning.

14

THE KÖNIGSSEE

Three days passed before I decided to go to the Königssee. It had been raining relentlessly and I knew I would not be able to enjoy my surroundings in such conditions. On the fourth day the sun was shining. Although I could not judge the weather from my room, once I had ventured out into the hallway I could see the snowy peaks of the mountains glittering in the sun through the tall windows. I hastily got ready, made my way to the electric tramway and caught one of the few trains that were still running. The journey was pleasantly quick, clean and free. It took me through a wooded valley, through which a mighty river raged. When I got to my destination I did not go straight down to the lake; I picked a path leading up a hill between houses so I could view my surroundings away from all the activity. It was incredibly quiet and peaceful. No police, no cars and no air defence. Country people, mainly women, were working the land with slow, heavy movements. The sky was light blue, dotted with fluffy clouds here and there, the birds were singing and the tips of the fir trees were nodding gently in the breeze. As the trees became less dense, the path led past fields and meadows, passing farms, large and small, the houses all neat with green shutters and flower pots in which the autumn flowers were fading gradually. A little murmuring stream accompanied the path, initially difficult to see as it was covered in vegetation. I went more and more slowly, so I could take in the pleasant surroundings, and also because I was not used to climbing up hills.

I was just taking a little break in front of a small house with a narrow front window that was dominated by a large tree. It looked to me like a walnut tree. Its leaves were starting to fall, leaving empty shells on its bare limbs. I had not encountered a single soul yet but now a little girl, perhaps 7 or 8 years old, was running out of the house. She was wearing the traditional long skirt and camisole typical of the Berchtesgadener peasant costume. Her bare little feet were scratched and not particularly clean. The child was carrying a large sheet of paper in one hand and a hammer and nails in the other. She was now attempting to nail the paper on to the post. I thought it a little unfair to burden such a young girl with such a difficult technical problem. First the nail fell down, then the hammer, then the piece of paper. At one stage it looked as if the wind was threatening to blow the piece of paper away completely. In the course of this procedure, the paper was losing its pristine whiteness.

'Can I help you, dear girl?' I asked, and bent down on my knees.

'Yes please, inspector!' the young girl replied, looking at me fearlessly with her large blue eyes. She would have never seen a navy blue uniform apart from on the electric tram.

I had an excellent reputation as a successful implementer of nails. I carefully extracted the exceedingly wrinkled piece of paper from her little hands and looked for the best spot on the doorpost. Although I was trying to be discreet, I could not help but notice what was written in large letters on the sheet of paper. It read:

For sale, unworn traditional costume. No textile supply certificates necessary (exception to 15b of the RWA (Reichswirtschafts Amt) viewings daily. Contact Theresa Pfnur, salt worker's widow.

'It won't be necessary to put this notice up because I'm interested.'

She didn't appear to understand and looked at me so sadly that I nailed the paper to the post anyway and knocked on the door.

'You are interested in the alpine costume? That was quick.' A striking woman had opened the door. She had the face of a Madonna but rough worker's hands. She looked a little haggard and was dressed shabbily. She explained: 'I'm so glad I was granted an exception to the rule. No one would use up a textile supply certificate for an alpine costume. The welfare centre looking after family members of those killed in battle intervened on my behalf at the RWA. I was given permission and hopefully will be able to get some money for it.'

At the window an old lady with snow-white hair and prominent cheekbones was concentrating on her sewing, mumbling: 'Our Theresa is always glad and happy. Everything is fine as long as it goes according to the Führer's plans. She is even grateful when offered some worthless good-for-nothing money for her last possessions.'

'Do not pay any attention to her, Herr Marineoffizier,' the peasant woman said. 'She is not quite right in the head and has no idea what she is talking about. I will show you the item of clothing if you are interested. However, I'm not sure it's suitable for ...' *Our poor soldiers on leave*, she was about to say but resisted out of politeness. Then she went on to tell me that so many fine spa guests visit the area from all over the world and that many of them would surely be interested in proper alpine costumes. Sadly, few of them visit this particular area.

I looked at my creased trousers and my dusty boots. I'm sure I didn't look like a gentleman of means who would be willing to pay a premium for the genuine article.

'Dear lady,' I responded. 'My appearance is misleading. I have recently inherited some money and I can well afford to spend some of it. Why should I save up for a rainy day? I am a member of the U-boat crew.' This did not impress her.

'My husband was with the SA,' she replied. 'Even at weekends he only ever wore the party uniform. We decided some time ago to get rid of these brand new clothes. My husband was one of the smallest in his team,' she looked at me sympathetically, but without malice, taking in my slight figure. 'I will show you his things.' She opened the doors of a farmhouse cupboard wardrobe which had flaming hearts painted on them and took out the following: a pair of lederhosen; a light grey jacket with green lapels and red-lined pockets; leather braces decorated with edelweiss embroidery and the inscription 'God bless Bavaria'; white knee socks with green stitching on them. The socks were more like white tubes with no feet – it did not appear that they would cover one's ankles. There were no shoes but there was a hat with eagle feathers and various bits of intertwined green rope.

'May I try it on?'

'Of course, I will step outside,' she replied. 'No one has touched these clothes since my husband went to Poland and …' The child with the dirty scratched feet and the fearless blue eyes had come into the room and caused her mother to stop mid-sentence. 'Who said you could come in here? Have you done your homework, Veronika?' she demanded strictly. 'If the Führer only knew that you were being lazy, he would not love you anymore!' The child burst into tears and left the room. 'I am trying to get her to only love the Führer,' she said in her fanaticism. 'But she is such a difficult child and keeps asking after her father. Yes, that's right, the shoes are not included. They would not have fitted you anyway and were not quite new anymore. My husband wore them to work. It is a little difficult with shoes. I'll go now. Do not mind the old lady at the window, my mother-in-law. She is a little confused and won't take any interest in you.'

It was a good thing I was not wearing my long johns, otherwise I would have looked even funnier in lederhosen. The clothes were not a bad fit, a little loose, but better than the other way around. The white socks gave me very shapely legs. I was a little surprised at first until I discovered their secret padding. I assumed these were meant for the tourists, known for the fill of their wallets not for the shape of their calf muscles. All in all I was quite pleased with the outfit. Someone with a big belly and sturdy legs would have looked ridiculous. There was no mirror in the room. I almost approached the old lady to ask her what she thought but she stared into the distance with an expression of such gloomy indifference that I did not dare. The young woman was looking inside to see if I was decent and then entered the room again. I would have been happy to pay twice the asking price if she had shown any signs of admiration, but she was a proud, unapproachable woman, selling clothes and not peddling admiring glances. She adjusted the braces a little and turned the hat slightly, but that was all I could hope to receive from her in terms of personal contact. And this in a situation where my heart was longing for some signs of sympathy and approval!

'What do I owe you?' I asked almost shyly.

'250 marks,' she said, defiantly at first, but then went a deep shade of red and started to stutter and explain why she had to ask for so much money. She seemed terribly embarrassed.

I decided to help her out.

'Here is the money,' I said. 'I don't think it is too expensive, dear lady. No. It's a bargain, really. Look!' I had purchased a brand new Baedeker guide to southern Bavaria and Tyrol, the latest edition, and read out to her: 'For a traditional alpine costume, handmade locally in a farmer's workshop, made with good quality materials, in brackets deerskin and original alpine loden, you can expect to pay between 240 and 260 marks, fullstop. Note: Be aware of the rules and regulations covering the trade of textiles issued by the RWA.' I was making all of this up. There was something completely different on these pages but the poor lady was reassured, and looked at me happy again.

'You see, my dear sir,' she said. 'Although we are not able to read such esteemed books ourselves, we are still aware of the true value of things. Would you like me to make any alterations at all?'

I looked down at my legs. 'The only thing I am not quite happy with, dear lady,' I ventured to respond, 'are these green bands woven into the material over the knee. I once saw a man from Styria playing double bass in a band in Hamburg. He had brass buttons on his lederhosen or were they staghorn buttons? Would that not look better? I would be willing to pay extra for these.' What I was demanding must have been a terrible offence against the traditional dress customs, similar to wearing brown sandals with a dinner jacket or a straw hat with a parade uniform. Whatever small amount of sympathy I had gained was lost in a flash, as I had evolved into an enemy and evil person.

'Buttons on the knee, in Berchtesgaden!' Her disgust was undisguised. 'That is not possible and I will not stoop so low. You may be able to find someone to do the deed but you will have to travel. I can guarantee that no one here would oblige.'

I was a little taken aback. 'Please, I was only making a suggestion.' She was inconsolable and I realised I was no longer welcome in her house. I gathered my things and took them under my arm. As a goodbye I tried tipping the large hat, but it was a little awkward as I was not used to the size of it. I could barely make out a thank you. It wasn't possible to put on my uniform – not that it was too cold to get undressed, but it was quite a public road. For the moment I could only see cows being led by children, but as a soldier there were certain rules of decorum that one had to follow. I rolled up the messy bundle under my arm and attempted to make a neat parcel out of it. The lake must be in that direction; there was a little stream leading to it. I thought it was unlikely that I would lose my way and I was right. Only moments later there was a signpost pointing in two directions: 'Field route to Seelände (short cut).' Then there was an arrow in the other direction: 'Shady promenade walkway to Seelände, 8 minutes.' I was not in a rush and chose the promenade route, although it was cold enough and I had no particular desire for shade. With my bare knees I was even a little chilly. I chose the longer path because I wanted to gather my thoughts in readiness for the hustle and bustle of the activities at the lake. I should be doing something for the benefit of all mankind, but my problem was I didn't understand them, although I was one of them. What else will mankind put up with? What will they take, how much more will they swallow? As they tend to say in certain areas of Germany: what else will they chew, and when will they finally start to resist? I was referring to the peasant woman and soldier's widow. That her husband had been taken from her and was shot in Poland in a war of aggression for objectives she did not share or understand

– that was okay. That she could not buy her daughter shoes and was doing all the hard work on her own, without help, making her hands bloody and chapped – that was fine. That the bread tasted rotten and was mouldy, even when it was only a day old – that was no problem. Her parents and grandparents and great-grandparents were pious and had always gone to church, praying to God and Jesus Christ. She no longer went to church but attended party gatherings. She was expected to pray to Adolf Hitler, a mortal person with a newfangled cropped moustache. That was fine, too. But that someone wanted to have buttons on Berchtesgadener lederhosen, where all of her ancestors had always placed green bands – that was quite definitely *not* okay. It was a disgrace and a damnable expression of wickedness!

Through the trees of the forest I could see a shimmering light green surface. That must be the lake. To the left and right there were little stalls, almost all of them closed. In the one that was open an elderly lady in a dirndl was wearing the full traditional gear, complete with a locked jaw. '*Grüss Gott* and welcome sir,' she called out loudly as I approached, hoping to find something worth buying. Unfortunately she was only selling quite useless things: walking sticks with handles made of goats antlers. Would that really be useful once I was back in my navy uniform? She also had finely carved stag heads with real antlers. I wonder if I could hang one of these in the *Torpedoanstossraum*, provided that I acquired the necessary permission and there was enough space to hang it. Then there were pictures of the Königssee in various different sizes and frames, long tobacco pipes – impossible with my uniform – and sunglasses. But they might be useful. I chose the biggest and most expensive model with blue, adjustable lenses and an imitation tortoiseshell frame. They were only 3 marks but the lady was pleased to get some business in the low season. I did not want people to recognise me, especially as it was forbidden to go out without uniform. I put them on straight away. With this purchase I also acquired the goodwill and pleasantries of the sales person.

'The gentleman cuts a fine figure in this costume!' she lied, flattering me. 'If I did not know for certain that all young mountain guides were conscripted, I would have taken you for an alpine guide.' I acknowledged that her intentions were good. It seemed to me that it was a true honour in these parts to look like someone who could be taken for a mountain guide. Her benign attention was now focused on my parcel; I had not quite managed to pack up my uniform properly – a few buttons were showing. 'The young man is a military man as well?' she asked, concerned.

I had to admit it. 'Would you do me a favour and look after my parcel here?'

'With great pleasure!' the woman answered keenly, 'and if I have to lock up before you get back I will leave it at the cloakroom of the Hotel Schiffmeister.'

That suited me fine because it would give me the opportunity to get changed there. She fingered my parcel, almost reaching into the pockets of the coat. 'A navy uniform,' she observed. 'There are some U-boat sailors here. I know they are here to visit the Führer. The poor things, it must be terribly nerve-wracking to have the Führer talk to you. I do not think I would survive the shock. It would be too emotional. I am not as brave as a seaman is, of course.' She leaned over the counter and whispered: 'One of them is meant to be a young man with fox-red hair whose eyebrows meet. His beloved is here, or is it his ex? She is lurking around, pretending to be one of the girls on the boats. By the way, she is a tall strong girl with a fine figure. The first few days (she has only recently arrived), she came by every day to ask whether we had seen a sailor with a fox-red mono-brow. In the party we were told that it was a disgrace to run silly errands for capable young ladies and to neglect our duties to the nation. But do you know ...' Here her tone became more intimate, 'we tend to be a little old fashioned in these parts. Every one of us here in Seelände would like to know if the girl gets the man with the funny eyebrows. Now, do you believe this can be true?' She continued, 'You must be a man with connections. In Berlin there is meant to be a scientific institute belonging to the party where they have developed a method to speed things up, if you know what I mean. That means that a pregnancy no longer takes nine months. Babies can be born only four months after the wedding night. Women would be able to give birth three times a year, but I do not know whether I can believe it. It is all the same to me. Those days are over for me but it could be useful for my husband. He manufactures cradles out of wood. It would be good business for him.'

'This plan is completely unrealistic in terms of party politics,' I explained. 'With higher birth rates the Hitler Youth would soon overtake all other party formations in terms of numbers. They could gain too much in influence or even try to overthrow the regime; this is something the others cannot risk.'

I felt I had had enough sympathy for my 3 marks, and said goodbye politely. Wearing my sunglasses and with my hands in my pockets, I sauntered the last 100m to the Seelände resort area. I came to the conclusion that most things in life required practice. Even walking around with my hands in my pockets was different, as the pockets in these lederhosen were cut differently to my usual choice of trousers. I was a little disappointed by the scenery. The water was picturesque, shimmering pleasantly in different shades of blue and green like an expensive polychrome print. Sadly, however, there was not much of a view of the lake and the little one could see of it looked like any old lake in a low mountain range. There were restaurants and kiosks in abundance making it look a bit like a fairground. My first thought was that there was so little to see because it was low season and they had put things in storage for the winter. Now I realised that it was deliberately constructed just so; the main resort started at the bend of the lake. When tourists arrived they would be obliged to take a boat and spend money if they wanted to see the lake properly. Now I could also see what the Seelände really was – a landing place for the numerous boats, the piers just wide enough for the many visitors to disembark comfortably. One of the kiosks sold tickets for the boats. On both sides of the piers wooden boat houses stood providing overnight or temporary shelter for the vessels.

The largest hotel was called *Zum Schiffmeister*. It had a large stone patio area to the front with cafe tables laid out for the expected visitors. Their number was not great, however. To the one side of the veranda there was a red wooden bench where the rowers were sitting, all in alpine costume and mainly females, although there were a few grey-haired men with what looked like arthritic fingers. The females were largely beyond good and evil but the younger ones seemed strong and looked fine in the flattering alpine costume.

I recognised Christine immediately because she was that little bit taller and more attractive than the other women around her. While the other girls were laughing and joking she was staring at the ground, lips pressed together. It appeared that she was staring at her shoes; well, my shoes really. These were the golf shoes she had given to me after our late-night rendezvous in her room. She had applied some decorative leather bits to them so that they matched the costume. Unfortunately, the long green linen skirt covered her shapely legs and the knitted Spencer jacket did not make the most of her top half either. Her nose was red and a little shiny, her pressed lips appeared pale, almost blue, and her lovely hands were rolled up in the apron. She was sitting a little apart from the other girls. It appeared this was a result of the mutual dislike and lack of acceptance.

There she sits waiting for her prey, I was thinking to myself with mixed feelings, some of them even sympathetic because I could see how bad she was feeling and how cold she was. I was not afraid; not for one minute did I think she would recognise me. She was expecting a sergeant with bright red bushy eyebrows – the one she had spied from the courtyard window. She must be thinking that her dear impoverished Wilhelm Andersen had been deported to Denmark by now. Even if the blue glasses had not covered half of my face, she would never have thought that the man in the alpine costume could be her lover. I did not want to press my luck too much so I kept my glasses on. And what was I to do now? Take the bull by the horns and go down to talk to her, I answered myself, to prove, once and for all, which one of us was the more cunning spy. So no one had ever been able to withstand her female wiles; well, I was going to be the first. I could not develop a strategy before gauging the situation, and the extent to which I would stick out in this masquerade. I did not need to worry. It appeared perfectly natural for the tourists to walk around like this. The locals greeted me amicably and the other tourists took no notice of me. I was not the only one walking around in such a costume. There was an elderly gentleman in similar attire, carrying a camera with a bright yellow leather strap attached to his grey jacket, umbrella over his arm and rubber galoshes on his feet. As he was passing me I could read what was embroidered on his braces: *Ein Volk, ein Reich* – one people, one empire. He proved my earlier point – that men with a big belly should definitely not wear lederhosen.

He addressed me briefly: 'Chilly today, isn't it?' he said and walked on.

I only gradually worked out how the place functioned as a business. The visitors that were spilling out of the buses and local trains were initially disappointed by the fact that one could not see the postcard view of the lake and began to ask everyone where the path was that would lead them around the lake to get a better view. The locals, used to these kinds of questions, would reply that there was no such path. At first the tourists did not believe this, then they would give in and buy boat tickets from the kiosk. They had a choice of two-, four- or six-seaters, whatever they wanted. Once a busload of tourists was ready, two of the boat girls would get up from the long bench, grab two oars and board the boat. The bigger and stronger one, or – in rare cases – the man, would row standing up, the older or weaker of the two would be seated. As they walked to and from the wooden bench, they joked loudly. I could not quite understand what they were saying because I wasn't familiar with the local dialect. Judging by their gestures, their comments were rude and only suitable for the open air. They would be quite out of place in a nice tearoom or coffeehouse. They seemed to stick to the order they were sitting in on the bench. Half an hour later Christine reached the end of the bench and it was her turn next. I had been walking back and forth along the landing area, hands in pockets, which again appeared quite normal. All the other tourists were just as cold in the chilly autumn breeze and kept on the move to keep warm.

Once I could see that Christine was next, I approached the ticket vendor and said, 'I would like a boat. Would it be possible to have one to myself? I would only need one person rowing and I'm not in a hurry.'

Behind the counter a miserable old man with bushy grey eyebrows looked back at me. He did not seem keen. 'With only one oarsman you will hardly move forward, it will cost you a lot of money as I charge by the hour. Why don't you join one of the bigger parties?'

My response was icy: 'I did not ask you to help me save money.' He grunted something into his beard, which if I could only have understood the dialect, could well have been offensive. He called out to the bench, I presumed to say 'Next please!' but it was just a noise to me. Christine tried to get out of it but the others would not let her. A storm of indignation ensued amongst the older and younger colleagues: '*Sacra Teif, gehst net zua, du Luader, du faules!*' (Holy Devil, get on with it, you crafty bitch, lazy thing!) Or something like that, I imagined. And even worse insults followed. She took her oar and marched defiantly towards the pier and the boat the man pointed to. She put the oar into a sling around her body which meant she was going to row standing up. All the while she did not look up from the ground in front of her, even when I brushed her skirt as I took my seat. The man gave us a hard push and we moved away from the pier at a snail's pace, through the rippled water that was crystal clear and shimmered pale green in the light.

The rowing boats used on the Königssee, called *plätten* by the locals, had a flat bottom and a curved bow like the Venetian gondolas, but they were difficult to row and not very stable. When there was only one person rowing, the oar had to be turned after every stroke which would slow down the boat. If you failed to compensate, then the boat would keep turning in a circle. Christine was standing behind me, while I was sitting on a low bench with a backrest. We both faced the direction of travel. I was still wearing my blue sunglasses and kept turning round, glancing back, enjoying the view of Christine and her rhythmical rowing movements. The water gurgled underneath the boat and the dark forests of pine were passing by along the shore. I had a bought a paper from one of the kiosks, a *Voelkischer Beobachter*, and I now used it to cover my bare knees. I had also managed to buy a few apples which came in a proper paper bag. I took a large bite. I did not particularly fancy an apple. I would have preferred a sausage, but I wanted to be able to talk with my mouth full so Christine wouldn't recognise my voice immediately:

If you have any queries regarding the flora, fauna or historic buildings of this traditional German alpine region, please do not hesitate to ask our oarsman who will be more than happy to help you.

I had read this on a sign next to the ticket office and I decided to make full use of my rights. We were passing a tiny island, full of both deciduous trees and pine trees with a picturesque stone image of a saint.

'Would it be possible to make a stop here, fräulein?' I demanded, my mouth full of apple.

'This island is private and off limits,' she rattled off. 'Docking and landing is forbidden and not recommended as poisonous vipers are to be found amongst the long grasses.' We continued and reached the western side of the lake where she stopped.

I took another large bite. 'Please, fräulein, would you please tell me a bit about this area? I am a stranger here.'

She recited: 'This part of the lake is called the *Malerwinkel*, the painter's angle. This is where painters come in all seasons to "angle". I mean paint the lake,' she corrected herself and continued, 'to paint the lake in oil or watercolour. Fine artistic renditions of this picturesque spot can be bought at the sales kiosk of Angerer Crescentia. Her prices are reasonable and she is open all year round, even in the low season.' This was the name of the lady I had bought the sunglasses from – my source of information and cloakroom assistant. She must be handing out commission to the girls who send business her way.

'The tourist board guarantees,' Christine continued, still reeling off facts, 'that all painters are of Aryan descent and all the materials used are made using guaranteed Aryan production methods.' In the short time she had been doing this new role she had memorised her facts well. We moved on, albeit slowly. Even the ripples we were creating were overtaking us. The water here was dark green and so clear that you could see the depths of the rock formations underneath us. Ghostly white branches of trees could be seen near the bottom of the lake and plump little fish swam amongst the white skeleton-like branches, their backs marked with black swastikas. No, that was just my imagination running away with me. They were black stripes that formed a similar shape in conjunction with their dorsal fins. Although the black insignia was to be found everywhere, and nature was lavishly decorated with them, the fish were not part of this campaign. This was not a matter of principle but more a technical difficulty, I thought.

The scenery changed once we turned a corner after the *Malerwinkel*. I now understood why the lake was famous. The further we went, the higher the cliffs became. Mountains, wild and beautiful, surrounded the lake. The view was breathtaking and in the background the pyramid-shaped peak was visible, covered in snow. A few miles in the distance a red dome could be seen with dark pine trees behind it, and surrounded by sheer limestone mountains.

'Here you can see,' my tour guide continued, 'the ancient pilgrimage church St Bartholomew. The lake here is stocked with *aibling*, or arctic char. Would the gentleman like to travel as far as the church?' This was said a little nervously with her natural voice. 'With only one oar this could take hours.'

I took another large bite of the apple. 'Just continue with the journey. I will let you know in good time.' We were steering to the other side of the lake and her strokes were becoming a little more laboured. Here the rock faces were very steep, almost like a fortress. There was no space to pull in at all. On the natural blank spaces there were rock drawings, old crosses and washed-out colours. 'These ancient petroglyphs depict the terrible fate of those caught in a storm on this part of the lake and who found nowhere to disembark with the steep cliffs surrounding them. The locals call them *Marterln*. According to local custom everyone who passes should say a prayer for the poor lost souls in purgatory. Storms can hit in a matter of minutes, especially in the autumn, and small single-oared rowing boats are particularly vulnerable. Would the gentleman like me to continue?'

'Yes please, fräulein, carry on,' I replied, still unfazed. She continued to push and pull the heavy oar through the dark green, still element. 'At this very spot,' she continued in her professional tone, but I could hear she was on the verge of tears of exhaustion, 'it is customary to fire a shot so visitors can hear the wonderful sound of the echo that reverberates from the cliff faces. Once the gunpowder reserves of our boat company are used up, this practice will cease for the duration of the war. We only fire a shot if the passenger expressly wishes us to. Most of our customers decline these days. The gentleman wishes also to decline?'

I took another bite of the apple. It was the last one. 'Dear fräulein, I have come all this way, from the other end of the Reich, only so I can hear the wonderful sound of the echo, so I must insist. Please fire the shot!'

This was the first time she looked straight at me, like a victim at the stake looking at their merciless tormentor.

She said, 'I am not very familiar with the workings of the equipment. My training was only brief.'

'If you prefer, fräulein,' I replied, 'we can return to the landing place and you can refresh your training, and we can come back here straight away.' The piece of apple in my mouth was by now quite small. She shook her head, her lovely eyes full of tears. She secured the oar, reached under the bench and pulled out an antiquated pistol so heavy she could hardly lift it with one hand. The barrel of this mighty gun was plugged with paper. She filled the gunpowder and lifted the murderous instrument high over her head. She hesitated a moment or two, struck with the dilemma of how to hold her hands over both her ears, while requiring one to pull the trigger. Her solution was not ideal. She lifted the gun as high above her head as possible and, pressing her arms against her temple and half-covering her ears, pulled the trigger. The explosion was hefty and sounded like the shot from cannon. I think she used a little too much of the gunpowder. The echo reverberated five times – six times – seven times – then there was silence. The pistol fell out of the girl's hands, scraped her knee and landed on her shoe. A lock of her hair was singed and her hand was dripping blood from tiny round black apertures. This was too much for poor Christine. Sobbing, she collapsed to the ground, a heaving mess of green linen, black wool and dishevelled blonde locks. My heart melted. I threw the blue shades into the lake and made my way towards the other end of the boat where the once proud girl had collapsed in a heap. I got down on my knees, which in this situation was not meant to be a position of reverence. As I had previously said, I was feeling sorry for the girl. By now, however, the boat was rocking so hard that I did not trust myself to walk upright. 'Christl, Christl, don't cry!' I tried to console her. 'Everything will be okay!'

She had pulled the linen fabric of her skirt over her head and I had to carefully unwrap her. She hugged me with such force that the boat tilted dangerously to one side. I freed myself and urged Christine, 'Please darling, stay calm. Do you really want us to die here and now, without having explained everything to one another?'

She was still holding my hand tightly. 'Wilhelm, Wilhelm, to see you here! Please don't look at me too closely. These barbarians don't let me wear any make-up, not even a little powder and lipstick because it is deemed bad taste. Please do go ahead and cover my legs again. I bet you would not have thought that I would be wearing two pairs of fustian long johns, but it's very chilly here and easy to catch a cold. Look Wilhelm!' She unbuttoned her jacket. She had pinned the brooch onto the floral winter dirndl. 'I wear it day and night, even pinned to my pyjamas or my night gown, depending on which one I am wearing. Ever since you gave me this I knew that you would not give up on me. You travelled all this way to find me. But who told you that I would be in Berchtesgaden? What a silly question! Of course – you have excellent connections. If I think how well organised the whole thing is. First you put me to the test but I passed, didn't I? I felt so sorry for you when you were poor, do you remember? I even gave you my golf shoes! Now I understand why you did not need to take them with you. But Wilhelm, I must say, your helpers were not that clever were they? If I had put up a little resistance then both of them would have been full of broken bones. I was the German jiu-jitsu champion of 1935! I would have made a knot out of the skinny one and with him tied the fat man's hands behind his back. But I was as quiet as a mouse when I noticed straight away that they were pinning something on to me. I had nothing to give them anyway. I had to put up a bit of a fight to make it seem real, so I screamed a little when they let me go. A bit like this, two soft little tones: *Heah – ho!* Even this was too loud. An armed constable was already heading towards us and I had to call out to your people, "Bye bye, boys, take care!" so that the policeman would not fire off shots in their direction. The constable grabbed me so hard by my wrists that you could still see the red marks days later. He shouted: "What's going on, were you attacked?"

'"Nothing is going on," I replied. "I was just saying goodbye to my friends, you heard me, didn't you? Now please leave me alone!"

'"Yes, you said goodbye at the end but before that you gave off a scream, I heard it loud and clear!"

'"A scream?" I said. "You are a rude man. Don't you know that the Führer expects the police to be civil to the German people, especially to women? I was singing a song from *Tristan*, a German opera. Listen: *Heah-ho!* We were arguing whether I was singing the right melody, so I told my friends that the shops were still open and to run and get me the sheet music so we could check if we had the right tune. And then they went off straight away."

'"You are under arrest," he said, gripping me even harder. "That will teach you not to ridicule the police." He reached inside my handbag and the first thing he pulled out was my duty pass issued by the Gestapo. "Pardon me, madam," he excused himself and then let go of my hand, saluting me reverently. We stood side by side for a while and then he accompanied me all the way home. He was good-looking really, and quite young for a constable.'

I was not really interested in her successes with other men. But there was no reason to be unduly jealous; I could sense that I was still her current favourite.

'Why don't you reveal your true identity?' she asked. 'I realise you are already my prince charming but are in fact a true foreign prince, perhaps a prince of Denmark? The brooch was so special and truly original. Is it an old Danish heirloom? Or something from the colonies in the West Indies? I'm so happy you finally found me; I will never let you go and I will always stay with you! You must understand, I need something more constant, you see, you never know how long the thing with the Gestapo will last. They are more and more out of favour with the people. Things are not as well organised as they used to be either. When I got here and reported for duty no one was in the picture and they only had two disguises to choose from – not enough for me to find something I can really work with properly. One of the options was to be a waitress in the *Hofbräuhaus*, in the restaurant; the other was to work on the boats on the lake. I thought the second option would be more pleasant. Men are always rude and a little forward with waitresses. You have to walk through the restaurant carrying drinks, giving ample opportunity for men to pinch you or grab you where they please as your arms are full. And you can see things are no picnic here on the lake either. I have no interest in tracking down the unattractive sailor anymore. They should have sent him by now but he still hasn't made his way to the lake yet. I think it would be best for me to give up the operation and move in with you instead. I can understand if you are unwilling to marry me, if you are of royal blood, but perhaps I could become one of your court ladies?'

I was tempted for a second and thought, *here is finally something I can use my money for*, but I decided against it. It was a cowardly solution.

'Dearest,' she continued. 'I will never leave you again. If you do not want me to kiss you now then we will find somewhere to disembark, not here of course, but just over there. There's a landing spot not far from the path leading to the *Gotzenalpe*. There's a little clearing and we can rest on the grass. It will be a little chilly and I will surely catch a terrible cold and it will be the death of me, but I don't care. That's a sacrifice I am willing to make for you. I love you so much that I cannot exist without you.'

It was time for me to interrupt her flow of words as I was starting to get a little uncomfortable. I did not have to wait long; we both saw it at the same time. A motorboat was heading towards us at great speed. I was sure that there were not supposed to be any speedboats on the lake. Two SS men from the *Leibstandarte* were standing upright – one of them had a blow-horn:

UNTEROFFIZIER GRIESEMANN REPORT FOR DUTY IMMEDIATELY!

Aha, I thought. *I assume it is time for us to meet the Führer and they have come to pick us up.*

'They're only looking for that sailor Griesemann,' Christine said. 'Coincidentally, that is the name of the man I am meant to be following. Don't worry too much. They should not concern you. As a Danish prince you are ex-territorial, are you not? Could you make sure they do not come too close to us? I do not want anything to do with them.'

'You are demanding too much,' I answered. 'I have no intention of scuttling the boat. The temperature is no more than 9 degrees and I am wearing brand new clothes that cost me 250 marks. I think it is more sensible to get up and do as they say. What will they think of us if they find us both lying here? I know well that I have behaved honourably. The boat was not very stable for one but I wouldn't want anyone to think badly of me.'

The motorboat was now at our side. 'You must report for duty immediately!' one of the men said to me – he knew me from sight. 'You must all be ready at 5 p.m. There will be a car waiting for you. Just jump over into our boat!'

I climbed carefully into their motorboat as it was quite unsteady. 'You sailors are always very funny,' said the other, 'but hurry up! We haven't got time for your jokes.'

'Who knows if he is having a laugh,' said the first one. 'I don't believe he is pretending, I think he really has got shaky knees. Have a closer look at the girl; you'll see why.' It was a cheeky thing to say and Christine went bright red. She was a little indignant that we were not giving her a lift, but there was nothing for it. She had to row all the way back on her own. 'Bye bye, sailor boy!' she called after me. 'Say hello to your mates!' It would be highly embarrassing for her to admit that she had been that close to her target without realising it. I doubted she would take action against me. Besides, she would be busy for a few hours rowing back, possibly taking even longer against the stream. Hopefully, by the time she was able to do anything I would have already spoken to the Führer. The two guardsmen hurried me along so much I nearly forgot to pick up my uniform.

15

A GUEST AT BERGHOF

I was lying on my back in the rear of the car trying to change into my uniform trousers. The car flew ahead, and with it my thoughts. My entire life passed in front of my eyes. I had been in several life-threatening situations in the past few weeks but never noticed my past speeding along via my thoughts; I was sure it had not happened before. As a result I have come to the following simple conclusion: when I am moving very slowly, say climbing a mountain with a heavy pack or behind a slow-moving plough, then my thoughts were equally slow. If I am in a fast-moving vehicle, then my thoughts are transported like a flash. I remember once knowing a poet who was only able to compose his poems in a taxi. This led to his financial ruin in the end.

With my life passing before my eyes, I was currently going through my childhood and youth, a state I was still familiar with. I was standing with my dear mother in the laundry room, 15 years old and on my holidays. I will not say where or which country so as not to give away any details that might endanger my mother. Laundry rooms and schools can be found almost anywhere in the world. I was helping my mother voluntarily, as I didn't normally have to do any work in the school holidays. My mother had sent me to the shops earlier on to buy some washing powder because we had run out. It was during the time when a particular advertisement was very popular throughout Europe (this much I can give away, we were in Europe). I will call it 'Pursol'.

The shopkeeper was trying to sell me some of this Pursol. 'It washes whiter,' he said. But my mother had told me to get the washing powder we always had. So I said, 'No thank you, I would like the usual soap flakes.' The shopkeeper was forced to concede.

As we were doing the laundry, there was a loud droning in the air. The laundry room was in the courtyard and had a covering but no walls, so you could go outside and look at the sky without having to open any doors. It was an airplane, not unusual in those days, but it was an old rickety model. It was pulling a banner. We could not tell what it was as it was the wrong way round, so we continued with our task. After a few minutes we heard the noise again. The airplane had come back and this time we could read the writing: 'Pursol washes whiter' were the words we could now read. 'What will people invent next?' my mother said, shaking her head. But at that moment in time we both lost our faith in the old soap flakes. We felt that our washing could indeed do with being a little whiter. 'May I light a cigarette?' I asked my mother. I was only 15 but I was on holiday and they weren't very strong. My mother answered, 'Just for once, but make sure that none of the ashes land on our washing.' I took out my matches. On the packet I found the words: 'Pursol washes whiter.' Since it was a fine day, we hung the washing out to dry in the courtyard. My mother said, 'That's enough hard work for today, let's go inside and you can read the newspapers to me.' We were both feeling a little discontented. I opened the paper and the first thing I could see was a full page with giant letters and a picture: 'Pursol washes whiter.' My mother had had enough of the paper and turned on the radio. We heard a few beats of dance music and then a voice said, 'Pursol washes whiter'. My mother sighed and looked outside where the washing was swaying in the breeze, commenting: 'Son, I don't think our washing looks particularly white today.' And I said, 'Mother, we don't know the maker of the soap flakes personally and we don't owe him anything. Do we have to resist any longer? Why don't we just go with the flow?' And my dear mother said: 'You are right, my son, the next time we do a wash, I will get you to buy some Pursol.'

This is the way advertising works, whether it be washing powder, toothpaste or laxatives, and this was how the Führer and his regime crept into our consciousness. He advertised himself and his ideals for so long and so consistently that no one dared swim against the stream and everyone just went with the flow. But let us not dwell on this now, the man is in power and could do as he pleased. If I manage to persuade him to rethink his ideals, then that would be true victory for humanity. As it stands the man is answerable to no one. I convinced myself that I would be successful. The forthcoming events presented themselves clearly to me in my mind. The structure was in three clear parts with a central image and two side panels, like an Italian altarpiece, a triptych. Only my mental pictures were much nicer than the old images since they were thoroughly modern. They were moving images and spoke to me clearly as in a film.

The first panel: I get separated from my comrades, evade all the policemen, sentries and the lifeguards. Crawling, creeping through corridors and slipping through doors, I reach the inner sanctum of the Führer. I'm not sure what his office looks like; light wood panelling with green carpets, someone once told me, lots of bookshelves and of course a desk with a telephone. It doesn't really matter what the room looks like – it was all about the man who sits there. I open the door so quietly that he does not notice me straight away – all this is in my head of course. He is restless and plagued by unpleasant thoughts. He is talking loudly to himself: 'Am I surrounded by crooks and fools, liars and sycophants? Is there no one who will tell me the truth?' I step forward – in my vision – and speak: 'Yes, my Führer, I am here. I will tell my Führer the truth!' I had to repeat his title. If I used the formal 'Yes, I will tell you the truth', *Ich sage Ihnen Die Wahrheit*, it would sound a little strange. If I used the informal form of address, the '*du*', as in *Ich sage Dir die Wahrheit* – how much greater would the impact be? How dare I use the informal form of address with the Führer? He would answer, 'And who might you be who professes to speak the truth?' I would turn a little so he could see my Iron Cross. He has one as well. That should be enough to forge a link between the two of us, being decorated with the same medal. 'I see you have demonstrated great bravery at sea for me and for the Fatherland. A man like you deserves to be heard. Speak!' He points to an armchair. I decline. 'No, my Führer, I would rather remain standing.' And then I begin my epoch-making, world-changing speech.

The speech itself is the centrepiece of the triptych. I do not need to think through this bit. The speech is ingrained in my mind. So I go on to the third panel, on the right. This is the most cheerful of the three as it signifies my victory and triumph. The Führer listens to the entire length of my speech, not once interrupting me. Every now and again he nods approvingly. 'Are you finished?' he asks. I affirm.

'Thank you,' he responds, 'you have convinced me', and he reaches for the telephone. He speaks clearly and calmly into the receiver, not too loudly and not too quietly. 'Put me through to the Head of the *Reichsdruckerei*, the national newspapers. I have some news.' It never takes more than six or seven minutes before he is connected. 'This is Adolf Hitler

... do you need me to spell it out to you? H for Hildebrand, I for Isidor, yes, that's right, it's your Führer and Reichs-chancellor. Please report immediately that all 4 million soldiers are to be demobilised as of now. End of conversation.'

'Chief of the navy?'

'Speaking.'

'All U-boats and minelayers are to sink all their weapons and return to their harbours. Chief of the army! Chief of transport! Chief of secret naval supply system!' And so it goes on, liquidating the elements of this unfortunate war. Then he moves on to foreign policy. 'Foreign ministry, please!' – even though he is the most powerful man in the world, he occasionally says 'please' – 'At 0610 I would like to see the American emissary, at 0625 the papal nuncio, 0628 the Dutch representative, 0630 the Belgian, then 0631 the Swedish emissary. All official representatives of those countries and powers who have been striving for world peace are summoned to the Führer's office immediately!'

Then he continues with home affairs. 'Chief of the propaganda ministry! Cease the anti-British campaign in print and radio. For tonight's programme, a sympathetic lecture held by a professor of literature or history on the life and work of Rudyard Kipling and Captain Scott's last journey to the South Pole. Chief of the Gestapo! Set all political prisoners free. Break the news gently to the old and infirm. Leader of the former unions, meeting tomorrow at 1130! For all those previously imprisoned – a hot bath, delousing and a warm meal beforehand. Ministry of the Interior: get me the rabbis of Berlin and Hamburg and the Palestine Office for a meeting tomorrow at 1145. No argument! Police Headquarters Lublin: be on the lookout for Jewish deportees, bring survivors back in ambulances and return them to the care of the Jewish community. Reichs-finance ministry ...'

'Should I be on my way now, my Führer?' I enquire quietly, as I do not want to be witness to anything too delicate or secret.

'No, stay here, young friend. Your clear head and critical intellect will be very useful to me …'

I was woken out of my reveries abruptly as someone was shaking me. The bottom of the car was littered with the alpine costume and I was back in my plain navy uniform. In the time I had got changed and been dreaming we had not only travelled from the Königssee back to Berchtesgaden, but were now already heading up the serpentine road to the Berghof. This was the Führer's residence. It was nowhere near five o'clock yet, but it was better to be early than risk being late. Edgar, our *Ehrenkavalier*, was waiting for the car outside the Berghof and took me straight under his wing.

'My only wish,' I told him – I already saw him as a friend and someone I could confide in – 'is to have a personal audience with the Führer.'

Edgar responded very quietly and returned the confidence. 'My only wish is to become a tour guide for foreign tourists in this ghostly palace when this business is all over. I speak three foreign languages fluently and it will be difficult for someone like me to find a good job when the war is over …'

This destroyed all my illusions and I needed a minute or two to regain composure and get back the sense of ceremony for this momentous occasion.

★★★

Edgar guided me past an immaculate stone terrace with a wonderful view of the mountains into a simply furnished room with low ceilings where the others were already waiting. They were sitting on wooden stools and stared straight ahead, waiting patiently. Everyone knew my outing to the Königssee had happened with the full knowledge and permission of the officials and they had no problem with me coming straight from there. Of course, no one had any idea how it had gone. We sat in silence. Finally we, the crew of U-boat XY, were summoned into the ground floor reception room. We formed neat rows of two and followed our patron saint. We did not march proudly like sailors in a parade. No, we were more like a group of orphans or little girls, none of us daring to tread too hard on the floor. The Baron and I formed the final row of two. Our shepherd remained standing at the door of a room on the ground floor, herding us inside as we marched past. The room inside was filled with comfortable-looking leather armchairs.

'Step hard on his foot,' I whispered to the Baron, 'but try not to break any bones. And don't make a fuss if you don't see me for a few minutes afterwards.'

'Don't be a fool, Gotthold,' the Baron demanded, feeling the apprehension that we all felt. But he did as he was told and stomped hard on the guard's foot, catching him as he started to fall and apologising profusely for his clumsiness. Just imagine how heavy the Baron was. In those few seconds in which Edgar could neither see nor hear I was able to slip out through another door. As this door closed I found myself alone in the hallway. Another step closer!

I had deemed it absolutely necessary to separate myself from my friends for this conversation. An audience would only have hindered me. I could picture my friends saying, as I got to the end of my ground-breaking, world-changing speech: 'Take no notice of him and his views. He is an okay guy but a little under the weather at the moment.' No, I had to see him on my own. Sadly, many things are easier when you imagine them. Breaking into and navigating an unknown house was more difficult than I had expected. We had all had a glass of beer in the first waiting room, so I thought it would be a good idea to go to the toilet before anything else. If I could find one, that is. Who knows how long my conversation would last if I really did manage to captivate his interest and, after describing my vision, he did make me his personal witness to the dispositions for cancelling the war. It wouldn't be appropriate for me to interrupt the earnest debate with the words: 'Excuse me, my Führer, I'll be right back. I'm just going to the toilet.'

I was still standing on my own, which was unusually lucky in this house that was fiercely guarded. On the other side of the hall there was a door covered in the same wallpaper as in the hallway, very discreet looking. I thought this must be what I was looking for. I also thought it would be a good idea to get as far away from the door to the second waiting room as possible. The shepherd may decide to count his flock and find me missing, and go on the lookout for me. I stepped forward and opened the wallpapered door. There was no handle but the door opened inward with a little pressure. It was not what I was looking for, that much was certain. It appeared to be a telephone switchboard. I forced my head and upper body through the small gap and looked around with great interest. In this tiny room there were three female operators on low swivel chairs. Just behind them there was a man on a higher chair with a backrest who looked like he was supervising them. They rapidly connected and disconnected the wire cords on the exchange switchboard, speaking in short monotonous sentences, no one raising their voice. I was trying to hear what they were saying as they were now talking about the Führer, but I was interrupted in a painful and surprising way.

The part of my body I had left precariously in the hallway was given a hard kick up the backside. I flew inside the cell, landing on my hands and feet. Tears of pain shot into my eyes. I could just hear a voice from the hallway: '*Schweinekerl*, you swine of a man! That will teach you to stop halfway through the doorway. You know we have visitors and anyone could have seen you.' The door closed behind me.

'Serves you right,' the *Ober-telephonist* remarked. 'How often have we told you all that no one is meant to find out about this door? But if you must insist that you know better then you need to feel the consequences.'

'But I ...' I wanted to defend myself. With a '*kusch*' he silenced me. 'You are seven minutes early. Stay standing and wait for your shift!'

The telephone operators were wearing dark blue overalls, not dissimilar to my uniform. But even if I had been wearing a suit of silver brocade they would not have noticed as there were no windows and only very faint lighting. Not one of them had turned around to take a closer look at me. They were fully engrossed in their duties. And very interesting their work was, too.

'*Achtung, Achtung*,' telephone operator No 1 said into his receiver. 'Armed sentry in the stairway statue. Take down your weapon, the Führer has passed your position.' There was no answer. I doubted there was enough space in the statue for a speech transmitter. 'Machine gun sentry near the stone balustrade,' he continued. '*Achtung, Achtung*, the Führer is walking past. Confirm your position!'

Telephone operator No 2: 'Stone balustrade reports: "The Führer is walking past, accompanied by an unknown man and an unknown woman, both in civilian clothes."'

The controller checked his slip of paper. He was short-sighted and had to hold the paper very close to his eyes. 'Neutral diplomat and his wife,' he read out. Visitor number 83 for 4.45 p.m.' He instructed telephone operator No 3 to check with the x-ray department. 'Hello, x-ray. Please report results for visitor 83.'

'Man carrying key-ring, wristwatch, two spare buttons on the inside of his lapel, one collar button, to the front fountain pen of unusual dimensions. Officially reported to the magician, because of fountain pen.'

Officially reported to the magician? Now I had it! I was beside myself with joy. One of the strange characters sitting with us in the first waiting room looked terribly familiar, and I was trying to work out where I knew him from and could not put my finger on it. Now I knew. It must have been from a circus somewhere in the world. When one travels around so much, it becomes impossible to remember the circuses one has been to. I now remember that it must have been a Sunday matinee performance. There was a magician who invited various gentlemen up to the podium and stole everything they had on them without their noticing. I had been called up too. He had nicked my India rubber and a small bag of malt sweets; there was nothing else in my pockets. Although I prided myself on being very sensitive, I did not feel a thing. And this man was now working here.

'Control to magician,' was the last thing I heard. It took a while for the magician to respond, as he was probably busy stealing something.

Then came his answer: 'Fountain pen passed to chemical inspection unit.'

'Control to chemical inspection unit.'

'No vitriol, no poison found; the ink is normal but of foreign provenance. Refilled pen and hidden in seat of the diplomat's car.'

'X-ray department reporting: diplomat's wife could not be screened yet,' telephone operator No 3 added. This caused much commotion and upheaval. Instructions went to all armed sentries in the park. 'Prepare to fire – keep your eyes on the diplomat's wife!' The three telephone operators repeated the command to the sentry posts: 'Position report!' All three repeated: 'Position report!'

The report from the sentry post stationed in a tree hollow came through: 'Führer leaving grid reference 13b and entering 15b. Woman walking to the right of the Führer, one metre's distance, man following three steps behind.' There was a map hanging above the switchboard, divided neatly into squares. If they had let us see the map in the beginning I would not have struggled to find the toilet in the first place and ended up here.

'Sentry post in the garden shed is asking to speak to you directly, sir!' operator No 2 said, passing her receiver to the supervisor. The man completely lost his composure. 'Arm in arm, you say! The lady and the Führer are walking arm in arm! No, you must not shoot. You might scare the Führer. No, wait for a sign from the adjutant. What are you saying, the lady has asked the adjutant to go and cut her a branch with fir cones? Shoo … No, wait a moment.' We all held our breath. Then came the release. 'Adjutant back in position. Group on their way back on the same route. Führer has let go of the lady,' the tree hollow sentry reported, and we all breathed a sigh of relief. 'Führer entering grid reference 11a.'

Things were improving. 'Sentry post in the bushes!' the supervisor demanded. He personally instructed, '*Achtung*, the Führer is approaching with his guests. Set the four blackbirds free, just by the side of the path.' There was a problem. He appeared to be scolding them. 'Set them free just by the side of the path, don't you understand? We only need one of them to hop into the path. Who cares if one of them got trampled last time; are they your blackbirds? What do you know about political tensions? If a single person has so much responsibility you can't expect him to always watch where he is going?'

'They want to speak to you,' said No 3. He took the receiver. 'Yes sir, Herr Standartenführer, leader of the guards; the child is indeed in the glass house and has been waiting there for three hours. I hope the flowers have not wilted. May I suggest that we do not always use the same child – even if it is good at what it does? The guests like to take photographs and then they end up writing books about it; it is easy to see it's the same child in all the pictures. Of course, Herr Standartenführer, no need to thank me. It was only a small suggestion in the interest of our service. There is no criticism.' It seemed to me that you had to be particularly subservient in this business. '*Jawohl*, Herr Standartenführer,' he said finally. 'I will make sure someone blows the child's nose before it walks up to the Führer to present him with the flowers. Put me through to the sentry post in the bushes.'

I had lost track of who was connecting who but it did not seem to make a difference anyway.

'Put your weapons down. Creep up to the glass house and go up to the child …' he repeated the command. 'What? You have the nerve to tell me that this is not what you are here for? You are here to kill, you say … not to train blackbirds or blow children's noses? So, since there's no one to kill this afternoon you think it's okay to refuse your duties? Understood; end of conversation.'

'Put me through to the leader of the guard again!' he said and reported the incident. 'Fine,' he said, 'I agree completely. You will put the man under arrest once he is relieved from his post. Of course you are right, Herr Standartenführer, why should we risk lives unnecessarily? I will make sure he is arrested after he has handed in his machine gun.'

This was fascinating. I could have listened for hours but then the door opened, closed again, and a man in a blue overall came in. 'Replacement for telephone operator No 1 reporting for duty!'

Now the supervisor looked at me more closely. 'What are you doing here?' he shouted. 'Caught you red-handed, you spy! This is the end for you!'

'You did not let me explain,' I shouted back bravely. 'I was pushed in here with force. Don't shout at me. I am a knight of the Iron Cross First Class, naval hero and guest of honour!'

'*Achtung*,' No 1 said, about to finish her shift. 'Waiting room No 4 on the ground floor is calling. One of the petty officers of the U-XY is lost. We have to patrol the hallway.'

'Tell them we have found him. His escort can come and get him.' He looked at me, his eyes full of hatred. I'm sure he wanted to kick me, but he was too lazy to get up from his seat. I wasn't sure if he was even allowed to leave his position.

Our friend Edgar opened the door, grabbed my sleeve and pulled me out into the hallway. 'The Gestapo has already instructed me to keep a close eye on you, especially here in Schloss Berghof,' he said, 'but you are worse than I thought. What on earth are you doing here? Oh, I see. Third door on the left. No, you may not go on your own. I am coming with you. It is nearly our turn, the others are waiting by the stairs but I would rather let them all wait than let you out of my sight for even a second. Let's go!'

★★★

'All follow me! Up the stairs, keep up and smile! Come on, smile! We aren't going to a funeral!' I was walking next to a sailor I didn't know too well. There was no point in sharing the fact that the bronze statue, complete with sword and hammer, was concealing an armed sentry. A plush red carpet runner was fixed with brass rods. Matching shiny red marble from Salzburg abounded in the staircase. We all held our breath at the sight of such magnificence. Even I was subdued. The speech I had prepared to change the Führer's thinking was composed in a relatively humble environment where cheap wallpaper and wobbly stools were the norm. It did not fit in here where expensive Gobelin tapestry adorned the walls with all the wood-panelling, the marble fireplace, priceless paintings in gold frames and wonderfully soft club chairs. Like sheep we were herded along, our feet sinking into the thick pile of the carpet. We were not even sure if we were staying inside or making our way outside. One side of the hallway had a glass wall. In the autumn light, the hallway was flooded with the afternoon sun's rays. Mountains and clouds seemed within arm's reach. Our personal guide and a few of his colleagues placed us around a circular table, where coffee and cake were served. They forced us into the soft armchairs while they remained standing behind us. No one touched a morsel for the moment.

I was sitting comfortably in a damask armchair. Next to me on a soft bench covered in brownish-gold brocade, the Baron, the Student and another sailor were seated, all waiting quietly and subdued as if they had been hit by a meat hammer on the head. 'Don't be shy, talk to each other, look happy,' our chaperone ordered, but no one could muster as much as a smile. The more cultured of us quietly discussed the blacksmith work and stonemasonry of the fireplace. The Baron was teasing the Student, who was eyeing the framed, naked Venus lounging on her purple cloak. It was difficult to hold a real conversation. We heard a movement behind us but no one dared to turn around.

Now our guard whispered to us: 'Stand up! Not all at the same time. Casually, one after the other. Look towards the window and stand to attention discreetly.'

There was an enormous mirrored table with no drawers. No one had noticed anyone sitting there when we entered the room. Now there was a broad-shouldered man, his head held unnaturally, browsing through books and papers. As soon as we were all standing, the man turned his face towards us, concealed in shadow, and his high metallic voice toned monotonously: 'My dear sailors, your Führer welcomes you!'

We no longer worried about what we had to do next. We were sure Edgar would tell us what to do in whispered tones. We were not let down. We heard a quiet 'Sit down again, one after the other. Look happy, eat, drink something; talk to one another. One after the other you will be called up to speak to the Führer.'

The hallway was enormous. There was at least 15m between the table where we were seated and the Führer's desk. I would be able to conduct my conversation relatively privately after all. As the others were sipping their cups of coffee, their hands shaking, hardly managing to swallow the bite of cake that was lodged in their mouths, I was staring unabashedly at the Führer. I noticed a very odd psychological phenomenon in myself. I had always been critical, harbouring feelings of extreme aversion towards the Führer, but ever since I had been in Germany and part of the military I could not help but feel a small fraction of respect. One cannot help but feel the influence of what is being said on the radio and in the newspapers. At this moment in time I also felt a strange warm feeling, almost like a childish reverence. I'm sure it had nothing to do with his greeting per se but was more to do with his nuanced delivery. The way he said 'welcome' with a long vowel, after which he blew out air from his nostrils into his moustache; all this seemed so familiar and even more disarming. I felt like a child again, sitting at the feet of the Führer. I'm sure I had been there before in a previous, more pleasant life, feeling happy and basking in his admiration. A voice interrupted my thoughts: 'We will start with the Iron Cross man.' A giant who towered over me, several feet taller than I was, grabbed me by the elbow and pushed me carefully, as one would handle a small child, in the direction of the Führer. He was the steward, or seneschal, as he was called here. He must have been used to dealing with people who, overcome by the sense of occasion, lose their composure and turn into bumbling idiots. He led me the entire length of the hall, the soft plush carpet swallowing the sound of our footsteps. The man sitting at the immaculately polished table was currently the most powerful warlord on earth. He had a few books, a folder and a pocket atlas spread out in front of him and he pretended to study these intently. It was obvious that it was not a working desk as there was not even a telephone.

The steward pressed me down onto a red upholstered stool. Taking a few steps backwards, he retreated. This was what I had been waiting for for so long.

The Führer smiled, showing a gap between his front teeth, numbers three and four, and his gums – this was by no means perfect dentistry: there should be no visible gap at all. I couldn't believe it! This must be a dream, a bad dream, caused by the days of anxiety and apprehension. Surely the Führer, who was one of the most powerful men in the world, did not have any false teeth, and if he did, they must be the most artful and perfect works of precision constructed by the best of all dental technicians. What I could see before me was a terrible fit, a truly botched job, but what really worried me was that I had seen it before, held it in my own hands. And even worse, it was my own work. It was my very first piece, and although it was a disaster and I was told to destroy the whole thing and start again, I didn't. It was not meant for a stranger. No, it was for a member of my own family – my Uncle Kassian who was also my foster-father. My uncle had decided to go with it even though it was a bad fit. This was partly so as not to upset me but, more importantly, he was given a special price and interest-free credit. This dental work brought my thoughts back into the real world. The man who had pronounced his welcome with the familiar long vowels, who had breathed so disarmingly into this moustache, this man was none other than my Uncle Kassian. The more I studied him, the more I recognised individual traits. These were his ears, his chin, here was his jaw line. His moustache was completely different and had been trimmed in the Hitler fashion. My uncle's moustache had been blonde and bushy. His hair had been dyed; around the eyes a make-up artist had drawn a few lines to make him look more like an intellectual and less like the farmer he was. With his back to the window and his face in the shade, he did resemble the Hitler I had seen on the many portraits in circulation. Without any doubt to me this was my uncle in the flesh. I had not seen him for at least five or six years. In the village where he lived he was known as the 'character', even though hardly anyone knew what a character was. He was known as this because he had his own opinions and did not put up with any nonsense.

We had been an unlikely pair in the past. He, a tall strong man, and I, a sensitive frail boy, but we stuck together like two close friends. I had often imagined what it would be like to see him again in later years. It was a major disappointment to me because it meant that the man I now had a private audience with was not in fact the Führer at all. This was putting an end to all my dreams and it appeared that all my efforts had been in vain. The man opposite was still smiling, all the while repositioning the bridge in his mouth and preparing to speak. I beat him to it.

'*Grüss Gott*; hello *Onkel*,' I said. 'How are you? And how is dear Maltschi these days?'

He showed no surprise, but this was typical of him. He had never been easily rattled.

Without batting an eyelid he responded, 'Thank you. Maltschi is fine' – Maltschi was his young and quite attractive housekeeper – 'Keep your voice down, you rascal. How could you have recognised me? I hardly recognise you myself. You are much taller than I remember. What are you doing in the military? And in the navy at that? You always used to be against the Nazis. But maybe you are not meant to be here, am I right?'

'You shouldn't be criticising me, uncle. I admit that I'm here in disguise, playing a role I'm not entirely happy with, but what about you? You, here in the Führer's residence? The last thing I heard from my mother was that you were a court usher in the county court of Txx., where all the judges suspended for drinking ended up. I thought you may have gone into early retirement but my mother never told me that you were now the leader of 80 million people!'

We must have forgotten the fact that he was now supreme commander of the army and navy, whilst I was only one of many mere tin soldiers. Perhaps it was the way we were holding our heads together, our regards too familiar, but in short the steward was not happy with the situation and made his way over to us. His voice was polite but there was an undertone of suppressed anger, 'Does my Führer request to see the next sailor?'

Uncle Kassian looked at him and said loftily, 'I request to be left alone.' With a gesture akin to shaking dust from a broom, he waved him off. Taking a few steps backwards the seneschal retreated. We were left in peace and resumed our conversation.

'That man is due a slap in the face from yesterday,' my uncle said. 'He insists on meddling and getting involved in things that have nothing to do with him. He is not even my superior. I am part of the Führer's personal security department not the household division. You know, my lad,' he continued, 'it is like this. Regrettably I am only of use in situations where I remain seated. I am around 7cm too tall. I hardly ever get to go in the car as there could always be a situation where I might have to get out and show my full height. But it is quite an honour, don't you think, to be given a talking role, to be used for a social engagement involving a private audience with individuals? Let me check what I was going to ask …' He looked at his notes, pinned to the cover of the atlas. 'Where were you born? I know the answer to that one. How long have you been on the U-boat; were your parents pleased with your decoration; are you happy with the catering? Etc. etc. The questions cannot be simple enough, my superior told me. And I have to agree with him. You would be surprised at how many of the soldiers and sailors forget the place where they were born when I start talking to them. They have to think hard before they answer. Thank goodness I do not need to remember or write the answers down. No one is interested. That's right, dear boy, I can see the steward is getting anxious but do not be concerned. I have just decided that he will receive a few slaps in the face when I see him later in the kitchen. I haven't seen you for so long, I want to enjoy our little conversation. The others can wait.'

I said to my uncle, 'You have a fantastic job. You must tell me more!'

'The only problem is,' he continued, 'when one of the party bigwigs needs to speak to the Führer immediately; having interrupted my conversation, they can see immediately that I am not the real Führer, but they have to play along and demonstrate the usual reverence and devotion. If this happens I have to make sure I don't run into one of them afterwards as they are likely to take out their anger on me. Of course, it is their fault because they should have planned the timing of their visit better. Surely they must have at least twenty secretaries who could have looked into it for them. You see, my boy, I do not have a single secretary and I have to plan everything myself. Sometimes this is difficult for your old uncle but in exchange I am now a civil servant with an attractive pension and have many important connections.'

'Do you ever see the Führer, uncle?' I enquired.

'The Führer? Don't be silly! Why would I want to? I am told he has a foul temper. I am happy with my well-paid post and the extras; the food is truly first class. I have heard that some people are struggling to find decent things to eat but they seem to make an exception here in Berchtesgaden – I cannot complain. You mustn't tell anyone I said this though. I could get into trouble. Your friends are getting impatient, that tall skinny one with the scrawny neck – don't look now, that would be too obvious. He keeps staring at us. If he forgets to breathe he might just keel over and die. Things like that can happen, I tell you. One thing I do want to know before you go: how on earth did you get into the navy? Don't get me wrong, I am very proud of you. It is quite an honour to receive the Iron Cross. But the navy? I remember that as a child you were terrified of water! But we are running out of time, don't tell me now. Be quick, is there anything I can do to help you now that you are here?'

'Uncle,' I said, a little dispirited, as everything had turned out wrong. 'I came here to talk to the Führer in private. I was hoping to convince him to change his mind. Of course, I am very happy to have seen you after such a long time but it was not what I was expecting.'

'You wanted to convince him to change his mind?' he repeated.

I nodded.

'To negotiate peace?' he enquired further. He was more intelligent than I had thought. I nodded again.

'You see, my boy, that's what I thought. If you had only said so at the beginning. Now things are more difficult and there is little time to discuss things properly. But listen, I am on good terms with the Führer's hairdresser. He is the chief-reichs-haircutter and an influential person. Every five or six days he cuts his hair and then has the opportunity to talk politics. I will take up your suggestion and see if he isn't able to lead the conversation in this direction and convince him it would be a good idea to make peace. Of course, I wouldn't mention your name. I have heard that there is no point in trying to be too direct with him. If you manage to feed him an idea without being too obvious then there is a chance he may pick it up and take it as his own. Let me make a note of it.'

Restore peace, he wrote on his white sleeve. 'I will not be able to let you know how it turns out but if you stay in the navy you should be one of the first to find out if peace has been declared. Then you will know where you are at and if the hairdresser was successful. And now ...' Here he raised his voice a little and acquired a tinny tenor; it was remarkably convincing. I leapt up and stood to attention. 'My dear petty officer, I thank you for your goodwill and brave deeds. My heart beats in time with the courageous men on the north coast fighting for the freedom of our seas, and winning. Next please!' This last sentence was read out word for word from his notes.

I clicked my heels, turned around and marched over the soft red carpet back to my friends, passing the sailor whose turn it was next. He was visibly shaking. I sat down next to the Student who was holding his watch in his hands, shaking so hard that the chain and the decorative anchor and buoy were rattling like an out-of-tune jazz band.

'Gotthold,' he whispered into my ear nervously. 'Twenty-seven minutes, do you realise that is how long you were talking to the Führer!' I pounced on the wonderful coffee and cakes, wolfing everything down and my comrades stared at me, dumbfounded.

16

THE RELENTLESS ONE

Although we were still meant to be talking to each other, looking cheerful and at ease, I didn't feel like talking to any of my friends. I could have whispered to the Student that the Führer was really my uncle. That would have been a great bit of gossip and the Student was one who enjoyed the sensational. But Edgar was keeping a close watch. The atmosphere in the hall was still strained and a little uncomfortable. The expression of the guardsmen, meant to convey a friendly but arrogant superiority, seemed particularly forced, but that must have been an integral part of their daytime uniform. The steward had whispered something into the Führer's ear and after this respectful command, the conversations became markedly shorter. Perhaps the hall was required for a different function?

I decided not to worry about it and continued to eat. It was doubtful that I would be offered such fine cakes again in the near future. There was a huge platter of them in the middle of the table and everyone could take as much as they wanted. How annoying, one of the raisins had lodged itself in my throat; they must have left on a bit of the stalk. I had to cough quite loudly and as a result everyone stared in my direction. Even my uncle stopped listening to what Anton the sailor had to say to him. I wanted to say to

Edgar, who was leaning over to see how I was, that I was fine; everything was okay, but it was a stupid idea to try and speak at this critical moment in time. The grape stalk lodged itself deep into my windpipe and I couldn't get any air and turned blue, my eyes bulging out of their sockets. Trembling, I got up and pushed my plate away from me.

Edgar, a frightened look on his hitherto calm and unruffled face, seized me by my waist and pulled me out of the hall. I tried to imagine my uncle – no longer listening to what the sailor seated on the edge of the stool had to say – following my movement with the utmost concern. If the seven guards had not been there watching, I'm sure he would have come over and hit me firmly on the back. This is something he had to do often enough when I was a child as I was constantly choking on things, but no one seemed to think of this simple solution. The pain in my breast was becoming unbearable and I already saw things ending badly. In a house like this they must have a doctor used to removing obstructions with a mirror and some tweezers. I could already see the headlines: 'Newly decorated petty officer chokes to death during his honorary visit to the Führer.' I would be famous but not in the way I had imagined.

Edgar pushed me forwards and I began to stagger, disoriented. I could sense that we were still on the plush carpet but heading down some stairs. This must have been the way to the doctor. It appeared that some of the air was still reaching my lungs otherwise I would have been dead by now. I could hear someone saying to Edgar: 'You are going down there at this time of day? You must be out of your mind.' Edgar kept mumbling, 'Hurry, hurry!' And to himself he was saying, 'What have I done to deserve this?'

I slowly regained my vision. A couple in civilian clothes passed us. The woman was saying: 'That was the best hour of my life. I swear I will never forget it. What a saint, and so intelligent and clever and his manners so kind! Did you hear what his evening meal would be? Spinach with a fried egg and some fruit juice!'

That must be the neutral diplomat's wife, but judging by her accent she was German-born. Her husband spoke German with a distinctly foreign accent. 'I wonder where I left my fountain pen?' Then he grabbed his wife's arm and said: 'Be careful Edeltraut! There's an epileptic having a fit. Come quick! You never know what he might do. We should get away!' They hurried past us.

I had to cough again, this time so hard that I trembled from head to toe and my eyes filled with tears. Through the haze I could now make out my uncle coming towards us. I knew I could rely on him. He was not going to leave his nephew and foster-child alone in a strange house when he was in danger of choking to death. Then, what a relief: the raisin flew out in a long arch, thereby freeing my windpipe. I was saved! 'Don't worry, uncle. I'm fine,' I was about to say, but the words remained stuck in my throat.

The man I was facing, eye to eye, was dressed in the same clothes my uncle was wearing, and although there was a close resemblance, there was also a marked difference. He was a little thinner perhaps, a little shorter, with an expression in his eye that was truly terrifying. Could it be the real …? I did not dare finish the thought. His grooming was immaculate. But what was that I could see? A thin, narrow black object had stuck in his side parting, ruining the effect. I looked more closely and held my breath. It was the stalk from the raisin I had expelled from my windpipe. Thankfully the dictator had not noticed.

'What is going on here? What are you doing?' he demanded of the guardsman. I was relieved that he was not speaking to me and even gladder that Edgar was able to answer and had not lost the ability to speak. He reported:

'Accompanying Iron Cross First Class U-boat *Maat* following his honorary visit.'

'U-boat *Maat*, that is very interesting,' the Führer spoke very quickly. He waved Edgar to one side. 'Tell me,' he began. 'Last Thursday you dropped a magnetic mine in the Thames estuary, what is your opinion as a knowledgeable petty officer? How can we best intensify this method?'

I didn't know what to say. Last Thursday we had already arrived in Berchtesgaden. I had been nowhere near the Thames estuary and out of principle I did not read the papers in Germany. Edgar answered on my behalf: 'Excuse me, my Führer. This man was not on the U-boat that infiltrated the Thames. He was on the U-XY, do you remember, three weeks ago they …?'

The Führer did not let him finish. He started to rant. 'What are you saying?' he shouted. 'These men have been dallying around on the mainland for three weeks? When every five minutes, every five seconds spent in enemy waters could create the deciding moment that determines the outcome of this war? It is not as if we have so many U-boats and crews that we can send some on holiday. This is outrageous! And a disgrace! Where is their captain?'

'He was called away. The Security Service ordered his return,' the unhappy Edgar announced.

The Führer became increasingly irate: 'I'll have you know, I will eliminate every single person who is responsible for this extortionate waste of our resources. Three weeks – that makes at least four merchant ships a day, let us say each at 3,000 tons; that is 12,000 tons a day or a quarter of a million tons of enemy matter in three weeks and these opportunities are lost through sheer negligence!'

What I wanted to say was: 'Don't shout at the poor man. He's only an *Ehrenkavalier*,' but I didn't dare. I thought it might harm the poor man even more, coming from my mouth.

'I will order the following,' the Führer raved on, 'that no U-boats will be allowed back into their home port except for emergency repairs. Auxiliary vessels will supply all the necessary: fresh ammunition, fuel, aspirin and Iron Crosses when required!'

I nearly piped up, 'You forgot to mention the post', but again I thought it better to keep quiet. Unfortunately, the Führer had noticed that I was about to say something.

'Go on, you have something to say!' he shouted.

This was the moment I had been waiting for. Now I could finally deliver my ground-breaking, world-changing speech, eye to eye with the Führer; his full attention upon me. But after all that, I decided not to seize the moment. I had already come to the conclusion that there was no point in persisting. This was not a man with an open mind who could be easily persuaded. I could see right through him. He did not care one iota about what anyone else thought and whether his people really wanted this war. His whole being was evil and he used his power to destroy and annihilate whatever crossed his path. Therefore, I gave up, right then and there.

'Reporting, sir. I have nothing further to add to what I said in the hall,' I responded briefly. I hoped that he would now regret not having spoken to all the sailors personally. Perhaps he would feel he had missed out on something important. But he did not seem bothered. He stormed up the stairs and took no further notice of us.

'I thought the Führer was a bit unfair to you,' I said to Edgar. He glared at me, cutting me short: 'I am not talking to you.' I think this may have meant the end of his career.

He must have spread the word about me to all of my comrades. Grimly we faced each other in the carriage of the train, not speaking a word. We set off that very evening to return to the naval harbour. We all knew what was expected of us. We were to follow this path of destruction and annihilation by order of the evil mind behind it all. We would be expected to continue on this futile course, following orders blindly until each and every one of us – or Hitler himself – fell victim to this terrible folly.

★★★

TRANSLATOR'S NOTES

In the novel, Gotthold Griesemann has been given the rank of petty officer, although he is referred to as Unteroffizier, Obermaschinenmaat, Obermaat, Torpedomaat and Maat. For the translations of the German ranks, see Jak P. Mallmann Showell, *Companion to the German Navy* (Stroud: The History Press), 3rd edn published 2009.

–maat	petty officer
ober-maat	chief petty officer

The dash is replaced by the individual's trade, hence:

Maschinenmaat	Petty officer of the machinist trade
Obermaschinenmaat	Chief petty officer of the machinist trade
Torpedomaat	Petty officer of the torpedo trade
Gefreiter	Able seaman
Maschinengefreiter	Able seaman of the machinist trade
Unteroffizier	Petty officer

Visit our website and discover thousands of other History Press books.

www.thehistorypress.co.uk